I0716550

HOODOO WAR

A TALE OF THE MASON COUNTY WAR

CRAIG RAINEY

Craig Rainey Creative, LLC
AUSTIN, TEXAS

Copyright © 2024 by Craig Rainey

All rights reserved. No part of this publication may be reproduced, distributed, or transmitted in any form or by any means, without prior written permission.

Craig Rainey / Craig Rainey Creative, LLC
Austin, Texas 78660
https://craigrainey.com

Publisher's Note: This is a work of fiction. Names, characters, places, and incidents are a product of the author's imagination. Locales and public names are sometimes used for atmospheric purposes. Any resemblance to actual people, living or dead, or to businesses, companies, events, institutions, or locales is completely coincidental.

Hoodoo War/ Craig Rainey. -- 1st ed.
ISBN 978-1-7371820-9-2

OTHER BOOKS BY CRAIG RAINEY

MASSACRE AT AGUA CALIENTE
STOLEN VALOR
DARK MOTIVE
REASONABLE SIN
SOVEREIGN RULE
NATIONS LAW
THE ART OF PROFESSIONAL SALES

For my mother, who introduced me to the story of the Mason County War without knowing she did. I am who I am because of her.

Getting away with it is not a long-term plan. It is a short road ending all the plans you made.

—CRAIG RAINEY

FOREWORD

I WAS A CHILD THE FIRST TIME I SAW the Mason County Courthouse. Like most courthouses in Texas, it sits in the original downtown center of the small town. I never paid much attention to it, no more than any of the other twenty or thirty I have seen in my life.

Since I was a boy, Mason was primarily a way point when my family travelled from my hometown, San Angelo. The town was always the first stop we made during our frequent journeys to San Antonio or Canyon Lake / New Braunfels.

My grandfather often stopped for a bite at the Hilltop Restaurant. My parents, preferring to waste no time, were satisfied to break at one of two convenience stores, a necessity when travelling with four kids.

Back on the road, our route through Mason took us around the perimeter of the town square. Its roof peaks finding the sunlight amongst the top branches of large pecan trees, the Mason County Courthouse stood, a monumental reminder of the history of Texas and the hard-won taming of a once lawless state.

As far as courthouses go, I had never seen anything unique or singular about it other than the architecture, and the sense of history and permanence it shares with any other courthouse – until a couple of weeks ago.

By chance, I read online the Mason County Courthouse had burned down. According to the story from TexasHillCountry.com*, County Judge Jerry Bearden said in a statement that the courthouse burned down on February 4, 2021. The suspect led police on a high-speed chase all the way to McLennan County where he was arrested on charges of arson. The judge is reportedly leading an effort to fund the rebuild.

The fire seemed to me a particularly personal travesty, an affront to Texas yes, but I took it personally. I hadn't realized the courthouse had become a fixture in my life, a monument to my childhood. Its destruction caused me pain and grief.

I expanded my search to learn more about the fire. What was the motive behind the arsonist's crime? Probably because of how recently the crime had been committed, beyond the TexasHillCounty.com article, I found little information about the fire or the arsonist. Instead, my research opened the door to a fascinating, and bizarre story I had not anticipated.

I found records and historical accounts including a complete history of Mason and Mason county. At first, I felt nostalgic as I learned of the founding of Mason, the German immigrants who settled the region, and references to familiar names and landmarks I had known all of my life. As I learned more, my nostalgic journey became a preoccupation - a consuming fascination.

I learned the courthouse had burned down three times since its original construction 174 years before. The first time occurred ten years after its original construction in 1877, the second was in the early 20th century. This latest time in 2021 was the third.

What were the odds one Texas courthouse would be destroyed by fire three times? My search led me to discover the story of one of the bloodiest range wars in Texas history, the Mason County War.

Being an eager and voracious researcher, I sought more information about the event. My research was not limited to web browsing. West Texas towns provide some of the best information resources in their ever-present hole-in-the-wall bookstores. My visits led to my discovery of many antique and out-of-print books. My favorite store is a musty smelling bookstore in downtown San Angelo where I discovered a section near the back wall filled exclusively with unknown Texas authors who wrote about their experiences in 1800's Texas.

My family is generations deep in Texas heritage, but even that did not prepare me for the realization the history of the state I call home is singular in its incomparable popularity with outlaws.

Some of the stories were told and retold in books, movies, and magazines. The untold stories of the most notorious outlaws and the daring lawmen who clashed here in Texas impressed me so much the ground beneath my feet seems wet still with the blood of some of the most compelling figures in history and their victims. I realized the most well known and most frequently portrayed villains in Hollywood films emerged from, and/or plied their dread skills, in Texas.

Wesley Hardin, Sam Bass, King Fisher, The Newton Gang (Newton Boys), and Bonnie and Clyde, are a few of so many whose stories helped create the state's reputation as a bastion for hardened but memorable outlaws.

Not so well represented in movies and books were the courageous lawmen and county judges of the 1800's who applied justice with a stern hand; or the rise of the Texas Rangers from failed efforts to establish a state police force.

As I conducted my research for this novel, I read first-hand accounts and historical narratives about the history of the region, I learned about the details of the Mason County War lasting from 1875 through 1876.

According to local lore, after the bloody conflict, an un-identified arsonist burned down the courthouse, ostensibly to eliminate all evidence of the range war and those who participated in it. The fire destroyed the courthouse on January 21,1877. The arsonist was never identified.

A half-hearted public outcry, and a few ineffectual calls to bring the arsonist to justice, amounted to no more than a meager attempt at propriety after the atrocities of the Mason County War. The weakly demonstrated fervor for justice died with little done to appease it.

As an excuse for their lethargic pursuit of justice, locals coined a phrase reflecting the weariness of a community wanting only to heal and move on. "The trouble is over, let it die."

Most of the evidence and recorded factual details of the Mason County War are lost or, more often, shrouded in mystery. The mystery was due as much to the stubborn silence of tight-lipped locals as it is to the evidence lost in the torched courthouse building. Embellished tales and disputed hearsay about the range war are all that remain today.

Within this novel, I depended upon what facts I could find. Many of the characters are true historical figures, others are of my own creation. I committed a significant effort towards authenticity as I portrayed an historic event I presumed would bear a personal stake with many who live in Mason County still.

As I wrote, I was overcome by the feeling my fictional characters walked amongst the ghosts of the past. Through them, I was able to see those men and women of Mason County firsthand. I feel fortunate to have been given the gift of the writer. Through it I was able to walk amongst those who before were only written names participating in fantastical events. I feel like I was there. I time travelled in a sense. I saw it all. I heard it all. I feel heartache and loss. I was there.

Like me in my boyhood, thousands will drive through Mason County, oblivious of the price paid by those early settlers, German immigrants, and the lawmen who civilized the region.

A brief description of the history of the courthouse is engraved upon a placard in front of the rebuilt structure. Unless you stop to read it, you too might pass by without guessing at the blood-tinged history lying behind the beauty of the quaint west Texas town.

From what I have been able to learn of the Mason County War and those who lived through it, I believe it appropriate the locals would create a nickname reflecting the pragmatic dismissal of the event as something to be disregarded and left behind.

They called it the HooDoo War.

1

HooDoo – (Slang) A hooded vigilante gang who takes the law into its own hands, hanging and shooting those it deems outside its own laws or counter to its opinions.

I T WAS MIDDAY IN HUNTSVILLE, TEXAS and the Sun's heat was a welcome discomfort for the near dozen men standing in the dusty street before the Walls Prison Unit. Some of those gaunt men had been separated only a few years from freedom. Others had been decades inside those tall brick walls. No matter the time in prison, each of them peered through squinting eyes, hands shading their tortured faces as they grew accustomed to the Sun's brightness and the idea they were truly free.

Jarvis Hutton cast a final look behind him as the tall steel doors locked with a clang. His time served at the Walls was finished. Twenty years left behind, nearly half of his life, and he was alone in a vastly changed world. He had changed also, though he was less aware of the differences the years in a cell had wrought.

He was lean as before, but this current condition was the result of a body suffering from disuse and decay. His sandy hair had weathered gray at the temples and thin atop his head. His visage was no longer chiseled and angular. His cheeks were sallow, his chin weakened by years of submission to the state.

The only feature of his face unchanged and still singularly bold were his clear eyes. They shone bright blue with an indominable eagerness; a hunger for those things he desired all his life. The years inside had not diminished his internal fire, but that fire had contributed to the deterioration of the man, drawing upon his very flesh in lieu of savage activity and fierce occupation of the mind and body.

Surveying those wretched souls nearby, he realized he was alone. So much had passed him by. His youth, and the years he might have invested in a wife and perhaps a family, were lost.

The War Between the States was waged and ended, largely unnoticed inside the prison walls, save for those newcomers incarcerated for post war crimes – often the only enterprise left young men cast adrift after their service to the southern armies.

His parents were long dead and buried in Nebraska. He knew of no one familiar upon whom he could call. The awaiting vastness of Texas was the only familiar thing; the only remaining constant since before his capture. Even his brother, dead now for seventeen years, added tinder to the lonely flame consuming the last of his good humor at his release.

The memory of his dead brother, and the circumstances leading to his death, drove Jarvis in a direction towards which he vowed to commit the rest of his days. He would follow this dread path to its unavoidable destination – murder.

Hutton frowned as he thought of his younger brother, Kyle. Their last moments together had been spent on one of his brother's rare visits to the prison more than seventeen years previous. Their final words were promises each made to the other. They would maintain contact no matter what befell either.

After that day, six months passed with no visit or news from or about his younger brother. Despite the faith he struggled to keep, Jarvis came to the disappointing conclusion Kyle had failed to honor his promise or had fallen afoul of the law and was confined to one of the many county jails in Texas.

State and county judges were strict purveyors of justice, handing out crushing sentences for even the lowliest of offenses. Those hard men of jurisprudence were said to be the thin line of the law, dispensing justice as they saw fit; a stern warning to others who considered committing a crime to think twice for fear of the price they would pay. Amongst lawmen and judges alike, it was believed respect for the law was preferred, but in its stead, fear was a sufficient motivator.

Lawmen and judges made the news of these harsh sentences public with a designed purpose, a deterrent to those who would enter the ranks of the lawless. It was clear if Kyle had been captured and convicted, Jarvis would have learned of it.

After another slowly passing year with no word, Jarvis suspected the worst. Even in the most secure prison in the territory, prisoners came and went. Huntsville was a small town, but the prison it served drew an element makng it as boisterous and busy as a gold rush town.

Whether interned or at large, the criminal element made up a sizable portion of the town's ever-changing population. The whereabouts or the condition of current and past prisoners were not guarded secrets. Conversely, word of an outlaw's death was disseminated as broadly and loudly as possible. Texas was a largely lawless region. Horribly detailed accounts of the death of an outlaw were freely broadcasted to the public.

Many of the lawmen, and a smaller number of judges, were recruited from the very class of outlaws they were sworn to bring to justice. News of successful apprehensions, the harsh delivery of punishment, and the brutal death of those who attempted to escape from lawmen, were heralded in the hope those stories would provide more discouragement to those beyond the grasp of the paltry number of law enforcement officials who dispensed justice.

Questioned by Jarvis, rustlers and highwaymen came and went from the prison as the law accorded with no word from or about Kyle.

One day a moment of happenstance put an end to the mystery. It was chance that brought them together. It was chance also that allowed Jarvis Hutton to learn of his brother's fate.

With a shake of his head, dispelling the dark pall of growing memories, Jarvis emerged from his reverie, standing alone before the prison gates. The others had drifted into town. Many of those newly released convicts would make their first stop one of the many saloons nearby. Others would rejoin families created by blood or by grim occupation.

Jarvis ground his teeth absently as the emotion of his brother's memory waned. He crossed the wide road separating the prison from the town. He entered the first mercantile he saw. He had twenty dollars in regional notes. With it he purchased hard tack, beans, and the makin's.

Outside the store he rolled a cigarette with one hand as he planned his next move. He needed a horse and a gun.

2

H E WAS DRESSED IN THE TYPICAL GARB of a German ranch boy. His hat had a tattered flat brim. His clothes were large for him in the waist but tight around the shoulders. He wore heavy boots more suited to work on the ground than in the saddle. He rode a roan gelding, content to allow the horse his lazy shambling gait as he took in the sights of the town.

Mason, Texas had remained unchanged for so many years, at the youthful age of seventeen he had seen as much change in the town as even the oldest residents had witnessed.

Fewer than a dozen permanent buildings comprised the total structures in Mason. The largest was the courthouse, constructed in the previous decade to aid in the distribution of justice on the Texas frontier. Next was the Southern Hotel, then Ranck's General Store.

Generally, the remaining structures were small but efficiently designed buildings including the post office, and the land office. The rest were small plank houses and a liberal array of dingy tents, often, only wooden frames covered with canvas sheeting.

There was little that was geometric about the central region of town, but the title Town Square seemed appropriate despite the shape. Most of the common buildings housing public commerce and official offices occupied the perimeter. The two-story brick courthouse fenced on all four sides was the centerpiece of the Town Square.

Arranged in clusters in cleared areas around the town proper were a handful of homes scattered around its outer limits, though the majority of the town's population lived just beyond, on small farms and ranches.

Prior to the courthouse's construction, criminal trials and other judicial proceedings had been conducted in the shade of an ancient oak tree. Similarly, as there was no official school building in Mason, lessons were taught where space was available. The locations had changed often throughout the years. It was common homes were made available for educating the local boys and the most privileged girls. For the current school term instruction was administered in the spacious lobby of the Southern Hotel.

The boy on the roan gelding, Boyd Wechsler was not much older than those attending school lessons. He was seventeen years old, but his broad shoulders and direct manner gave him the appearance of a grown man. Making his way past the courthouse, he guided his mount towards a point in front of the hotel. As he drew rein, he watched from horseback as three boys surrounded a small tow-headed boy. The boy was Boyd's younger cousin, Hans. Although smaller, with none of the might of his elder cousins, Hans faced the three larger boys with a fearlessness Boyd did not understand but admired despite its foolhardiness.

The hotel was empty of all its school goers and patrons, including schoolmaster Ellis, gathered outside to witness the inevitable destruction of the German rancher boy.

Boyd remained in the saddle, curious to see how long his cousin's courage would hold. He wasn't eager to allow little Hans to be injured, but his fascination with the courage of the diminutive sprat stayed his succor.

If Wolfgang Wechsler, their grandfather, learned of Boyd's delay, he would reward the hesitation with a leather strap across his backside. Doubtlessly, the old man would read into his grandson's tardiness a reluctance to intervene, rather than assigning the delay to fascination or curiosity.

The Wolf, as Boyd's grandfather was sometimes called, would assume Boyd acted upon cruel intentions. Possibly he would see the delay as recompense for the Wolf's more astringent punishment he paid Boyd than he did to Boyd's three cousins.

Even at the range worthy age of seventeen, Boyd was a frequent target for his grandfather's discipline. There was no small amount of irony involved when it came to the old German rancher's penchant for violence when dealing with Boyd. Although in his teens, Boyd was no stranger to the duties of adulthood.

He had grown up with the bloody violence of a war fought between friends and brothers. His experience was of blue coats inflicting postwar cruelty upon southern folks despite participating in military service or not. Even the foreigners, Germans immigrated to Texas to claim awarded land grants, were not immune from northern brutality. Boyd's grandfather had suffered the loss of cattle and supplies, taken by Union Army Peacekeepers in claimed support for the army's protection. Most Union Peacekeepers were civilian volunteers, pilfering a profit from war weary, and male depleted settlers along the frontier.

On frequent occasions, Boyd had joined the men as they pursued rustlers and thieves. Despite his participation and his sharing in the bloodletting with the men, the Wolf showed no deference to him. Instead, the old man continued to thrash him for his misdeeds as he did the younger children in his family, like a schoolboy.

Two of his three grandsons were Gerhart and Chlodwig, the sons of the Wolf's eldest son, Klaus. Hans was the Wolf's youngest grandson, from his younger son, Ernst. Boyd's mother, Emma, was the middle sister. Boyd had never known his father, who died before he was born.

The dark thoughts faded as Boyd's attention focused upon the conflict growing before him. The three Städtbewohnen boys; that is what the German ranchers called the Townies, closed upon the painfully thin Hans. As the larger boys moved gradually closer, Hans turned in a slow dusty circle, fists balled in white-knuckled readiness.

Boyd was acquainted with Hans' three assailants. Two were the brothers, Pogue and Gayle Spears, nearly Boyd's age. He guessed Gayle was perhaps a year his junior. There was little doubt they were the catalyst for the conflict. The Spears brothers reminded Boyd of a pair of stray dogs, filling their loafing boredom with violence, ganging up to inflict cruelty upon the helpless.

The third boy was Trace Worley. His father was deputy John Worley, trusted second to Mason County's Sheriff John Clark.

Like his father, Trace was a blind follower, easily led if the result elevated him or his status. Trace's penchant for cruelty was exclusively exercised when following the lead of others. Alone, he was a shy and cowardly boy.

Pogue's lantern jaw jutted ahead of his tall knobby frame, daring Hans to take a swing at it.

Gayle leered cruelly, restraining himself from launching a sneak attack.

Trace Worley kept a cautious distance, content to follow the others' lead.

"I heard you been jawing about us," Pogue lied, spit carrying his words across the distance between them.

"You square heads think you own this town. I got news for you. You don't."

Hans watched Pogue carefully, familiar with his penchant for surprise attacks. He knew it would come, and he was certain he could not avoid it.

"He ain't denying it, Pogue," Gayle said with an accusing hiss.

"Ain't no denying it," Pogue agreed, though he shook his head as if he didn't. "Everybody knows him and his kind don't belong here. No piece of paper can say otherwise."

Boyd scanned the area nearby. He was certain no aid could come from the surrounding school children or School Master Ellis. The teacher would not involve himself in Townie matters when they included the handling of a German rancher.

During the two years Boyd was allowed to attend school, he endured his share of encounters with Townies. The teachers never failed to side against him with the Townie boys or their parents.

Beyond the small group of school going spectators, some half dozen Townies observed the conflict from the street. The Anglo Townies hated the Germans who they believed received the finest ranch land through foreign land grants. They viewed the arrangement as unfair and offensive. Those watching would undoubtedly side with the bullies against the German boy.

Oblivious to the crowd, Hans said nothing in reply to the Spears' comments, choosing instead to save his energy and his attention for the violence ahead.

Pogue nodded as though Hans had indeed made a retort. He aimed a fast-moving fist at the smaller boy's face. The impact sounded like a stone thrown against a rotten tree trunk.

Hans went down in a heap, rising again with remarkable agility. With unexpected courage, he drove his slight frame against Pogue's larger physique, delivering a flurry of rapid but ineffectual lefts and rights.

Released from his restraint, Gayle stepped forward and hit Hans hard in the face.

Hans' head jolted violently under his snapping white hair.

Boyd dropped lightly from the saddle, dust puffing beneath his heavy boots. He moved through the crowd with long strides, arriving at the fray as Trace Worley moved in to join the Spears brothers in the beating.

Boyd grabbed a handful of Trace's curly hair and yanked him away from the fight, flinging him onto his back in the dirt. Pogue turned to counter this new threat and Boyd backhanded him across his nose. Blood spurted in a wide arc, staining the ground in a thick red line.

Gayle aimed a hard fist at Boyd's face.

Boyd bowed his head, taking the blow on the crown of his skull. Gayle's knuckles collapsed against the hard bone. He yowled as he clutched the injured hand to his chest.

Boyd blacked his eye, then dropped him with a punch behind the ear.

Despite being rescued from a certain beating, Hans repaid Boyd's heroism with a dark look.

Boyd gripped his arm, dragging the resistant Hans through the crowd to his horse.

"Let off me, Boyd," Hans complained as he was dragged along. "I can't run from this."

Boyd made no comment as he released Hans and mounted, beckoning Hans to join him astride the horse.

A freshened commotion erupted amongst the dusty, yelling, and milling school children. Pogue emerged from the throng like a ship emerging from a dense fog bank.

"You ain't been dismissed, Wechsler," he called to Boyd, wiping blood from his nose with the back of his hand.

Boyd gave Hans a stern look.

Pogue moved rapidly towards Boyd.

With a single stride Boyd was off his horse, moving towards the elder Spears boy.

He intercepted Pogue at the halfway point between the crowd and his horse. Pogue staggered from a quick pattern of alternating left and right punches. Each struck his face. Each drew blood and conjured discoloring marks. A fresh flow of blood leaked from his nose.

To the onlookers, the spectacle was a bizarre one. The silence of Boyd's assault, and the moist staccato impacts of his fists against Pogue's face, presented a scene of surreal horror.

Boyd Wechsler was known for saying little when in public. Many townspeople interpreted his silence as the conduct of a halfwit. Until recently, when he sprouted the last eight inches he would ever grow, he was a popular target and easy game for town bullies. Because of his reputation for silence, a favorite game amongst bullies was beating Boyd with the promise to continue until he cried out.

Boyd never gave up and he never cried out. Defeating him was rarely achieved without a cost to his attackers. His toughness was secretly admired by many, although few would ever admit it.

On occasion, some of those who admired his toughness were heard to admit quietly, "They may take his breakfast, but he's sure to get at least an egg off the plate before they do."

At his fully attained height of six feet, he was formidable. His formerly narrow and stooped shoulders were broad and thick. His long bony hands were hardened with a firm muscled padding.

Under the tutelage of Simon Martinez, formerly one of the hands on his grandfather's ranch, Boyd acquired a considerable skill in a fight; accuracy and speed when shooting; and a reasonable ability in tracking game and performing outdoor craft.

Boyd admired the elderly Mexican. He was silent like Boyd but took a liking to the youngster. Perhaps the old man's connection with the boy was the bond of a fellow outcast, or perhaps he too admired Boyd's toughness and desired to even the odds for him.

It was rumored Martinez was a former gunfighter, working on the ranch to hide from his enemies. The ranch hand mentioned to Boyd in rare and often vague comments his father was a Vaquero, and his mother was Comanche. Her kin were fierce and untamed Indians born in a time when they ruled the rugged Texas frontier.

Their blood flowed in Martinez's veins and much of their wild spirit remained in his make-up. Boyd took to his instruction as if that same blood flowed in his veins. Martinez found Boyd's easily attained skills uncommon for a German ranch boy.

Gayle hollered his rage as he sprinted to add his will to his brother's conflict. The Spears brothers fought with a pack mentality, preferring overwhelming numbers to any formal tactical plan.

Boyd sidestepped the second brother's plunging leap, curling him into a ball in the dust with a knee to the ribs. He glanced towards the crowd, ascertaining Trace Worley's intentions. When the Deputy's son failed to appear, Boyd returned to his horse, sparing no further attention for the Spears brothers.

Hans saw in his cousin's face a dark look discouraging him from presenting any further efforts to argue his point. Instead, he climbed onto the horse behind Boyd's saddle.

Neither spoke as Boyd clucked to the gelding. They rode away, the Städtbewohnen watching in silent judgement.

Boyd set his teeth against his sense of dread for the response his grandfather would levy when he learned of the fight. As for the Townies, the Spears' defeat would not go well with the boys' father and clan patriarch, Russel Spears. Boyd had no doubt the father Spears would not let his sons' defeat go lightly.

Boyd felt a more concerning sense of danger from his grandfather's response to the fight. Wolf Wechsler was clear those in his charge and in his employ shall avoid trouble with the Anglo townsmen. When the Wolf dispatched

Boyd to town, his instructions were clear. Collect Hans from the hotel and return. There would be no quarter given him for protecting his cousin.

3

EMMA WECHSLER WIPED TEARS FROM HER eyes, dropping another onion into the tall pan. She glanced at her mother to see if she had seen the tears. Her mother peeled potatoes in silence, giving no indication she had noticed. Despite the entire clan feeding at the main house, Emma's two sisters-in-law rarely participated in the evening meal preparations. Their domains were deliberately limited to the houses they kept at the far ends of the home pasture.

Emma's father and brothers would be late arriving, well after nightfall. These early spring days during calving season were the longest. Since their arrival from Germany when she was still a girl, rustlers had plagued them like mosquitoes on a still summer night. Calving season kept German ranchers out late, protecting their stock and branding those steers old enough to take the scar.

Everyone knew the names of those who rustled livestock. Sheriff Clark and his deputies had thus far refused to side against anyone who plagued the operations of German immigrant Ranchers, even going as far as to deny the guilt of confirmed cattle thieves.

Most of the rustlers were townies, Städtbewohnen. It was common knowledge amongst the German immigrants

Mason was a haven for those who stole their livestock and would destroy them if they were able.

German immigrant ranchers were the primary targets for cattle thieves. Little was done about it. The laws pertaining to rustling were lax and their interpretation depended more upon the honesty of the thief than the rightful possession of the ranchers.

Her father, Wolfgang Wechsler, due to the failure of many of his fellow immigrants over the last few years, had acquired ten additional leagues of prime pastureland. His larger than typical ranch supported thousands of longhorns and beef cattle, the most of any single German rancher. He controlled more than 6,000 acres of fertile grassland on Comanche Creek. His stake included some of the finest grazing land in the region. His good fortune and growing wealth drew the ire of envious town folk who would see the granted property in Anglo hands.

Emma frowned at her thoughts as she deftly cut away the heart of an onion, hoping to limit its blinding vapors.

Her father's success was the siren song for countless rustlers, seeking quick and easy profits from the theft of poorly protected stock.

Accepting the smaller losses was an unavoidable part of ranching. During calving season, the Wolf committed an extraordinary investment of manpower and precious time to safeguarding his herds. Unbranded cattle were easy prey and once lost were rarely recovered.

Emma heard the muffled thuds of a horse's hooves on the packed dirt outside the kitchen door. She rinsed her knife in a water filled basin, brushed crisp onion rynds off her apron, and went to open the back door.

Outside, her son Boyd helped Hans down from his horse. The youngster's left eye was closing from a fresh blow, and dried blood was caked under his nose. Boyd appeared uninjured.

She feared the worst as she rushed to Hans, inspecting him for additional wounds.

"Did you hurt your cousin, son?" she asked Boyd dreadfully.

"Townies," Boyd replied, ignoring the carelessly delivered accusation. "Spears boys. I expect Russ Spears directly."

"What did you do?" she asked her son.

Boyd showed the slightest sign of impatience with her preconceptions of his role in the fight.

"They were gonna hurt little Hans..."

Hans kicked the dirt, his tow hair covering his eyes as he stared at the ground.

"I ain't little, Boyd. Don't say otherwise."

Boyd regarded his cousin mildly. Hans' irritation with him lightened his mood.

"The Spears boys are a little worse for wear right now," Boyd added.

"We don't need no more trouble from the Städtbewohnen," his mother scolded him.

Boyd made a face at the German term.

Instead of commenting further, he led the roan gelding to the stables. It was late; too late to join the others for calving. He would join the calving detail in the morning. His grandfather would be hard on him for missing the rest of the day, but with the Spears clan out for blood, Boyd didn't want the women or Hans left alone.

Boyd stabled his horse then returned to the house where he ate an early supper. He drew one of the carbines from the gun rack in his grandfather's office and returned to the stables to await the Spears' arrival.

Before dusk faded to darkness, five riders appeared at the break in the tree line where the road made its way to the ranch house. They travelled at a rough trot. The elder Spears was certainly angry, apparent by how hard they pushed their mounts. The riders carried side arms and rifle butts protruded from saddle scabbards.

Alone against so many armed riders, Boyd was at a great disadvantage, but the rifle's weight promised reliability, bolstering his confidence. If he fell, it would be after he shot Russel Spears.

Boyd levered a cartridge into the carbine and stepped onto the narrow roadway. The Spears men pulled up short, a few rods distant, spreading out in a loose semi-circle.

At the center of the group was Russel Spears, a large raw-boned man with a red face, sitting a big bay gelding. He glared at Boyd who stood wide legged in the middle of the lane.

Pogue and Gayle Spears sat their horses on either side of their father. Pogue grinned cruelly, anticipating the punishment due to Boyd for his part in the fight. Gayle watched his father carefully, waiting for any cue to act.

Two others, most likely volunteers from town, watched silently. Their manner clearly identified them as townsmen backing a native comrade against a Square Head rancher.

"You're gonna come with us Wechsler," Russel Spears ordered Boyd with a tone of moral authority.

Boyd made no move to comply. He merely watched the group, his carbine poised for quick action.

"Did you hear what I said to you?" Spears asked, louder this time.

"He heard you, pop," Pogue explained. "He's a little simple. He don't talk much."

Gayle and the two Townies laughed.

The elder Spears leaned forward as if to dismount.

"Get off that horse and I'll kill you," Boyd warned.

There was a steady timbre to Boyd's voice that froze Russel Spears' motion.

Spears returned to his seat in the saddle, shifting his weight to bring his pistol into a more available position. He considered the boy before him with a more serious attention. The deadly threat from a mere boy was an unexpected response. Spears struggled to reframe his impression of what appeared to be a schoolboy. The kid who stood before him talked like a full-grown man.

"Did you just threaten murder?" he asked, as though Boyd were on trial.

Boyd said nothing.

The kitchen door banged open. Hans emerged, his varmint gun in his hands. He ran to take a position beside Boyd.

"That pea shooter ain't gonna work against us," Pogue said with disdain for the small caliber rifle - and for Hans.

Spears surveyed Hans' bruised face. He deduced this was the boy who started the fight.

"You two boys drop them weapons," Russell Spears barked. "You're in enough trouble already. Don't make it worse for yourselves."

Hans' aggressive demeanor sagged, and he lowered his rifle to a less threatening posture.

Boyd displayed no change in his posture, nor did he make any move to obey.

Movement behind Spears and his men drew Boyd's attention and he glanced briefly from Spears to identify the source.

Behind the Spears group, Wolf Wechsler and his men approached, returning from calving, the sound of their advance muted by the lush grass bordering the lane.

Wolfgang Wechsler and his men stopped their horses behind the Spears group. Pulling his rifle from its scabbard, Wechsler rested it over the pommel of his saddle.

"What's your business here, Spears?" he asked.

Surprised, Spears jerked his head around. He surveyed the men behind him. He was outnumbered and out-flanked.

Wechsler's men continued to fan out to either side of the Wolf, surrounding the Spears group. There were eight men in the Wechsler band. Wolfgang's sons, Klaus and Ernst, sat beside their father at the center of the group. Two others were temporary hired hands from one of the other German families nearby. The Wechsler brothers' sons Gerhart and Chlodwig were beside them.

The last man was Verner Koenig, a young German immigrant who had remained in Mason County after Wechsler purchased his granted property from him. He was a diligent worker and fiercely loyal.

Klaus motioned to his boys, Gerhart and Chlodwig to move a short distance to the side, out of the field of fire, in case it came to that.

"Your boys jumped my sons in town," Spears complained, the authority in his voice replaced with a whiny tone. "The bigger one is a grown man. He can't have his way with schoolboys."

The Wolf shook his head with disapproval. Spears might have thought the gesture for him, but Boyd knew the head shake was meant for him.

"He is seventeen, not much past his own school days," Wechsler said. His tone hardened as he addressed Boyd. "Why did you hurt these two children, Boyd?"

"We ain't children," Pogue complained. "If he wouldn't have surprised us, I would have finished him myself."

"Shut up, Pogue," his father said. To Wechsler he said, "Your boy has to answer for his actions."

"He is my grandson, and it sounds like your boy is willing to settle it now. What say you?"

"It ain't going to go that way," Spears growled. "This is a matter for the law. Your grandson has to come with me. I'm taking him to the sheriff."

"Not today," the Wolf said. "Get off my land. The sheriff can come for him personally if he sees fit."

Spears stewed for a long moment. His stained teeth bit the air and his lips contorted with unheard protests as he struggled to maintain control of his frustration.

Finally, he yanked the reins.

With a frightened snort, his horse reared and wheeled around.

"Expect the sheriff soon," Spears screamed as he spurred his horse to a gallop, passing by Wolf Wechsler and his men. He stormed into the darkening night. His horse's hoof falls grew fainter as Spears fled the ranch.

The remaining men in the Spears group hesitated, silent, unsure how to proceed. Finally, as one, they loped their mounts after their leader. They avoided looking towards the rancher or his men. Their will to fight seemed to have fled with their leader.

Once the group was underway, Boyd lowered his rifle, releasing the hammer carefully.

Wolf Wechsler rode forward until he towered over Boyd. He glared at his grandson.

"Why do you have to cause trouble for me? I asked you to do one thing, and you had to do it the hard way. We don't need any more trouble with the Städtbewohnen."

Boyd's eyes lowered until he looked at his dusty boots.

Hans watched the conflict between his grandfather and Boyd fearfully. He was a continual source of punishment for his elder cousin. He worshipped Boyd with the adoration of a hero. Now he suffered, knowing Boyd would pay for championing him in a fight he caused through his own mischief, likely with severe punishment from their grandfather.

Wechsler reached out a bony hand.

"Give me that rifle then help the men with the horses. We'll talk about this later. I'm tired and hungry."

Boyd handed the carbine to his grandfather, moving to obey. He stopped short of leaving.

The old man held the rifle in a manner that kept Boyd's grip upon it. He favored the youngster with a withering look. When he spoke, his voice quivered with anger.

"You could have gotten Hans killed. For some reason he looks up to you. He armed himself against those men. What if he had been shot?"

Wechsler glared at Boyd with real hatred.

"I don't want you in the house tonight," he said. "You act like an animal; you will sleep with them. Komst du, Hans."

As the old man turned away, Boyd watched his grandfather, trying to understand why the old patriarch felt such hatred for his own grandson.

Finally, Boyd turned away. His shoulders hunched with his discomfiture, and his heels dragged the ground, raising a small dust cloud as he headed towards the stables.

Hans dutifully followed his grandfather into the house, casting guilty glances over his shoulder towards Boyd.

4

TIM WILLIAMSON SMILED AT WILLIAM Scott Cooley who sat across from him on his porch. The broad-shouldered young man sipped strong whiskey with a careful steadiness, indicating he was unfamiliar with spirits.

Williamson was in an unusually fine humor. To his eye the day was bright, and he shared a rare moment with a long absent trail partner.

His companion grinned sheepishly through the vapors of the liquor.

"What is this stuff?" he asked. "Kerosene?"

"Kerosene's kissing cousin," Williamson replied with a teasing smile. "I'm pleased you never took up drinking. The good Lord knows you had every right."

Cooley surveyed the ranch house, nearby stables, and the paddocks beyond. Cattle grazed in an adjoining pasture.

"You've come a long way, Tim," he observed, taking another gingerly pull from his glass.

Williamson lifted his glass, consuming its contents with a gesture.

"Billy," he said with pride. "Our path is the same. I am only a few miles further along the road you yourself are on. I've always believed in you. I even agree with your reasons for leaving the Texas Rangers Frontier Battalion. You needed room to grow into those shoulders of yours."

Williamson favored the younger man with another toothy grin. His was the manner of a proud parent.

"I see great things in you – Mary does too. She said so just now when I fetched the bottle from inside the house. You have always been like a son to me – and her."

Cooley ducked his head at the praise, a flush reddening his suntanned skin from his forehead into his shirt collar. It was obvious he was uncomfortable with the attention and the praise.

"You know the feeling's returned, Tim," he said almost boyishly. "You believed in me when no one else would. You took me on my first trail drive, taking Army beeves into Kansas. You made a full-fledged cowman out of me. You have always been fair and even handed, no matter that I was green. For that you will always have my loyalty and support."

"Well, you ain't green anymore, Billy, but your words mean everything to me."

Williamson leaned back to survey the handsome youngster. Cooley had changed much since he last saw him. He was no longer an awkward boy. He was a tall, rawboned cowboy with big, calloused hands, and a labor hardened frame.

Williamson poured another drink as he looked Cooley over critically. He leaned back, satisfied with what he saw. He raised the glass to drink, pausing at the last moment.

"I am happy you moved back, even if you are a full day's ride away."

He emptied the glass once again.

"You'll do fine in Menard County," he said, his throat tight from the bitter drink. "At least you're closer than Kansas, or Oklahoma, or even Jack County."

"Like you said," Cooley agreed. "Maybe I can make a go of the cattle business like you have."

"Maybe make a go?" Williamson scoffed.

He leaned closer, his face serious, his tone confident.

"William Scott Cooley. That is a name we will all come to know in time."

"Let up on me now, Tim," Cooley begged. "I can't take much more without bustin' out in tears like a schoolgirl."

Both men laughed heartily at the idea of big Scott Cooley weeping about anything.

"Alright, alright, son," Williamson said, wiping tears of mirth from his own eyes. "I can't help myself. I often think about our adventures together and here you show up like a specter from a dream."

Williamson sighed as he caught his breath from the laughter. He looked askance, gathering his wits. When he looked at the other again, mischief was clear in his demeanor. He feigned pity for the other.

"Mary will have supper on soon enough and you'll have more to hear from her," he warned the other jokingly.

"Good god," Cooley exclaimed, extending the empty glass. "Pour me another, Tim. I'm gonna need it."

Williamson filled the glass to the top. He eyed Cooley for a long moment with a singular intent, his humor sobered for the moment. Refilling his own glass, he leaned back in his stiff-backed chair.

"I gotta know, Billy. Your uncle told me once, when I met you, you and him, and his brother were trailing a couple dozen Indians for horse stealin'. I can never keep it straight. How many of them Injuns did you scalp? Beau said all of 'em."

"Why do you always ask me about that time?" Cooley complained with real embarrassment. "I've told that story to you at least ten times."

"And the tally changes every time," Williamson replied, failing to hide his efforts to tease his friend. "You said none the first time, and that number has moved around between one and eight over the years."

"Well, whatever I told you the last time holds true today," Cooley replied stubbornly. "How's that do for you?"

Cooley's manner changed and he displayed a curious gravity as he spoke.

"I don't do that no more, Tim. I'm ready to let the past stay in the past."

"The work you did with the Rangers ain't gonna stay in the past, Scott. Last time I saw Captain Dan Roberts in town, he asked after you. He retold that story about how them Indians ambushed your unit at Lost Valley. Despite your watering down the details, he claims your actions saved a lot of men that day. He said you rushed into that Indian camp like a banshee – that's his word – and single handed spoiled them redskins' will to continue their war party on them settlers from Nebraska."

Williamson's gaze rested upon Cooley as he emerged from his reverie.

The younger man's expression was much changed. His smile was gone. In its place was a dark look. The target of his frown was not his companion. Rather, he seemed to look within himself, disliking what he found.

Williamson cleared his throat in an effort to soften the edge to his questions.

"Maybe the past is the past, Billy," he agreed sympathetically.

A long silence followed until Mary opened the door a crack. She peeked out past the door at the two men. Seeing she wasn't interrupting, she stepped onto the porch.

"Supper is ready. Come and get it before I throw it out."

Cooley's manner changed immediately. His smile returned, pulling his face into its previously beaming visage.

The men followed Mary into the house. The table was set with candles and a spray of wildflowers in the center.

Dinner was a simple affair of steak and greens, but it was received with hearty appreciation and approval, their former joviality returning.

Cooley swallowed a big bite of steak.

"I hear the Germans are getting tired of the Anglos rustling their cattle," he said. "I've seen some questionable brands as near as Menardville. Them cattle thieves are getting mighty bold if they are selling stock closer than Kansas

City. You reckon the Dutch will form an association like the ranchers in Menard County?"

Williamson shrugged, shoveling a large slice of juicy steak into his maw.

"They tried to put one together last year," he said through a mouth full of food. "It didn't go well with the former county sheriff. There are more rustlers than there are cattle to steal. No one sees much in it – except them Dutch invaders."

Mary cleared her throat, wiping her mouth with an embroidered napkin.

"That's no kind of talk to have at the dinner table, Tim."

She cleared her throat again. Her focus shifted to their guest, her attention fully upon Cooley.

"Scott, have you met a nice girl since you moved to Menardville? I can make some introductions if you like."

"Let the boy be, Mary," Williamson scolded with no heat to his words. "The best girl from these parts is already spoken for."

Mary blushed, covering her face in embarrassment. She smiled into her napkin, her eyes wide with pleasure.

"Some things never change no matter how long I'm gone," Cooley observed. "You two still talk like you just met. If I had designs on a girl, she would struggle to meet the standards I see with you two."

Williamson nodded at his wife.

"You're right Billy. There is only one, and I'm glad she made the promise before she knew about all my bad habits."

Cooley grinned at Mary's discomfort at being thrust into the center of attention. He rescued her from further embarrassment.

"I have enjoyed your kindness and hospitality, but I must return to my ranch."

Williamson looked up in surprise.

"It's a late start," he warned. "You're welcome to stay the night, Billy."

"Thank you for the offer. I was passing through when I decided to stop. With a new ranch and pressing business needs attending to, I must get back."

Mary stood. She smoothed her dress then stepped forward, taking one of Cooley's big hands in hers.

"Promise me you won't wait so long until your next visit, Billy."

Cooley nodded and Mary released him. He donned his hat, beaming at her.

"I promise. Thank you for your kindness and hospitality."

He looked at Williamson.

"Both of you," he added.

5

Hans opened the window to his bedroom. He ground his teeth at the slight noise the movement caused. His senses were heightened because of the rules he broke by leaving the house after dark without permission. He scanned the dark paddocks and outbuildings beyond the ranch house. Stealthily, he crept along the side of the ranch house, moving forward in a crouched posture. He gave no thought to why he moved along in that manner any more than he considered the possibility of being caught out of his room so late at night.

He rounded the corner of the house, passing by the kitchen door with a fearful glance, as if an unseen sentry might leap from cover with a loud triumphant yell. Instead, he continued towards the stables with silent steps.

He released the wooden catch and pushed the stables door with a steady pressure. The hinges groaned under the ponderous weight of the large door. Hans opened the door only wide enough for him to slip inside. He entered the deeper darkness of the stables. He spied the glow of a lantern radiating dimly from the mow above the stables. A horse blew as he approached the ladder leading to the mow. Hans climbed the ladder, peeking over the top edge where Hans saw Boyd working at something, sparing him only a casual glance as the youngster gained the planked floor of the mow.

At closer range, it was clear to see Boyd cleaning a black Colt revolver, The worn leather holster lay nearby, the bullet loops filled with extra ammo.

Hans took a seat beside Boyd, leaning against the wall as did his elder cousin. He plucked a hay straw and stuck it in his mouth. He considered Boyd's labor over the pistol for moment before he broke the silence.

"Is that Martinez's old gun?" Hans asked.

"Grandfather will tan you for coming out here after dark."

"Only if you tell him."

"I should after all the trouble you cause me."

"You're right to say so."

Boyd gave Hans a covert grin as he loaded the pistol and returned it to the holster. Boyd sat back, his thoughts his own for the moment.

"Do you still practice with it?"

Boyd watched Hans for a moment as though he struggled to concentrate on the boy's words.

Finally he replied in a way that seemed like he sat his thoughts aside for the conversation.

"Not enough to talk about."

"Do you miss him - Martinez?"

Boyd looked at his bare feet, dusty with hay dust.

"Sometimes."

"He liked you."

Boyd thought about the old Mexican gunfighter turned ranch hand.

"Is that right?"

"He said so."

Boyd rubbed his eyes, fatigue reaching for him.

"I liked him too," Boyd said with a yawn.

"I wish he taught me fightin, and shootin, and trackin."

Boyd roughed Hans' hair affectionately.

"I'll pass on what he taught me when you're big enough."

Hans bristled, sitting straighter. He gave Boyd a hard look.

"I am already big."

"Compared to what?"

Hans struggled as he conjured someone with whom he could compare.

"I'm nearly as big as Chlodwig."

"Your cousin is nearly twice your size."

Hans pouted as he returned to his leaning posture.

Boyd grinned at him again, again unseen by his cousin.

"But he doesn't have your sand. I'd lay to that with anyone."

Hans smiled beneath his unkempt locks, obviously pleased by the limited praise.

"You'll see someday, when I pull you out of a tight spot. I'll save you someday."

Boyd didn't register enough seriousness at this bold prediction, causing Hans to pout once again. Boyd leaned towards Hans, speaking in a serious tone.

"Maybe Hans. Like I said, you got sand, I'll give you that."

"Hans!"

Both cousins stiffened at the sound of a woman's voice, surprisingly near the stables.

"That's ma," Hans whispered.

"Hans. Get to bed - now."

Hans grabbed Boyd's hand.

"I ain't small Boyd. You'll see."

"Go to bed before we both get in trouble."

Hans squeezed Boyd's big hand before disappearing down the ladder.

Boyd heard the stables door swing to then footfalls as Hans returned to his house at the near end of the home pasture.

6

RUSSEL SPEARS AND A SMALL contingent of townsfolk milled around the front of the court-house. The morning was cool for early Spring, but the fair weather did little to brighten the foul mood of those gathered before the courthouse entrance.

Sheriff Clark entered the fenced boundary of the court-house property. At the front door, he reined in his mount, looking over the group with a suspicious eye.

Without a word, he stepped down from his horse and moved to the front door. He entered then moved to an in-side entrance with a wooden painted sign over it reading 'Sheriff.' He unlocked the door to his office and entered, closing the door behind him.

Outside, Spears raised a hand at the rising protests from his companions.

"It's best if I go in alone," he said. "The sheriff is their man, but he's fair. I'll holler if I need help."

Spears climbed the steps and went inside the court-house. He entered the Sheriff's office. Clark was busy sweeping the floor in front of his desk.

"I heard about the fight yesterday," the Sheriff said by way of heading off the conversation.

He continued working the floor over with the wispy broom.

"Morning, Sheriff," Spears said as if he hadn't heard him. "I need your help."

"Why don't we just let it drop?" Clark advised, pausing in his labor. "Boys will be boys. Besides, I heard your two sons was with John's boy, ganging up on that little tow-headed German sprat. If things had gone different, I might be calling on your house this morning."

"That Wechsler kid is a full-grown man. He jumped my boys from the crowd. You ain't gonna allow a man to beat on schoolboys, are you?"

Clark resumed his sweeping.

"Boyd Wechsler is a troublemaker," Clark agreed thoughtfully. "But he ain't more than a kid himself."

Clark again paused in his labor to look Spears in the eye.

"What do you want me to do, Russel?" he asked gruffly. "Arrest him?"

"That's exactly what I want you to do."

Sheriff Clark leaned the broom against the wall and took a seat at his desk. He leaned back in the stiff-backed chair, stretching the early morning out of his joints.

"I'll send Deputy Worley out to the Wechsler place. He'll have a talk with the old man and his grandson."

Spears snorted his ridicule of the idea.

"You ain't even gonna go out there yourself?"

"Russel, I'm a busy man. I was elected to put an end to this rustling problem. I don't have time to get in the middle of a schoolyard scuffle."

"We know you were elected by the goddam Germans, John. But we got just as much right as they do. If you won't uphold the law, we'll have to do it ourselves."

"Don't talk to me that way, Spears," Clark said with unmistakable gravity. "I am a duly elected peace officer. I will dispense the law around here."

Spears' jaw worked as he tried mightily to control his temper.

Clark watched him suffer for a moment before he finally said, "Alright, I'll drop out there this afternoon."

"I want him in jail," Spears said bitterly. "At least make a show of upholding the law, even if you don't feel the need to enforce it."

Clark rewarded Spears' disrespect with a dangerous look.

Despite his ill temper, Spears felt his short hairs stand tall. The look in the lawman's eyes seemed cold and deadly, more like a criminal than an officer of the law. Spears, like many others in town, knew nothing of the man's past. He arrived one day with the support of the German ranchers and won a steeply one-sided election. His penchant for siding with the German immigrants when enforcing the law smacked of paid favoritism. None of this was provable, but Spears' suspicions were aligned with Anglo sentiment in town.

Spears' thoughts were interrupted by the growl of the Sheriff's next words.

"I've been about as mannerly as I am going to be. I heard your complaint and I have agreed to act on it. Get out of my office, Spears."

It was midafternoon when Sheriff Clark arrived at the Wechsler Ranch. He tied his horse to the rail at the front porch of the long house. He cast a look around the ranch buildings, noticing there was little activity near the paddocks or the cattle pens.

Emma Wechsler appeared in the doorway as the Sheriff approached.

He paused at the sight of the blonde daughter of Wolf Wechsler. He was smitten with her, had been since his arrival to Mason, but his advances had thus far been summarily rejected.

From habit, she wiped her hands on her apron and tucked an unruly hair strand behind her ear as she waited for him to mount the stairs to the porch.

Instead, Clark waited at the bottom of the stairs, giving Emma a long look.

She was relieved he came no closer, but his lingering gaze caused her discomfort. She was aware of his desire for her, and even if his reputation as a man who took advantage of women was not known, something about him was repellant to her. Her instincts compelled her to avoid the man or, when she was unable to do so, maintain a vigilant caution around him.

"How are you, Ms. Wechsler?" he asked with a solicitous smile. "I guess the men are working the young stock today."

She was uncomfortable with Clark calling out her vulnerability. She was alone and helpless. She attempted to comport herself with direct talk, taking comfort in the distance between them.

"They are indeed, Sheriff. What can I do for you?"

"You are looking mighty comely this morning, Emma. You could invite me in, and we can talk inside the house."

Clark had been accused recently of a questionable encounter with a neighbor, Beatrice Upton, whose husband was away on business. Emma knew Beatrice Upton as a loyal and kind wife, and a devoted mother to her four children.

Upon returning, her husband, Quinn Upton, confronted Clark who admitted he and Beatrice had been romantically involved. But Clark insisted the interaction was not forced nor unwanted. The result was Upton beat Beatrice and ran her out of the county.

"Did you come here to insult my honor, Sheriff? I don't invite strangers into my home unattended."

"I'm hardly a stranger, Emma. Besides, I don't see how you could take what I said other than complimentary."

"There are rumors about your conduct around unprotected women."

"Don't tell me you are like them gossipy biddies who believe that was against her wishes."

"This is not proper conversation, Sheriff. State your business or leave now."

Clark was silent for a moment, his smile fading at the bald-faced accusation. He felt a strong attraction for Emma. He believed he could win her over if given a fair opportunity.

As he delayed, Emma grew more uncomfortable with the way he looked her over, and the time he was taking to make up his mind to do whatever he was considering doing.

She was an instant from slamming the door in his face and arming herself at the rifle case when he finally spoke.

"Is your boy about?"

"He's with the hands. Only us women and children are left here. Is there anything else you are needing?"

"I wouldn't say no to water, thank you."

Emma looked at him with measured caution. Against the urging of her instincts, she chose courtesy over defense.

"Take a seat on the porch and I'll bring you some."

Emma disappeared from the doorway as she moved to fetch the water. The urge to arm herself was almost irresistible. She felt a moment of panic as she filled a tin with water from the stone drinking crock. Steeling her resolve, she returned to find Clark had not moved from his position near the stairs.

Relieved he had not advanced onto the porch, she regained some of her fading confidence. She stepped onto the porch and handed Clark the tin of water.

Clark drank the contents dry, appraising her over the rim of the cup. With a contented sigh, he lowered the empty cup.

"Now did that hurt one bit, Emma?"

Emma frowned at his familiar manner. She received the cup and retreated to the comparative safety of the doorway.

"Is this about Hans and the Spears boys?" she asked.

"This is about your boy. He jumped them two Spears boys. Russel Spears is up in arms about it. He asked me to do something."

Emma considered the Sheriff's words. Neither Boyd nor Hans had spoken of the fight, but she doubted it had occurred as the Sheriff claimed.

"What do you plan to do?" she asked.

"I ain't decided yet, Emma. Maybe we can work it out now and avoid any unpleasantness."

"Work it out now?" she asked with renewed anxiety.

"I don't want to cause you any trouble, Emma. You know how I feel about you. I only want what's best for your son."

"It sounds like you are looking out for your own interests, Sheriff."

"That may be a small part of it, Emma, but I still have a job to do. I can't show any more favoritism than I already have."

"What favoritism do you think you have shown to me or my son, Sheriff?"

"Oh, come on Emma. Your boy has earned a reputation as a bad seed – or at least everyone thinks he is headed that way."

"That is just talk, John…"

"Thank you for calling me by my given name, Emma. Talk is how laws are made. Talk is how guilty verdicts are found. And talk is the reason you stay away from town. Talk is all we got in this part of the world. I'm just saying I can't protect you and yours if you don't allow me to."

"I am not going to be able to help you as you think I should. I don't feel that way about you. I never will, John. I don't mean to put a hard edge on it, but I have to be true to my feelings."

"If not me, then who, Emma?" he asked with obvious exasperation. "You're gonna go to seed out here alone with no man to look after. You don't want to end up with one of Wolfgang's saddle tramps, do you?"

He looked at her with a stern and meaningful expression.

"Your reputation will never die," he said, pausing for a moment before continuing. "But I don't care about any of that. The past is the past. I'm an important man. I've got position and title. No one would dare say a foul word as long as you were my wife."

Emma took a sharp breath. She was struck off balance by his candor and direct manner. What must he think of her feeling comfortable talking about her reputation so openly? She had born Boyd out of wedlock and the Sheriff, who only arrived to town recently, spoke of her reputation as if it were as casual a subject as bad weather. He discussed her shame without regard for the hurt it caused her. The idea he thought to rescue her with a marriage proposal was not just insulting, it mocked her and anything she may have accomplished despite the stigma of raising a bastard child.

"I'll tell my father you came by Sheriff," she said coldly. "Is there any other thing you want me to tell him?"

Clark shook his head.

"I'm trying to be a good man to you despite your foolish mistakes. You won't find anyone else of station who will treat you like a regular woman considering your tainted reputation."

Emma's mouth fell open. She could conjure no words to counter his insensitivity. She felt as humiliated as if he had forced his way upon her.

"Leave now," was all she could utter.

"I gotta see Wechsler and talk to your boy before I go back," he said, disregarding the gravity of their conversation. "Are they in the south pasture?"

Emma was stunned how easily he altered his manner. One moment he claimed to be deeply concerned about her, making callous observations, and offering marriage as a solution. At her refusal, he reverted to his former casual self, returning to business as usual with no consideration for how he had hurt her.

She fought tears, her face a frozen mask.

"The creek pasture, west of here," she said woodenly.

Emma turned to leave.

"Emma," Clark said to her back.

Emma paused, turning towards the Sheriff. Her tears were near, and couldn't be denied much longer.

"You are a fine woman. I think about you often. At least give us some thought when you're not so unsettled about your son."

"Good day, Sheriff," she said, passing from the door and into the house, sobs finally taking control.

Clark easily located the calving party. The young herd and the laboring men kicked up a tall cloud of dust. As he got closer, the cattle's bawling and crying sounded like the hoarse voices of anguished children.

He spied Wolfgang Wechsler in the saddle, pointing and yelling at his men. Clark watched as grunting, sweating riders pulled calves to the branding fire where the livestock bawled in pain as other men put the iron to them, burning away hair, and cooking the brand into their flesh.

Clark pulled up beside the rancher who seemed displeased with the scene.

Wolf glanced at him briefly but remained focused on the activities around him.

"Get those few into the squeeze chute," he ordered one of the men. "We're running out of daylight."

"Herr Wechsler," Clark said. "We need to have a talk about your grandson, Boyd."

Wechsler looked at the Sheriff again with the same passing glance before once more surveying his men.

"Herr Wechsler," Clark continued "He's not a child anymore. I can't sit by as he goes to town and fights with schoolboys. A large group of townsfolk were at my door when I got there this morning. They are in a lather for me to do something about the fight."

Wechsler nodded.

"What do you plan to do, Sheriff?" he asked without looking at him.

"Not much," Clark replied mildly. "How does a night in the jail sound? The Townies will see I did something, and the boy learns a lesson he'll take into manhood."

This time, Wechsler gave the Sheriff a long look, weighing his words. Finally, he answered, changing his grip on the reins.

"Take him, then."

Clark hesitated for a moment, thinking Wechsler was baiting him. He hadn't expected so easy a time in collecting the boy.

Wechsler touched a spur to his horse. Clark followed him towards the milling activity near the branding fires. Boyd stoked the flames, heating the branding irons until they were red hot. His uncle Ernst worked the fire beside him. Verner Koenig returned from the squeeze chute for a fresh iron, looking curiously at the Sheriff.

"Boyd," Wechsler commanded in a stentorian voice. "Collect your horse. The Sheriff needs you to go with him to town."

Boyd stood up straight, a poker stick in his hand. He assessed the Sheriff with a critical expression.

Clark didn't like the look the youth gave him.

"Step to, son," he said with authority. "I don't want to be out after nightfall."

"Sir," Boyd said to his grandfather. "You're going to see me arrested because I stood up for your grandson? Do you know what they would have done to little Hans if I didn't step in?"

The old man shook his head, unsurprised but weary at the boy's disobedience. He leaned forward in the saddle towards Boyd and spoke with an intolerant tone and menacing glare.

"Don't sass me, boy. Get to it."

Boyd dropped the poker, pressed his hat tighter on his head, and moved to his horse.

He swung into the saddle, the gelding stepping out as he did. Clark nudged his mount until they rode abreast of one another. They rode to the edge of the fenced pasture in silence.

Boyd opened the gate then closed it once they passed through.

Clark observed the youth who paid him no mind. Boyd rode along as though he hadn't a care. Perhaps he understood the uselessness of arguing, or maybe he failed to understand the gravity of his deeds.

"You shouldn't have beaten the Spears boys," he said.

Boyd made no response.

"Russel Spears wants your hide nailed to the courthouse wall. There's no telling what he is trying to get the town folk to do about this."

To the Sheriff's surprise. Boyd snapped an angry look at him. His voice came with a bitterness more suited to the situation.

"I defended my cousin against three boys who thought they would bully a German kid hardly big as a girl. What was I supposed to do, Sheriff?"

Now it was Clark's turn to be silent.

When Boyd and the Sheriff arrived in town, the dusty streets of Mason were dark with the shade of dusk. Clark led Boyd into his office, locking him in the first of the two barred cells. Boyd moved to the back wall and leaned against it, scowling at the sheriff.

"I'll stable your horse for you," Clark said mildly. "All you got to do is cool your heels for a day or two and you'll be back home."

Boyd made no comment to the announcement. Instead, he pulled off his hat and mopped his brow with a sleeve.

Clark left the office to care for the horses.

A plate of food was delivered from the hotel restaurant. Boyd ate in silence, awaiting nightfall. He dared not relax his vigilance as long as the hour was early. At least after dark the townies would no longer worry him, and he would sleep.

7

JARVIS HUTTON SAT THE SADDLE OF A lump headed, bald faced gelding. He peered into the darkness towards a distant ranch house. His men rounded up a half dozen yearlings in the small pasture beyond the little house. For he and his men, this was an often-repeated operation. With this experienced crew, he anticipated nothing that would alert the occupants in the house of their presence, but he was careful by nature.

There was no talking amongst his gang of rustlers. They knew their jobs and went about their work with practiced efficiency. The terrain was clear of brambles and limb falls which might otherwise cause a horse to stumble or falter. The cattle were docile as pets, making them easy to drive.

In anomalous silence the rustlers moved their gathered stock past their leader and towards a dry creek bed some fifty yards distant. Jarvis took his place at the rear of the herd, staying far enough back to avoid eating too much trail dust.

Their work this night was one of many repeated as often as they were able to sell their pilfered stock. He and his gang worked their enterprise west and north across the Texas frontier.

Jarvis maintained a consistent direction of travel, despite the misgivings of his men. He alone knew their destination. He alone understood the grim task ahead of him. Authorities or a posse using their predictable path to capture them was a secondary consideration. North and west took Jarvis and his men where he would find Wolfgang Wechsler, the man he would kill for the murder of his brother. Nothing else counted. Nothing else was important enough to move him from his path.

As it so often did, the memory of his dead brother again caused him profound grief. No matter how he resisted the weakness of useless emotion, he again felt anger warm his insides. It did not serve him to waste time and effort on a discomfort he would remedy soon enough, but he could not control the memories or the familiar bright flash of desire for revenge; a restless impatience for the day his anguish would end in the death of the man behind it all. The pain drove him to exhausting his days with a tireless energy. As always, he experienced an internal unrest of cold emotions combined with hot rage. His inner turmoil stung him like a dervish wind, lifting and driving particles of sand and nettle spines, prickling his insides.

He gave only a small portion of his attention to the slow movement of the cattle herd as it descended into the draw. He detected no sign of alarm from within the ranch house nor any sign of a covert pursuit. His men would push the stock all night. By the time the rancher discovered the loss, the yearlings would be stalled in a holding pen, ready for shipment north.

In a returning reverie, Jarvis recalled the day he began his confinement in the Walls Prison in Huntsville. Kyle had gripped his older brother's hand as two Texas State Police officers dragged Jarvis towards the prisoner transport.

"I won't forget what you done for me, Jarvis," Kyle promised. "I'll stay by your side until you get out."

"Step back," one of the officers commanded Kyle, successfully pulling Jarvis away from his grasp.

Jarvis never expected Kyle to honor that pledge. His younger brother was driven by the same weaknesses, driving Jarvis. Their shared urges were the chief contributors to his conviction and incarceration.

Kyle killed a cow puncher over a back-room card game. Jarvis' habit of protecting his younger brother and his participation in the coverup created an environment where the evidence pointed to Jarvis as the killer.

The pronouncement of a twenty-year sentence was unusually lenient in a murder conviction, but the victim was a known thug and gunman and there was some doubt whether self-defense could be argued in the case. As was typical in a Texas courtroom, without the death penalty as an option, the judge handed out a harsher than usual sentence to dissuade others who might take a life, no matter the provocation.

For a time, Kyle managed to make every visitor date without fail. The Walls Prison allowed one visitor day each month. Kyle was his only outside contact.

During those visits, their time together was precious to Jarvis, filled with his younger brother's recounting of his exploits and near catastrophes with the law. The visits passed as quickly as the ill-gotten gains Kyle received from the execution of the crimes he detailed in his many wild stories.

Those precious visits continued uninterrupted for two years until one day Kyle failed to show. As Jarvis saw it, his brother's missing a visit was long overdue. Kyle's adventures took him far afield. His livelihood was not a long-term proposition at a distance, much less near a busy prison town. Travel was arduous even at close hand. If an exploit kept his brother far afield, it was sensible he might miss a visit.

Kyle's previous visit was filled with stories of a surplus of beeves, ripe for the taking in Mason County. Also, there was a girl. Jarvis knew from Kyle's narratives that Mason was several hundred miles distant from the prison. The travel time combined with the increased complication of a love interest nearly guaranteed missed visits.

So, with understandable forgiveness, Jarvis accepted his brother missed their visit because of his preoccupation with this new love. Despite his years in prison, Jarvis clearly remembered the power of the fairer sex and its effect on a young man.

The first missed visit from his younger brother stretched into two, then six until the interval equaled a year. Jarvis' worst fears seemed to have come to pass. He had taken the blame for his brother. He served his brother's sentence. How easily had he been discarded. No more than the tug on a heartstring by a pretty girl had been enough to dislodge the weight of the debt his brother owed.

A slim shadow of a doubt held Jarvis back from the precipice of despair. He drew a strange comfort from the possibility Kyle had been arrested, or worse. At least that outcome would exonerate his brother from a less honorable excuse for his absence.

As the years passed him by, and those moments came when Jarvis felt the most betrayed, his suspicions Kyle had come to grief at the hands of the law buoyed his flagging confidence in the mettle of his younger brother.

Sadly, there was an almost quixotic aspect of a Texas prison he could not deny. Huntsville was a town built upon the convoluted relationship between lawmen and the lawless. He learned early in his incarceration that there were no secrets kept when it came to the fate of an outlaw. If Kyle had fallen to the law, or perished at the hand of a lawman, Jarvis would have learned of it in short order.

Despite his confidence the eager reports of boastful lawmen, and criminals brought to justice, would bear some news of Kyle's fate or whereabouts. Years of silence passed before Jarvis finally discovered what had become of his brother.

One Summer afternoon, more than a decade prior to his release, Jarvis loitered in the temporary confines of a holding cell. He awaited an audience with the warden. It was a rare occurrence that a housed inmate was held in the prison's receiving area, reserved for newly convicted criminals.

Jarvis was known as a compliant inmate, seldom causing trouble. He was popular amongst the guards and prison staff due to his light humor and genuine manner. In reward for his exemplary conduct, he was to meet with the warden for the likely approval for a trustee position. Although the trustees position involved continuous labor and enough exposure to freedom to torture the prisoner, the scant privileges of a prison trustee was preferable to the life of the unrewarded inmate.

While Jarvis awaited his audience with the warden, Captain Leander McNelly of the Texas State Police brought in a man named Clarence Karnes, suspected in the widely publicized killing of the Freedman, Sam Jenkins.

With the newly signed Emancipation Proclamation dominating the news of the day, the killing of a former slave was handled with remarkable political expedience.

Captain McNelly remanded the suspect to temporary custody at the Walls, returning to his manhunt in pursuit of three additional suspects in the murder. Karnes was placed in the holding cell with Jarvis.

The accused suspect, Clarence Karnes, voiced his displeasure at his arrest and imprisonment. He took advantage of the company of his lone cellmate to lodge his objection to being detained.

Like everyone imprisoned there, he denied any wrongdoing. Unlike most inmates in the Walls, his claims of innocence proved truthful, and he would be released soon after the other three suspects were captured and confessed to the crime.

During his brief time with Karnes, Jarvis endured an unwelcome narrative where Karnes expressed his innocence at length and at a volume sufficient to inform all in the front offices he had no part at all in the crime. At length, a threatening word from an irritable and particularly formidable looking guard reduced the ferocity of the newcomer's passionate outcry and he begrudgingly resigned himself to settle in for a prolonged stay.

With a forced calm settling over them, Jarvis was surprised he relished the conversation. Even as it was tedious, Karnes' unceasing narrative helped pass the time, a benefit rarely enjoyed by a prisoner.

It took little prompting to encourage his new cellmate to take up other subjects, to which Karnes complied with equal zeal.

Pleased with his cellmate's display of interest, he favored Jarvis with tales of his travels around the region, recounting his many exploits.

As much as Jarvis at first craved the time eroding talk, after hours of Karne's nonstop chatter, Jarvis again grew weary of the incessant prattling of the new man. Jarvis regretted encouraging him as much as he had, though it took little to get Karnes to open up.

How long could the man talk? If he would not tire from wasted energy, would he not run out of stories to tell, or lies to make up?

Although Jarvis suspected his next actions would ruin his chances for a desirable trustee position, he was maddened by the man's babbling. He desired a return of peaceful conditions. He was willing to pay any price necessary to put a violent end to the man's babbling monologue. The sacrifice seemed worth the satisfaction of silencing the garrulous newcomer.

Jarvis rose from the hard wooden bench, teeth set behind working jaw muscles. He moved stealthily, approaching the talker whose back was turned, quietly ready to attack.

Karnes' next words froze him mid motion.

"The best place for an ambitious man to make an easy score is in Mason County."

Jarvis' mouth worked silently as the name Mason sparked a long-unspoken memory. He remembered his brother mentioning Mason County while recounting his many exploits.

The tales Kyle recounted were many and told with a fire, driving them into Jarvis' memory as if they were his own. Hearing a stranger summon the same name in a conversation was not to be dismissed.

With a conscious effort, Jarvis relaxed his aggressive approach. He stood straighter – less threatening.

"Did you ever run into a man named Kyle Hutton during your time in Mason County," Jarvis asked as casually as he could.

Karnes turned, surveying Jarvis who unexpectedly was on his feet. Dismissing his fears, Karnes' mouth contorted around missing teeth as he struggled to recall.

Finally, he shook his head and said sadly, "That name don't ring a bell. Sorry pardner."

Jarvis was reluctant to miss this rare opportunity to learn the fate of his long absent brother.

"Maybe you saw him then," Jarvis said hopefully. "He's about my height but younger. Dark hair, bright blue eyes, almost like a girl's."

Karnes squinted, studying the other's face as though he read a book with small print. Finally, he slapped his knee as he remembered something.

"I worked calves with a fella that had them kind of eyes. He went by the moniker KB."

"Kyle Boyd Hutton," Jarvis filled in. "Middle named after his uncle in Nebraska."

Karnes beamed an ugly smile and nodded his pleasure at the newly found connection with this formerly silent stranger. Secretly, he had suspected violence from the man rather than pleasant conversation.

"That boy was a rare hand with a runnin' iron," Karnes said proudly.

Hunching his shoulders, Karnes looked around as if someone unseen to them might act on his information. He continued his narrative in a low conspiratorial voice.

"He could work a brand so slick even the owner couldn't positive identify his own mark in the new one."

"A runnin' iron," Jarvis repeated thoughtfully.

In their days of crime together, he and Kyle preyed upon unsuspecting travelers and held up the occasional mercantile. Rustling had never been a part of their work.

"Yeah," Karnes said. "He claimed to have learned it from some southern soldiers on the run as deserters. He told the story them troops was captured and hung."

Jarvis considered this new information silently. Finally, he spoke again.

"I heard he had a girl too."

"My my, she was just a doll," Karnes said wistfully. Then he added sadly, "Too bad she was his undoing."

"What do you mean?" Jarvis asked a bit too pointedly, causing Karnes to give him a more careful scrutiny.

"You ain't his uncle or something are you?"

Jarvis thought it best to continue cautiously.

"Sorry," he said as casually as he could. "Just an interested party. What became of KB?"

Karnes' enjoyment of sharing a tale with an interested audience overcame his caution.

"It looks like we got time for me to tell you the whole tale. KB and us, there was five of us altogether, but KB tended to take the lead; we worked the German ranches from Llano, to Loyal Valley, to Menard County. The richest haul was from them Pontotoc German Ranchers. Most of 'em got land grants near Comanche Creek and the Mason River in Mason County.

"None of them ranches are very large. Most run a couple dozen steers on small spreads. We weren't the first to get there, neither. Them German settlers had been rustled since before the war. During and after the war, vagabond southern soldiers took up the trade. Hell, before that, a goodly number of Indians had their way with Prussian beeves.

"KB decided we would follow suit. The problem with fishing a pond that's been fished out is them Germans committed a lot of work to keeping what was left of them herds safe. The herds was small enough the ranchers kept their cattle close to their houses, sitting watch all night. Them cattle was calm as house pets. The commotion of moving them tended to rouse the house. Our first tries went poorly.

"The worm turned when we came across one of them square head ranchers who built up his holdings through buying up failed land grants from other German settlers. He grew himself a respectable sized ranch off the misfortune of his foreign brethren. That old man - Wechsler was his name - has a few thousand acres on Comanche Creek. He runs thousands of beeves.

"Over the years, them Germans got deed to the finest grazing land in the county. Having to settle for poor ranch land didn't sit well with the native Anglos. The foreign ranchers weren't very popular with the native settlers and the law more often than not was Anglo men.

"We were one of a few crews working calves and yearlings out of his herd. Some of 'em got caught, but it was so common an enterprise for so many years nothing serious ever resulted. The customary practice was to let the rustlers go, maybe with a beating – sometimes not. Them Dutch ranchers were careful to limit their efforts in taking out their anger on the Anglo rustlers. Anglo lawmen punished rough treatment of rustlers with loss of Dutch stock and horses.

"We kept pretty flush in those days. KB had the dangerous habit of living it up in town, flashing his prosperousness as it served him. He raised a few eyebrows, but he never came to grief. One day he was in Ranck's Store when he met Emma Wechsler, pretty, blue-eyed daughter of old man Wechsler, the same rancher whose beeves we made our money from.

"If there was ever such a thing as love at first sight, this was it. Over time, she learned more about our operation from that lovestruck KB. At Emma's insistence KB slowed his work on the old man's herds. That didn't go well with the boys, but no one dared make a fuss to his face. He was not one to mutiny against. As you may know, he was hip deep in sand and pretty much fearless in a fight.

"One day KB showed up in camp with some unwelcome news. He said he was running off to San Antonio to elope with the Wechsler girl.

"Hell, we knew that was the end of the gravy train. He wasn't just the leader, KB was the heart of our gang. He planned everything and led the jobs. We stayed clear of posses mainly because he had a nose for trouble - which is the main reason the other gangs got pinched instead of us.

"As you can guess, the boys raised hell. We was all cashed out with no new job to refill our pockets. We ain't bankers in our line of work. We never saw the need to save our pennies when we had a steady diet of German cattle to keep us flush. No one could have predicted the breakup and we was all flat broke.

"It took some doing, but we finally talked KB into pulling one last job before he ran off with that Dutch girl. Looking back, maybe his nose for trouble failed him on that one.

"KB rushed together a plan to grab a few head before week's end. At first everything went as planned and we cut out a goodly sized herd when suddenly, we were surrounded by some twenty men.

"Well, they had us dead to rights. We was afraid. but didn't fret too much. We knew as long as we kept respectable in our talk, keeping our hands out where they could see 'em, everything would work out.

"Old man Wechsler himself was there. We was a little worried the old man was there personally. He was king of the German ranchers, and he wasn't afraid to rough up rustlers more than the other ranchers might. We expected a rough time of it, but instead, he let all of us go without a fuss, except for KB. We protested some because we suspected he was singling out our boss for good reason.

"They ran us off with threats to give us what KB was gonna get. We lit out, knowing what they would do if we stayed. Like I said before, rustling was common as sin, and if every rustler was hung, the Indians would have the frontier all to themselves in a week.

"I sneaked back and hid in the bushes. I arrived just in time to see the end. Wechsler told KB his daughter would never end up with a – he called him some German name – then he had one of his men toss a noose over a limb. They hung KB on the spot."

Jarvis paled noticeably but said nothing as the shock washed over him. He stared at Karnes with unseeing eyes, his imagination recreating the scene of his brother's murder.

Karnes seemed oblivious to the dramatic change transforming his companion. He scratched his head as he turned from Jarvis, leaning against the cell bars, looking down the narrow hallway towards the steel door at the end.

He spoke with his back to his cellmate.

"Later on," he continued casually. "I heard the old rancher was tipped off about the raid by one of his hands, a man named Koenig. Apparently, he had designs on Emma. She jilted him, passing him over for KB."

Jarvis collapsed onto the bench, overcome by grief. He looked at his hands helplessly as the story washed over him like a black wave. His brother was dead. He would serve the remainder of a sentence for the deeds of a dead man. He would have no reward for his sacrifice. He would never see his brother again.

After a pause, Karnes concluded by saying, "I also heard she was with child at the time. Maybe that was just a rumor, but it could be why the old man killed KB. I don't know for certain. Sure is sad."

Jarvis rose from his seat on the hard bench, unfurling like a serpent. He uttered a string of growled curses.

"You just left him there to die?" he snarled at the new-comer. "You cowardly snake."

Karnes turned a fearful face towards Jarvis. It held a look of dreadful expectation, a grim understanding of the error he had made in trusting to the safety of a shared story with a fellow sufferer. Realization of his vulnerability to ret-ribution in so confining an environment chilled him with foreboding.

Jarvis attacked Karnes with a deafening cry of fury. He rained blows upon the man as though Karnes were the cul-prit who had ended his brother's life. His bellowing cries drew the attention of the guards who rushed into the hold to restrain him, but not before an enraged Jarvis Hutton heaped upon the storyteller sufficient abuse to confine him to a hospital bed for a fortnight.

That new infraction eliminated any chance of the inmate becoming a trustee. Conversely, for his crime, the warden added two years to his remaining sentence.

Jarvis' dark recollections were interrupted as he helped his gang arrange the small herd for night travel. The wan-ing quarter moon provided scant light, but the country was wide open where they pushed the cattle through a broad grassy valley.

With an effort, Jarvis pushed from him the rising rage so often his companion when he fell into his frequent brown studies. He turned his attention to his crew.

To the left of the herd were the two Baccus brothers, Elijah the eldest, and Pete. Both were skilled at rustling. Jarvis brought them on in San Antonio de Bexar.

Riding lead was Caleb Hall, considered second in command after Jarvis. His preferred vocation was a highwayman, supplemented by the occasional second story job. Jarvis recruited him in a saloon in Blanco County.

Right of the herd rode Abe Wiggins, a tough raw-boned outlaw, known for his drunken rages. Beside him was the only member of the gang who was friendly towards him, Tom Turley, as mild as Wiggins was violent. Both were killers who said little about their past unless it was something they shared privately between themselves.

Jarvis and Charlie Johnson rode drag, pulling from a nearly empty whiskey bottle. Charlie was the most tenured member of the gang, falling in with Jarvis in Huntsville.

Jarvis drove the herd west by northwest towards the village of Loyal Valley. They travelled to a region known for its plentiful cattle, and a buyer for loose stock. The man they sought was a rancher named Williamson. They would sell the rustled stock to the rancher. As always, their route took them directly towards Jarvis' destiny, Mason County and the German rancher, Wechsler.

Jarvis again conjured the grisly image of his brother's death at Wechsler's hand. How the old man must have experienced a grim pleasure as Kyle kicked the air, twisting and writhing as he suffocated, his arms tied behind his back.

The image nearly drew a primal yell from the old outlaw. He yearned to feel the old man's throat in his hands. He would rip him to shreds with his bare hands.

8

IT HAD BEEN TWO YEARS SINCE EMMA WAS last in town, and only her second time in Mason since Boyd reached his mid-teens. She kept her eyes on her horse's bobbing ears as the reliable sorrel mare made her slow way to the jail house. Emma dismounted before the front door, tying her mount to the hitching post.

Emma was loathe to enter the Sheriff's office. Her emotions were occupied on one front by the many undisguised dark looks from the Städtbewohnen, and on the second, the questionable incarceration of her son. She most particularly dreaded continued entreaties and unwanted advances from the sheriff.

Fear gripped her as she entered the courthouse.

Sheriff Clark rose from behind his desk as she entered his office. He removed his hat reverently, his eyes searching her up and down.

She was a handsome woman, retaining her shape despite the hardships she bore on the ranch. Her blonde hair was tied in a bun and her blue eyes shone brightly with some as yet unrevealed emotion. Clark made no effort to hide his desire for her.

Boyd stood at the back of his cell, leaning against the brick wall. If he noticed, he gave no indication he was aware of the attention the Sheriff paid his mother.

"How do, Ms. Wechsler," Clark greeted her. "Aren't you all cornflower and goldenrod today. Your boy's safe and sound as promised. Did you give any thought to our conversation yesterday?"

"May I have a moment alone with my son?" she asked, ignoring his query.

Clark frowned at her disregard for his compliment. His manner sobered as his disappointment grew.

"I can't allow you to be alone with a prisoner, Emma…"

"He is my son," she cried, already at the end of her patience with the Sheriff's sham. "You said yourself you have him here for show. He is not a danger to you, me, or anyone else. Give me time with my son, Sheriff."

"Keep yourself in hand, Ms. Wechsler," he demanded, recovering some authority by donning his official mantle. "I'll grant your request this one time."

He retrieved his hat in an uncertain grip, then left the room by the front door.

Emma moved to the cell.

Boyd approached her, grabbing the bars in two big hands.

"Boyd, I'm sorry. Your grandfather is a stern man. He thinks you will learn a lesson from this."

"What do you think, Ma?"

Emma looked into her son's troubled blue eyes. His tone seemed to convey a deeper meaning. She knew instinctively he wanted to know how deeply she supported her father's decisions. She defaulted to the customs and dogma of her upbringing.

"I see some merit to his sentiments, but I don't agree with his methods."

Boyd leaned back from her. Disappointment was obvious in his expression.

"Besides," she said dismissively. "This is all a performance for the Städtbewohnen."

Boyd leaned towards her and spoke earnestly as though he alone saw the truth.

"This ain't gonna amount to anything with these Townies. They'll see this as less than a small atonement for us settling their country. The full price will be more than Grandfather - or you - are able to pay."

Emma grimaced.

The humiliation, which had built up over the years, overcame her. Boyd looked so much like his father. It seemed like Kyle spoke to her through him. She felt angry for bearing the brunt of what they had done together. She saw in her vision, a dead lover blaming her – leaving her alone to live a life of shame.

Tears welled in her reddening eyes, giving them an unnatural shine.

Boyd was surprised at his mother's sudden show of emotion. She was no stranger to the trouble boys got into. She was uncommonly strong, bearing life's hardships with little complaint. He was alarmed raw emotion betrayed her now. What was behind her discomfiture?

"I've already paid more than you will ever know," she cried softly. Her brow softened as she once again saw only her son. She extended a hand through the bars, touching his cheek tenderly.

"Please quell your anger, Boyd. Do this thing and return to the ranch. Just come home. I know what they have done to you. I see how it hurts you. You are not a child anymore. Everyone sees you as a man."

"Not Grandfather," he disagreed dejectedly.

"He sees you as a man too. Make no mistake. He treats you as he does because of what he sees you may become."

Boyd shook his head, backing away from his mother's touch.

"Promise me son you will keep your temper in hand. Promise me to come straight home after."

Boyd said nothing. He watched his mother, his expression changing to that of a dispassionate observer. He was confused by her varying moods. He needed distance between them to determine the truth behind her words.

Emma was experienced with his moods and his willful fits of independence. She accepted there was no remedy. He would make his own way, no matter her wishes or council.

She composed herself, ashamed of her weakness.

"Do you need anything?" she asked with improved decorum.

He remained silent, his thoughts his own for the moment.

Finally, she said, "I will see you in a day or two."

Emma turned her head as the front door opened. With the bang of the door and stomping of heavy feet, Russel

Spears entered ahead of Sheriff Clark. The latter was mid-admonishment as they arrived. The sudden increase in din filled the formerly quiet room.

"This is a law matter Spears..."

"Shut up Sheriff," Spears exclaimed with a violent gesture, dislodging Clark's restraining hand.

He approached the cell, ignoring Emma Wechsler.

"You're not getting out of this so easy," he yelled at Boyd. "We have you here and you ain't going anywhere until we are finished with you."

Emma stepped back from the big man, who crowded the cell front.

Boyd eyed Spears with a grim turn to his mouth. He watched Spears like a panther who sees raw meat.

"Mr. Spears," Emma began. "My son..."

Spears grabbed Emma by her dress collar and drew her close.

"Shut your mouth, you whore. We know all about you..."

Boyd leaped to the cell door, reaching for Spears. With his right hand, Boyd grabbed the back of his neck and slammed his head into the bars. With his left he pummeled Spears' face with four quick hard blows.

Emma was slammed against the bars in the fray, bumping her head soundly. She pushed away from the struggling men, straining against the bars. She fell to the floor, a red mark on her forehead.

Clark rushed to the cell, drawing his pistol. He trained the weapon on Boyd.

"Let go," he yelled. "Let go or I'll shoot."

Boyd didn't hesitate. He shoved Spears from him. The man fell inertly to the floorboards, blood dripping from his nose and mouth.

"Do you know what you have done?" Clark asked Boyd. "This can't be undone, Wechsler. You were on thin ice before…"

Boyd turned from him, returning to his leaning position at the back wall of his cell.

"Get him out of here before I kill him," Boyd warned with a tone carrying no anger. His advice was a matter of fact, not an impassioned threat.

"Nobody talks to my Ma that way, not in front of my face."

Emma rose from the floor. She shook her head and covered her mouth with a pale hand. She dared not trust herself. Instead, she fled from the room, leaving the front door ajar.

Sheriff Clark helped Spears to his feet.

Spears' red face was bruised and bloodied. Upon it was an ugly look the wounds could not hide.

"I'll kill you for this," Spears muttered, his hand dabbing at the blood under his nose. "Mark my words, these are your last days above ground."

Boyd watched the man with a fearless sneer.

Clark attempted to guide Spears with a clandestine pressure on his shoulders.

"Let go of me, Clark," Spears warned dangerously. "I ain't forgetting your part in this."

"What are you talking about, Russel?"

Rather than reply, Spears collected his hat from the floor and stormed out of the room.

Clark watched Spears depart, walking to the open door. The front door to the courthouse banged audibly as Spears stormed from the building. Clark closed the door quietly, drawing a deep breath before he turned towards Boyd, who watched impassively from his cell.

"You got your wish," Clark said. "There is no place left for you here in this town. I wouldn't risk a wager on your chances even on the ranch."

Obeying an impulse, Clark moved to his desk. He produced the jail keys. He returned to the cell and opened the door.

"Your horse is in the livery. Go home. Tell your grandfather what has happened here today. My advice is you get away from this place. You are old enough to go it alone from here. Maybe things will cool down for you in time. As I said, I wouldn't give a plug nickel for your chances if you stay."

He unlocked the cell door, letting it swing wide. He stepped aside, clearing the way for his prisoner.

Boyd left his office, then the courthouse, without a word. Outside, he saw no sign of his mother. She had mounted and fled the town without delay.

The Sheriff appeared on the front steps as Boyd walked away towards the livery stables.

Boyd looked back at the lawman but said nothing.

Notably, Clark detected no fear or regret in the youth. Rather, there was something of an air of calm confidence about Boyd. Where did it come from? The Sheriff tended to mark it up to hubris, the arrogance of a prideful child, ignorant of the dangers he faced.

Clark mused softly to himself, "That boy will end up at the end of a rope or the target for the bullets of a vengeful shooter."

Clark wanted to feel pity, but he couldn't.

He turned to the front door.

On a whim he paused, turning once more towards the youth. He watched the boy make his way across the expanse of the Square to the stables.

An insight struck him like a brief flash of light. He was suddenly consumed with a sense of prescience – a wave of inspiring foresight.

Was there more to this boy? Could the calm confidence he assigned to hubris be something more? Was the Sheriff's opinion the product of the prejudice of age, blinding him to a dawning reality? Was he witness to the beginning of something that would find record in campfire lore?

Clark shook his head at the foolishness of his passing fancy. More likely this Wechsler boy was just another bad seed, destined for an early grave.

Clark mused he was the product of a violent and unforgiving life. His pragmatism was rarely puzzled by a persona, and he was rarely given reason to doubt his intuition. Something about the Wechsler boy inspired both conditions. He felt a certainty Boyd Wechsler would come to no good. Many would pay with their lives when he realized his full potential as a bad man.

Clark loitered at the front of the courthouse, watching the few visible residents as they went about their business.

Boyd entered the stables, emerging moments later astride the roan gelding. He loped the horse casually out of town as if he hadn't a care.

With a shake of his head, Clark returned to his office.

9

LOYAL VALLEY WAS SO NAMED WHEN THE town leader and community Patriarch, John Meusebach, took control of the little German settlement of Cold Springs by founding a general store. He allocated a portion of the hastily built structure for use as a saloon and hotel.

His typical patron was any of the many locals comprising the growing number of German immigrants settling the area. He entertained the trade of the occasional passerby with equal familiarity.

Building the first and only commercial enterprise in the small village allowed him a measure of autonomy to mold the community hub to his liking.

Being a Union loyalist, he renamed the town to demonstrate his devotion to the principles of the north. The German immigrants shared no stake in the politics of the day and made no protest. Those who offered an opinion tended to agree with his loyalist views.

He faced no opposition in the renaming particularly because the name Loyal Valley summoned a pleasant vision of what the region could grow to be. To some, the new name was a prophecy. Most of those who populated the town arrived fleeing the atrocities of hostile Indians. Their wishes were clear on the vision the name conjured: may it become a reality.

Jarvis and his men tied their horses before the saloon entrance, making their way inside the cool narrow room. Jarvis and his half dozen men filled the simply furnished bar from end to end.

Meusebach placed short glasses before each of them. The idea of matched drinking vessels, much less those made of glass, was a rare treat for those weary travelers. Each glass was filled to the rim with amber liquor. Jarvis dropped coins on the bar as he and his gang lifted the whiskey to their eager lips, draining the contents instantly.

Meusebach poured them another round.

"You anteed enough for a second," he explained with a broad smile under his thick moustache.

Jarvis nodded his thanks, and they drank once more.

The group fell silent as three strangers entered the saloon. The newcomers hesitated at the sight of so many occupying the limited confines of the small room.

The leader of the newcomers was an ordinary looking man in a fresh suit of clothes. Behind him followed two men in typical cowpuncher attire, carrying pistols. One was a whipcord lean man in his early thirties. The other was a kid in his middle teens wearing a two-gun pistol rig seeming nearly as big as he was.

"Come in Tim Williamson," the saloon owner said to the newcomer. "Is that Skeeter Collins with you? I can serve him but not the kid. This ain't no haven for juvenile delinquents."

Williamson approached the bar where Meusebach poured two more drinks. Williamson paid, and the newcomers lifted their glasses to the bartender. The kid hung back near the door, a black look on his face.

"Mr. Meusebach is known for his hospitality and friendly ways," Williamson commented for the other patrons' benefit.

"So it seems," Jarvis agreed with uncharacteristic amiableness. "A crowded hole in the middle of the day will start the talk."

"No talk will come from this hole unless you stop the flow," Meusebach said as the goodwill in the room took hold.

Williamson laughed at the jest. He glanced at Jarvis before turning towards him.

"I'm not one to inquire of a man's plans," Williamson said. "Are you men passing through or would you be looking for some work?"

Jarvis downed his drink.

"Well, that's an interesting question, Williamson. We are here on business."

Jarvis understood the question for what lay beneath the words. His vocation required the ability to recognize the interest of others in the trade without alerting those who were not.

"We consider ourselves men of the road with an eye towards an opportune moment."

Williamson touched the side of his nose with a knowing wink. To Jarvis it seemed almost the gesture of an Irish imp.

Williamson indicated a table near the corner of the room.

"Perhaps we should repair to a more sober locale in which to discuss our doings."

"Another round for the boys," Jarvis called to Meusebach.

He and Williamson made their way to the table, sitting with their backs to the room.

"Like the man said, my name is Williamson. I heard only I was meeting a crew with loose stock. Can I know yours?"

"Jarvis Hutton, and you heard right."

Williamson regarded Jarvis for a moment. His impression of the man seemed to settle his worry. He nodded his silent understanding.

"How many head you got?"

"Not many," Jarvis said casually. "Less than twenty in all."

"That's not much," Williamson agreed. "I could make the risk more worth your while in the future if you're game."

"Tell me something new."

Williamson nodded, patting Jarvis's arm.

"I'll buy your stock today," he assured him unnecessarily.

They tossed back their glasses to seal the deal.

"How much do you know about the Prussian home-steaders about?" Williamson continued.

"I know enough," Jarvis answered with a hint of serious-ness. "What do you know about them?"

"They got way too much livestock for my liking."

"So I noticed," Jarvis agreed, warming up to the direc-tion of the conversation. "We have some experience in the matter."

"As for something new, with a goodly sized crew, we could help with their livestock worries to the tune of a hun-dred head of loose stock."

Jarvis shifted in his chair at the number of beeves indi-cated. "Loose Stock" meant unbranded yearlings and calves.

"When would you need a crew for the work?"

"It don't get easier with time," Williamson replied.

"I have one piece of business I need to undertake before we do the other."

"Maybe we can work together on both," Williamson of-fered ambitiously. "Do I know the other?"

"What do you know about a German named Wechsler?"

Williamson shook his head and grinned.

"It just happens your business is our business after all," Williamson said. "It's of his stock we're talking. A hundred head should take care of both."

"He is going to pay a steeper price for what I want from him."

"I'm the first to say a man's business is his own, but with so much on the hook, may I inquire if there is a place we can work together and get what we both want?"

Something about Williamson set Jarvis at ease. He decided to provide an insight into his intentions. Maybe he could glean something new about his brother's death.

"I reckon you have been around long enough to know about the history here."

"Been here since before the Fort at Mason was abandoned and they used the remains to build the town with."

"You ever hear of, or worked with a young fellow named Hutton?"

"KB," Williamson said with a frown. "I knew him only by name. he worked with a crew of former Confederate vagabonds. He was good with an iron I hear. How did you know him?"

"My last name is Hutton, same as his."

"Brother?"

"Was," Jarvis replied with pathos. "Wechsler is going to pay for his handling of my brother."

"I heard about that," Williamson said seriously. "I would want the same thing if he was my brother. I know a lot about that old Prussian, and I know this. He cares a lot less about his life than he does about them cattle. If you want to hurt him, take your revenge by the pound. Take the rest after."

Jarvis considered Williamson's reasoning. His path had been set for so long change was not an easy consideration. Vengeance allowed little room for compromise.

"I can see you are a man who takes his commitments seriously," Williamson continued. "After you turn this little trick and live through it, what will your next step be? You might need to make it heeled."

Jarvis gave his new acquaintance a hard look. His ire was up, but not for his new companion. He was struggling to get used to the detour he was being asked to take.

"Your men will move the cattle. My men will help. I will provide the plan and the holding pens to brand them, then I'll arrange for the sale locally."

Jarvis made no rejoinder.

Williamson suspected the other was more interested in revenge than a small piece of the job.

"Normally," Williamson continued. "I would offer a fifty-fifty split, but you have a lot of mouths to feed, and I sense you wouldn't accept that offer."

Jarvis' eyes narrowed as he listened to the other.

"Tell you what: I'll offer you sixty percent."

"Our number is seventy-five percent, and we'll do the heavy lifting ourselves. I don't have a man that don't know how to handle himself in a scrape."

Williamson was silent.

He didn't favor the counteroffer, but he found some benefit to risk-free gains. Besides, he thought. This would be a good first effort. They could renegotiate on the next

Williamson extended his hand.

"I believe we have reached an agreement, Mr. Hutton. I say we go tonight."

10

WOLFGANG NODDED WITH A LOOK conveying no pleasure at the accuracy of his predictions. Since Boyd emerged from his daughter's loins, there was no doubt he would follow the path his father trod. The narrow but cleaner path the old rancher followed allowed little room for foolish and prideful actions.

With begrudging reluctance, the local folk had learned to accept the old rancher's place in their midst. Acceptance was not assured, and his progress had been won through patience and persistence.

All of the hard-earned favor he had won from the ranching community was now lost. The favor had been slight but noticeable. In an instant his adopted grandson had returned the bubble to dead level, maybe below.

He surveyed his daughter with a critical eye. He knew how difficult it must have been for her to face the townspeople again after so long an absence. The dishonored reputation of an unwed mother was a lifelong mark, never to vanish.

"There was no business for you in town, daughter," he said bluntly. "What good did you expect would come of it?"

Emma watched her father silently, knowing he would never hear any defense she offered. Secretly, she guessed his opinion of her was nearer that of Spears than not. He had maintained for years she was to stay away from town. She had brought the life sentence upon herself with a rash and ill-advised relationship with a base rustler. She dared not tell her father of the pain she felt. She could tell no one.

"Spears will kill him, Emma. Ready yourself for that inevitable truth. He is a boy, nothing more. He is hardly a capable hand around my ranch. It is my opinion he lacks the courage or the strength to stand against a man like Spears."

Wechsler watched his daughter. He was not waiting for a response. He measured her commitment to the folly of her belief Boyd still had a place among them.

"What does he believe will sustain him?" Wechsler continued. "Bearding the lion ends one way, no matter the lies we tell ourselves."

"You will do nothing?" she asked, knowing his answer.

"What would you have me do?" he asked, looking at her in bewilderment. "Am I to fight his fights for him? Am I to show support when the reason he is in this predicament is because he disobeyed me? It is in his nature to disobey."

The Wolf shook his head and closed his eyes.

"Good riddance."

"He is your blood – at least in part," Emma pleaded.

The Wolf glared at her.

She picked at a painful wound which he knew would never heal. He felt an uncontrollable rage at her attempt to create a bond he knew did not exist. He despised her self-serving tactics.

He rose from his desk chair. He towered over her, his anger causing her real fear for her well-being. His eyes blazed with fury. His voice came as a low hiss.

"The rustler's blood flowing through his veins overshadows any small trace of Wechsler blood you may have shared with him. Press your will no longer, woman."

Emma fled from the room, a hand to her trembling lips.

Boyd rode in just before midday. He stabled the roan and completed the daily chores he typically performed. He entered the kitchen door of the ranch house. As he expected, his mother sat at the small table mending an article of clothing. Her fingers moved deftly as she manipulated the needle and thread with practiced efficiency. She looked up at him for only a moment before dropping her glance back to her work.

"The Sheriff released you today?" she asked without looking up again.

"I need to speak to grandfather," he said.

"He won't help you, Boyd. He can't," she said with a tone void of emotion. She continued her work on the garment.

Boyd remained where he was, putting this latest information in order. He wasn't asking to speak to his grandfather because he wanted help. He felt it necessary to explain his role in the conflict and offer a solution. His mother's summary rejection indicated there was more to the problem than he knew.

Boyd noticed a slight discoloration above his mother's right eye, a result from her impact with the jail bars during the Spears conflict at the jail.

"Are you hurt, mother?"

She looked at him in confusion for a moment. As realization dawned upon her, she touched the bruise.

"This was not your fault," she said. "It is nothing."

"There seems more wrong here than just a bruise," he observed with a thoughtful tone. "What did you do, Mother?"

She glanced up from her sewing with a sharpness he found troubling.

"What are you asking me?" she snapped, the patience gone from her manner.

Boyd considered her for a long moment. After the emotion he witnessed at the jail, then her current stoicism abbreviated with a sharp rebuke, he was certain there was more going on than he knew.

As his silence continued, she saw him transformed from her son to the man she saw more often these days. He became the silent observer, judging those around him by a metric with which he alone knew the quantity of measure. She felt herself left wanting in his estimation.

She tried to change the subject, softening her tone.

"I am pleased the Sheriff decided to release you so soon."

Boyd's voice held no emotion as he responded.

"The Sheriff advised I leave Mason County, maybe Texas."

She seemed surprised by his admission, but she made no comment.

"I will speak with Grandfather," he said with finality, striding from the kitchen.

He found his grandfather in his vestibule office. The room was an oddity on the Texas frontier. Bookshelves lined an entire wall, filled with the rich browns, reds, and golds of stiff-bound tomes. His desk was of a Prussian craftsmanship exclusive to the old world.

He had paid dearly, financially and in suffering, to bring it with him: a single remnant of his former life, other than his treasured collection of stately books.

The old man scrawled upon a lined ledger book as Boyd entered, hat in hand.

Boyd waited respectfully in the doorway as his grandfather completed his commitment of information to the accounting journal.

Finally, the Wolf leaned back in his chair, considering Boyd critically.

"What is it, boy?" he asked curtly.

His voice held no real coldness, yet there was no trace of warmth, or the welcome of a grandfather to a grandson, only inquiry.

"I am surprised to see you here so soon."

"The Sheriff released me. He advises me to leave the country immediately."

Wechsler searched his grandson's face as though the solution to the puzzle of the Sheriff's advice would appear on Boyd's face.

"Russel Spears came to the jail this morning. Mother was there. He laid hands upon her and called her a vile name. I was able to stop him from my cell."

"You were able to stop him," Wechsler repeated.

"Yes, sir."

"So, you not only attacked his sons, you assailed him also?"

"Yes, sir."

"Is it your intention to see me hauled from this region on a rail, tarred and feathered, and dishonored?"

"If that is the response of the Townies to protecting a woman from the insulting attack of a strange man, then I suppose your fate is set, Grandfather. I don't see how you would have reacted differently, yourself."

"Don't sass me, jungen."

"Would you have seen little Hans beaten and maimed? Am I so different from you that…?"

"Silence!"

"Yes, sir."

"You are bringing trouble down upon yourself – and this family. There is a bad seed within you that will grow into a pernicious weed: a damnable force which will ultimately destroy you and those around you."

Boyd took this harsh observation with a shock he tried to conceal from the old man. He was unsuccessful.

Wechsler watched him with the grim satisfaction his words had found purchase. Strangely, he felt a small measure of sympathy for his illegitimate grandson. His thoughts arranged the matter in that way. Boyd was illegitimate and the spawn of an evil outlaw.

His feelings concerning the welfare of the boy emerged from a stern understanding of the creature before him, and the determination the boy would suffer, but by no fault of his own. He would pay in blood for the blood which flowed in his veins. His empathy for the boy's plight was a cold regard tinctured by the certainty of the sad but inescapable fate awaiting him.

"I will do my part in the matter you have created. I can do no more for you. My concern is for those in my family who have no part in this yet stand to suffer because of it."

"I am nothing to you, grandfather?"

"You are something to me, boy. You are a continual source of strife and a highly conductive conduit for attracting trouble and conflict. You cannot help who – or what – you are. I cannot do but what must be done as a result. Even then, after January, I wash my hands of you."

"Yes, sir," Boyd said.

Throughout his life the same date had come up often with the same claim of its significance. Boyd now considered it a statement of hyperbole, a vague threat of something to come for which he had no control.

"I have grown weary of our time here. I see you have much upon which to reflect."

Boyd hesitated for a moment, watching as his grandfather returned his attention to his accounting. Although he was no stranger to the stern attention of his grandfather's ire, Boyd had never suspected the depth of the disfavor the old rancher bore him.

He turned on his heel and left the room. He returned to the kitchen, passing his mother, still at her sewing, and left by the back kitchen door.

He felt a hot flush on his face. An exquisite ache gripped his heart. He felt a tormenting sense of confused displacement. If he didn't belong here, then where? What about him elicited this singular contempt from his grandfather? His cousins were treated with none of the dismissive disregard he received. Was he different in some way? Had he made some huge misstep of which he was unaware?

Boyd was almost to the stables when he halted abruptly. Something his mother said at the jail returned to him.

'I've already paid more than you will ever know.'

Boyd turned his head towards the house. The urge to press his mother on the matter was nearly irresistible. What did she mean, she had already paid? Why did she choose that moment in the jailhouse to make such a claim? Was there some secret she kept? Why couldn't he ask her to clarify her words?

Perhaps, he guessed, it was his reluctance to harm her any more than he had when she was thrown against the jail bars during the fight. He continued to the stables and saddled the roan gelding once more.

Once the gelding was saddled, Boyd moved to the ladder leading to the hay mow above the stables. He climbed up to the loft and quickly located the hiding place amongst the framing of the roof. Removing a flat plank, he found his worn gun belt holding a single action colt pistol.

He strapped on the gun rig and descended the ladder. He led the roan outside and latched the stables door. He mounted and headed the gelding towards Comanche Creek.

He had no definite plan, but he believed it better to travel armed in case he encountered Spears or someone loyal to Spears. His grandfather's words confirmed the Sheriff's bleak forecast for his future. Advice, even from those who care little, is often accurate. He didn't recognize much in his favor. He would have to adopt a habit of self-reliance if he were to avoid a helpless fate.

11

WHEN WILLIAMSON ARRIVED AT THE rustlers' camp, Jarvis and his gang lounged within the cover of a grove of Live Oaks. The setting Sun's intense rays reached for the men with a final effort, as if it resisted extinction from the approach of the darkening twilight sky in a wash of reds and orange hues.

Williamson, his man from the store, Skeeter Colins, and the young kid with the bulky two-gun rig, dismounted at the edge of the copse, entering amongst the lounging outlaws.

Williamson handed Jarvis folded cash then accepted the proffered whiskey bottle in return. He squatted on his heels and took a large pull. He passed it to Collins as he looked around at the rough-looking group.

Jarvis nodded at his men.

"This is my gang," he said, pointing to each man in turn as he introduced them. "Abe Wiggins, Tom Turley, Charlie Johnson, Caleb Hall, and the brothers Eli and Pete Baccus. All capable men, and good with rope and gun."

"Pleased," Williamson said, nodding his greeting. "You already know Skeeter Collins, here. The kid is Allen Bolt. He's young but handy."

"How does this thing come off?" Jarvis asked.

"The cattle are north of us. The Wechsler hands are gathering their horses to return to the ranch house. They will leave a single sentry to watch the cattle. Just after nightfall we will capture the guard and make off with the stock. I count some fifty head of loose stock."

"That's half of what you claimed before," Jarvis said without temper.

"That's what I wanted to discuss," Williamson said. "Skeeter here is a hand with the running iron. Wechsler's brand is easy to change. If we take the newly branded beeves with the unbranded, we will have our hundred head."

"What's the difference then?" Jarvis asked.

"Working the brands will slow down our money. We'll have to drive the cattle to my ranch in Loyal Valley, work the brands, then drive them to Menardville where I have arranged a buyer who sells to the Mexicans. If we all pitch in, the cattle will be headed to points unknown before anyone knows they're gone."

Jarvis received the bottle from Skeeter, keeping an eye on Williamson. He offered it to the kid, who covered his grin at being included in the drinking.

"You been planning this for a while, I see," Jarvis commented, returning his attention to Williamson.

"That's why I make my share in this. I arrange the details."

"How much longer will it take to work them brands?"

"Wechsler's brand is simple, not like the XIT brand, which is nearly unworkable. The fifty head of marked stock are freshly branded. Our new brand won't look added or worked later over a scarred brand: if we all pitch in, maybe another day of hard work."

"That's a long delay," Jarvis said with a shake of his head. "Plenty of time for following our trail."

"If we were anywhere else, I would agree. Them Prussians have been rustled since the Indians plagued the land here. They accept they have to allow for the loss. They elected their new sheriff to stop the losses, but I doubt he will go against the town folk to support the Prussian invaders. If we are followed, it will be by the rancher and his men. If they manage to keep on our trail over unfamiliar country, a bunch of saddle-sore Germans won't be no match for a hard-edged group like this one. We'll post a guard down the road, so they don't catch us unawares. Besides, you might get the chance to settle both accounts at once."

Jarvis grunted.

He liked the prospect of killing Wechsler sooner than later. He considered the details for a moment more.

"Alright," he said finally. "Let's take all of 'em."

Chlodwig Wechsler chewed on tough hardtack, pulling from his canteen to combat the salty thirst it caused. He felt at ease with his carbine near at hand and the comfort of leaping flames licking at the Mesquite limbs in the fire nearby.

His horse nickered, ears erect, eyes searching towards the western darkness. The mare's attention was focused just beyond the light circle from the fire.

Chlodwig grabbed his rifle and approached the horse. His grandfather had been clear about the danger he might face if rustlers decided to take the stock. His heart raced at the prospect of facing outlaws alone. He froze at the sound of a voice behind him, near the fire. How had someone sneaked into his camp undetected?

"Lay the rifle on the ground, son."

Chlodwig stiffened as he stoked his courage to resist the command. The voice was familiar, but he couldn't place it immediately.

"No point dying on such a fine night," the voice urged. "Set it on the ground and get on your belly."

The boy obeyed with stiff movements. He made a point to avoid looking at his captor. When he was prone the stranger stepped close, collecting the carbine. His hands were bound behind him with rough cord. His captor covered his eyes with a stiff length of cloth. He heard the stranger step away into the darkness towards the direction where his horse's attention had been drawn.

Some moments later Chlodwig heard the sounds of multiple horses, then a large number of cattle moving slowly away. He lay for a long time in the dust, the night sounds returning to normal around him.

He awoke with a start. His covered eyes were of no help to him. A sound had roused him. He heard the fall of an approaching horse's hooves. The horse halted near his camp. He heard boots strike the ground as a rider dismounted. Footfalls approached and he was released from his bonds and the rider lifted the rag from his eyes.

Chlodwig squinted the blur from his vision, recognizing Boyd.

"The cattle are gone," Boyd informed him pointlessly.

"Rustlers."

Boyd nodded, looking around him into the darkness. He turned on his heel, returning to the fire where the roan gelding shook his head, rattling tack.

"You going after the rustlers?" Chlodwig asked, noticing Boyd's side arm for the first time.

Boyd was younger, but Chlodwig addressed him as a superior. The seventeen-year-old possessed an authority which transcended age and station.

"Nope."

"Why are you here, then?" he asked tersely.

"Just happened along."

"Just out for a lark? We gotta get on their trail."

"How many rustlers would have to be in a gang able to steal that many cattle?"

"I didn't see 'em. I heard a few horses. Maybe a half dozen or more."

"You want to brace a half dozen outlaws in the dark?" Boyd asked with a condescending smile. "If I help you kill yourself, your grandfather will hang me."

"Our grandfather," Chlodwig corrected him.

Boyd grunted, his understanding of the situation greater than his cousin's.

"Gather your pack and mount up."

"I ain't going back without them cattle."

Boyd moved swiftly, his face registering frustration and pain.

He grabbed his cousin by the shirt and shook him violently.

"Get on your damned horse and follow me. I'll bust you up if you argue with me. You don't know what you are saying. I won't let you die out here."

The other retreated before Boyd's passionate display. He didn't understand any of this. He had never known Boyd to duck a fight. Instinctively he knew it was not fear that moved his cousin. What compelled him remained a mystery.

He looked again to Boyd's waistline. It seemed odd he wore a gun belt strapped to his lean hips. None of the German ranchers or their hands carried weapons other than the occasional saddle gun, or perhaps a shotgun for hunting. He wondered why his cousin was armed in such a way, but he lacked the courage to press Boyd on the matter.

Silently, Chlodwig gathered his pack, mounted, and followed Boyd back to the ranch house.

12

DAWN BRIGHTENED THE HORIZON ahead as Williamson and Jarvis' gang secured the last of the young beeves within a protected pasture on Williamson's ranch. Jarvis joined the rancher as he returned to his house atop the hill overlooking his place.

"Come in Hutton," Williamson welcomed him. "Mary Elizabeth will have coffee ready for us."

Jarvis removed his hat as he entered. As promised, a lean woman, her hair tied in a bun, brought in a tray with two cups of hot coffee. The men took seats at the kitchen table.

Jarvis nodded his thanks to Mary Elizabeth as he received the steaming cup.

After she disappeared through the far door, leaving the men alone at the table, Williamson sipped gingerly at his coffee, eyeing Jarvis across the table.

"I sent young Allen Bolt along our back trail. He will keep an eye out for pursuit. We'll get right on the branding and be out of here by nightfall. Rest your men in shifts if you like."

"They are used to long hours during a job. It's best to keep them close in the case of trouble."

Williamson nodded his agreement, sipping once more from the cup.

"We'll start the work right away. We'll rework the branded stock and save the unbranded for last. We will move them out once the brands are worked."

Jarvis nodded.

The dawn brightened the few windows in the little ranch house. The men sipped coffee silently, their thoughts on the labor ahead. The workday would prove long, but the short-term discomfort would be a small price for the long-term gain.

They finished their coffee.

Jarvis returned to his men. All were bedded down around the barn, snoring, and mumbling in their exhausted slumber.

Jarvis rolled a cigarette and leaned against a fence post. He pulled smoke deep, exhaling with a noisy sigh. His wakefulness was forced upon him by thoughts of Wolfgang Wechsler, and the hope he would come for his cattle.

He allowed his men a respite no longer than it took him to finish his cigarette. He tossed the butt and stood straight. He moved among them, kicking the men awake with a rough call to action.

"On your feet, men. One last push for riches. You can rest when you're dead. Rouse up boys!"

His gang rose slowly, moving like gaunted up old men, stretching and complaining. They regained their resolve by degrees, their motivation, their commitment to the reward at the work's end.

Mrs. Williamson arrived on a buckboard driven by Tim Williamson. She brought coffee and a cold breakfast of biscuits and bacon. The morning meal was a quick one which emptied the wagon of food and coffee. Soon the branding began in earnest, the men grim-faced and stern.

"Hutton," Williamson said. "I'm gonna fetch some grub down the trail to the kid. If all goes well, we should be on the move by sundown."

Jarvis nodded, moving towards the sound of curses from the working men, most already sweating, even in the early morning coolness.

13

RUSSEL SPEARS LED A LARGE CONTINGENT of Town Folks into the clearing beyond Wechsler's ranch house. In all, there was a total of fourteen in his cavalcade. All appeared ill-tempered and purposeful. They passed a pair of Mexican laborers tending the large vegetable garden as they made their way along the narrow lane to the ranch house.

Unlike the previous visit, members of the household did not meet him. He and his men passed by the long stables, undetected by anyone within the house.

Spears lifted a hand as he pulled up before the kitchen door. Emma appeared in the doorway, surveying the riders with apprehension.

It wasn't Spears who spoke first, but rather a stout man with large sideburns, astride a barrel-chested black horse; apparently one of the few mounts capable of bearing his weight for so long a journey.

"We are here for your son, Ms. Wechsler," the stout man announced evenly but firmly.

Emma recognized the speaker as Wilson Hey, presiding judge in Mason County, and unelected leader of the town of Mason.

"He isn't here, judge," she said flatly.

"Where is he?"

"I'm right here," replied a voice from the direction of the stables. "Go inside, Ma. This isn't your affair. I've already seen how these Townies treat women. Let's see if Spears has the sand to front me outside of prison bars, without the cover of a woman to protect him."

"You are a blackguard liar…," Spears growled, his hand gripping his pistol.

"Russel," the judge interrupted. "This is a matter for the law, not vigilantes."

Boyd watched the conversation carefully, unsure how to act with a judge participating in what he considered to be a personal vendetta.

"Now, young man," the Judge continued in a reasonable tone. "The allegations against you are growing at an alarming rate. These latest charges levelled by the law-abiding citizenry, combined with your past misdeeds, warrant my involvement today. Sheriff Clark is unavailable, so I recognize my participation as being a bit outside of normal procedures. Nevertheless, I need you to surrender yourself to me and these men and return to jail until we straighten out this matter."

Wolfgang Wechsler appeared in the doorway. He laid a hand on his daughter's shoulder, easing her away from the door. He stepped onto the porch.

"On what charge do you arrest this boy?"

Boyd failed to cover his surprise at his grandfather's intervention on his behalf.

"Wolf," the judge replied with a polite smile. "A charge is not required to secure a suspect in an investigation, particularly if I am unconvinced he will not flee the jurisdiction."

"I'll need an accounting of potential charges if I am going to release him to your custody, judge."

"You ain't entitled to a reason," Spears said loudly. "You got no authority to resist an officer of the law."

"Shut up, Spears," Hey said with uncustomary heat. "Wolf, this boy has attacked three members of the Spears household and pulled a rifle on a group that visited to handle this matter peacefully. One of his attacks was upon a man in the Sheriff's office. The Sheriff had to quell the attack at gunpoint. Your daughter even participated in the assault."

"Where are you getting your information, Judge?" Wolf asked with dismay registering on his face.

"I will hear from all sides in this matter. I intend to end this thing peacefully, with those responsible accounting for it in the eyes of the law. My participation here today is to ensure the peace is kept and the matter is handled properly."

Wechsler considered what he heard.

"Come now Wolf," the Judge urged. "I know you. We have always seen eye to eye when it comes to right and wrong, good and bad, legal and criminal. I am counting on your equable nature in this matter."

Boyd waited silently, his fascination with the conversation overriding any instinct to intervene. The Judge's accounting of the events of the past few days were, in the least, over simplified, and at the most, one-sided, and self-serving. Boyd believed there would be an opportunity for his response no matter how the debate ended.

"I appreciate your consideration of my sense of reason and fair play," Wechsler said slowly, measuring his words. "It is true we have seen eye to eye in the past. I think you may remember dealings singularly from long ago. Since then, I trusted you and the law to deal fairly with me when I brought you hard evidence of those who rustled my cattle, only for you to release them on a twist in the wording of the law.

"I recall one of my men went to town after collecting his wages. You may remember him. He was beaten within an inch of his life in the hotel saloon for being an outlaw and gunman. He was there, unarmed at my insistence. That man is no longer in my employ, gone for parts unknown to escape the death those men attempted and which he narrowly avoided.

"I see here among you several of those same men who attacked him that night. They were never arrested, nor was anyone arrested in the case. In another instance, you awarded a rustler one of my prize horses when my son shot his from under him as he attempted to make off with my cattle.

"We elected a Sheriff who swore to bring these rustlers to justice, and you say he is not here to do his job."

Wechsler placed his hands on his hips as his two sons emerged from the door behind him, rifles in their hands.

"Our days of like minds are a part of history now, Judge. Bringing this large a group of men to my ranch seems a mite heavy handed if your aim is to enlist my assistance. You will forgive me if I say I feel a bit pressed by the number of men in your troupe today. Not a one is one of my people. Not a one is friendly towards me or mine."

Judge Hey colored red from his cheeks to the top of his shiny balding head. He cleared his throat as he gathered his composure.

"What you don't know," he said. "Is that I have sent a missive to Governor Coke requesting Ranger assistance with this rustling problem. Now the law may not work on your schedule, Wolfgang, but it does work."

The German rancher seemed unimpressed.

"Get off my land, all of you. The boy stays here."

Spears leaned forward dangerously.

"I will have satisfaction, Wechsler," he growled.

Wechsler's eyes flashed as his temper got the best of him.

"Is that what you are after?" Wechsler shouted, his temper lost. "Well, there the boy is. Face him and end this like men. He doesn't seem afraid to meet you here and now. How about you Spears? Are you afraid of a boy?"

"Damn you and your spawn," Spears shouted with unpent fury. "I have no fear of any of your blood, much less a snot-nosed kid."

Wechsler levelled a look at the Judge.

"What say you, your honor? A duel is archaic, but not illegal if it is mutually agreed and witnessed."

Judge Hey shook his head helplessly. The accusations leveled at him by the rancher occupied his mind at present. His official composure was abandoned, superfluous in the face of irrational men.

"If we have a willing accord," he acquiesced wearily. "Then I will not intercede."

Spears dismounted with a bound. The others withdrew to a safe distance, creating a straight perimeter in line with the two duelers. Spears showed surprise when he noticed the pistol strapped to Boyd's waist.

"I see the boy is heeled," he said with a hardly discernable note of doubt.

Like most Anglos, he was accustomed to the typical German rancher who wore no side arm. Their habits tended towards passive acceptance of the actions of others, depending upon a manner of imperturbability and self-possession in matters of confrontation.

The boy wore his pistol low with an unmistakable comfort causing the elder Spears a twinge of uncertainty.

"A Dutch gunfighter," he said in ridicule. "You'll die before your pistol clears leather. Say when."

As he spoke, Spears' confidence grew. Whether his resolve was manufactured or real, he appeared committed to his course.

Boyd pulled the hammer strap loose from the black pistol and turned sideways to his foe, left side forward, reducing the size of the target he presented.

Spears recognized the tactic from stories he had heard about notorious gunfighters. He wondered how the kid knew about it. Was he only imitating what he had heard or was he practiced in gun craft? His reason overcame his pique with the assurance the kid was a German ranch boy. He was no gunman.

Boyd glanced at his grandfather. Was this what was required to earn his respect or was this a ploy to end him and quell the hatred he felt for him?

The old man watched him dispassionately. He could as easily have been watching him ride a rough horse. There was no alarm or concern on his face. He revealed no surprise at Boyd wearing a side arm.

Boyd inhaled and released the breath, feeling a calm wash over him like a warm wave. All of the practice; the tutelage under Simon Martinez, the man beaten in town by many in this very group, calmed him with a confidence he did not expect.

Judge Hey cleared his throat.

"Men, when I drop this kerchief, fill your hands. I will personally gun down the man who pulls early."

He conjured a small revolver from somewhere within his clothes and cocked the hammer.

The group was silent as they awaited the signal from the Judge.

Suddenly a cry rang out and Emma burst through the kitchen door. She rushed to where Spears stood in the dusty road. When she arrived, she shoved him, grabbing his pistol from his holster.

"You will not kill my son here today," she shouted, pointing the pistol at his face. Her visage was remarkably changed from her previous calm demeanor. Her eyes flashed, tears reddening them at the edges, and her lips were wet with moisture, a fleck of white at the corner of her mouth. Her body shook, and her fingers clutched and unclutched the pistol as her passion overcame her.

"Get your vigilante posse off our land or I'll kill you myself."

"Emma," Wechsler said with force.

"Hush, father," she said without taking her eyes from Spears. She cocked the hammer. "Get on your horse now!"

Spears paused no more than a second before retreating to his horse. He mounted, and similarly to his first visit, yanked the horse's head around, leaving the others behind as he spurred the horse, galloping away from the group.

The remaining members of the posse waited, unsure what to do.

Judge Hey considered Emma for a moment. Seeing her attention was reserved solely for Spears as he rode away, he eased his mount towards Wechsler, tucking his pistol and his kerchief back in his clothes.

"As far as the law is concerned," Hey said. "This matter is not concluded. I will, however, delay taking the boy into custody with your word he will not depart the jurisdiction."

"It is given, Judge."

Judge Hey turned his horse, leading the remaining men from the ranch.

When the last of the townsmen departed, Wechsler walked to where Boyd stood, remaining in his draw ready position. As if emerging from a dark reverie, the boy relaxed his stance at his grandfather's approach.

"You may think you are a dangerous gunfighter because of a small amount of guidance from Martinez, but I assure you it is not enough. Simon Martinez told me of his tutelage, and I recognize his gun and belt. You will not wear a sidearm on my ranch. Am I understood?"

"Yes sir."

"Put it back in the stable where you hide it. We will talk more of this later."

Boyd turned on his heel, returning to the stables, his mind full of questions and doubts.

Wechsler turned to his sons, who watched with interest.

"Get on your horses. We will delay the pursuit of our cattle for the moment. I want every rancher here tonight, is that clear?"

His sons replied together.

"Yes, sir."

The last of the German ranchers arrived an hour after dark. Emma and her mother served hot black coffee and buttered bread.

The Wolf took his place before the broad fireplace. He raised his hands to quiet the men. When the other voices grew silent, he spoke in a normal tone, as if he addressed only one or two men, not a room full of German Ranchers.

"Last night more than one-hundred head of my cattle were rustled from my lower pasture. They overpowered and tied up my grandson as they did it. We were readying to go after them when we received visitors from town.

"A large contingent of Städtbewohnen came to my home today to take my grandson by force. Judge Hey was among them. Sheriff Clark was said to be in dispose. We supported his campaign and ensured his election with his promise to end the scourge. He has not honored his word. We have very few avenues afforded us in the matter. I propose the reformation of the cattleman's association. Alone, nothing will change. In this matter we are brothers united by a common cause. As one, we have great power in both number and in might.

One of the German ranchers, Bernard Keiferstein, shook his head.

"What say you, Bern?" Wolf asked of the rancher.

"After the last hanging," Keiferstein replied. "We agreed to disband and never to gather again without a vote and a quorum for that vote."

"There will be no vote. There will be no quorum. There will be no debate about how we rid the range of these thieves. If you will not join, leave now."

Keiferstein's eyes did not drop from the Wolf's gaze. Not one man looked around. Not one man left the room.

"These thieves are likely gone beyond our grasp. I feel certain they are local men who know us and the country around. We will post sentries at all quarters. From this moment forward we will maintain a patrol on horseback day and night.

"If our sentries see a group of men who seem suspiciously intentioned, they will send word to the patrol. The patrol will react accordingly. Henry Pluenneke will lead the primary patrol. Pick your best men and be ready. Peter Bader will lead a second patrol."

The announcement drew hushed conversations from those in attendance. Most remembered the first Association. They disbanded after several ranches burned, and entire herds of cattle were butchered and left in the pasture to rot.

Wechsler's comments about Sheriff Clark gave them no confidence. If the new Sheriff was unwilling to do what they had elected him to do, what prevented them from suffering the same fate as before?

Wechsler knew what they feared and called for quiet again.

"I know what you are worried about. I am also aware you have no faith that John Clark will do what we are paying him to do.

"I am not asking you to trust Clark. I am asking you to trust me. I have spoken with him. I will do so again - soon. Assemble the patrols as I ask. I will do the rest.

Though remaining doubts lingered, Wechsler's assurances seemed to ease some of their fears.

The men remained for a time, catching up on old news and eating bread and butter sandwiches. They hadn't gathered as a group in years. The event was a call to war. But that didn't diminish the good cheer of a long-awaited reunion.

Boyd watched from the back of the room. His mother appeared from somewhere within the house and placed an arm around his shoulders.

"I love you son," she said in his ear.

"I know, Ma. I love you too."

14

J ARVIS, WILLIAMSON, AND THEIR MEN remained at the ranch near Menardville only long enough to collect and distribute their gains. To a man they were bone weary, but their fatigue was eased by the weight of currency in their pockets. Already in the works was a new plan for additional gains.

Jarvis received a shock while he distributed shares to his men. When he came to Charlie Johnson, his oldest friend outside of prison, he handed him his earnings.

"This is it for me, boss," Johnson told him. "I ain't never been comfortable with cattle work. I've got a stake that will buy me a place west where I can settle down and go straight – if you'll let me."

Jarvis nodded knowingly.

"So that's why you've been hoarding all your money, Charlie. Well, I guess this is so long then."

He extended his hand.

Charlie took it in a firm grip.

"You can come with me, Jarvis," he said warmly. "I know you want blood for your brother. Maybe you can find peace with an old friend and honest work. This here trail ends only one way. I can't bear it may be your final one."

Jarvis showed no temper to his old friend.

"That means a lot coming from you Charlie. I have to see this thing through. Here's wishing you good luck."

Charlie lingered with their hands locked. Finally, Johnson released his boss and trail partner and turned to his horse. He mounted and with one last look at the men he left behind he touched his hat brim.

"Good luck men,"

Charlie Johnson headed west as the others returned to Mason County.

They were within five miles of Mason around mid-afternoon when Williamson called a halt.

"Skeeter, the Kid, and me are headed back to Loyal Valley. We'd best let this one die down before we take on another job."

Jarvis scratched his head thoughtfully.

"Do what you think is best Tim," he said. "The boys and me will head back to camp and lay low for a few days. We'll send Caleb in for whiskey tonight though."

"Let's meet up in fifteen days at Meusbachs'," Williamson said.

"We'll be there," Jarvis agreed.

Williamson and his men rode away from the others.

Caleb sidled his horse closer to the leader's.

"A night indoors would do us all some good, boss," he said. "We've been drinking whiskey on the ground for months it seems. A hot meal and one night in a bed won't kill nobody. Besides, who is to say we didn't earn our money honestly?"

"It's risky," Jarvis began.

"We're with you no matter what Jarvis, but the kid is making a lot of sense to us," said the normally silent Tom Turley.

Jarvis looked at the others.

Eli Baccus shook his head.

"We ain't risking it, boss. Pete and I are staying out of town for a few days.

"Hell boys," Caleb said. "If the Baccus brothers ain't drinking with us, who can I make fun of? Besides, I'm buying the first round."

"Alright," Jarvis agreed. "Don't flash your loot. The first sign of trouble and we slope – no arguments. Agreed?"

His conditions were met with nods and murmurs of agreement.

Williamson, Collins, and Bolt travelled the road to Loyal Valley at a leisurely pace. The day was clear, and the south-easterly breeze bore a pleasant coolness, rare that time of year. They hadn't gone far when the youngster pulled up.

"I think I might drop into town for a little visit."

Williamson and his companion drew rein, eyeing the boy warily.

"That's not a good idea Allen," Williamson said with the warning tone of a father to a son. "If you get a drink or two in you, you don't want to get gabby. It would be best if you stayed near the ranch for a few days until things cool down."

"Mr. Williamson," Bolt said with a crooked grin. "I ain't a kid no more and I ain't gonna say nothing to nobody about any of this. I just want to spend a little money is all."

The other two reacted to this with darker frowns and deeper consternation.

"How are you going to explain the money?" Collins asked.

"Explain the money to who?" was the youth's reply.

"Anyone who asks how a kid got so flush when he is known for never hitting a lick since he got fired from Lehmberg's place."

"That wasn't my fault."

"Just the same," Williamson added. "There will be questions."

"I'll say I worked for you at your ranch."

Williamson shook his head. After a moment of silent reflection, he held out his hand.

"Give me what you have saving a couple of dollars. I'll give it back when you return to the ranch."

"Aw, Tim," Bolt whined. "I don't want to."

Williamson waited patiently with his hand extended.

Finally, Bolt emptied his pocket, handing over the bills and coins.

Williamson counted out four dollars. He gave the money to Bolt and pocketed the remainder.

"When you return," he repeated, patting the pocket containing his money.

Bolt nodded then rode back towards town. He waited until he was out of sight to pull out another cache of money hidden in a leather purse in his other pocket.

Jarvis and his men sat in the back of the hotel saloon which served as a dining room during daylight operations. They dined on thick beef steaks, potatoes, and warm bread. They filled their glasses in turn from the whiskey bottle going around the table. From the lobby, they heard the sounds of the school master and lessons conducted.

The meal began with reverence for the classes beyond, but the more rounds the bottle made, the less respect was given to the brightening of young minds. With the completion of the meal came an increasing frequency of glasses filled.

The aproned bartender, who also served as the kitchen staff, was on the verge of cautioning his guests when the appearance of a boy wearing a two-gun rig occupied his attention.

The six rustlers watched as the kid, Allen Bolt, leaned on the bar and ordered a whiskey.

The aproned bartender moved behind the bar, positioning himself before the youth.

"We don't serve kids in here," he said with finality.

"I ain't no kid," Bolt argued.

"If I was to serve you, which I ain't," the bartender said testily. "How do you plan to pay for it?"

With a flourish, the kid reached into his clothes and produced a leather bag. He dropped it on the bar where it landed with a solid thunk, coins jingling inside.

"Now pour," the kid demanded. Fishing out a coin from the bag, he slapped it on the bar.

His back was to the men at the table, or the kid might have taken note of the reaction his dramatic outburst elicited from them. They paid with small denomination coins and cleared out of the hotel, taking the bottle with them.

Outside the hotel, they mounted their horses, heading them out of town. As they passed the courthouse, none other than Clark himself stepped out of his office. Deputy Worley emerged next. Both lawmen watched the half dozen men with keen scrutiny, taking note of every detail of the riders. They stepped onto the sparse grass of the courthouse yard and strode rapidly to the fence line at the roadway.

As they watched the lawmen approach, Caleb Hall leaned towards his companions.

"It looks like things may be hotter here than we guessed. I'm for putting miles behind us until that beehive settles back down."

Clark stepped onto the dirt of the road, bringing his pistol out. Worley stepped forward, a rifle at the ready.

"You men hold up for a moment," Clark commanded.

The lawmen's trained weapons dispelled any ideas the outlaws harbored to attempt a hasty escape.

"What's the trouble Sheriff?" Jarvis demanded with as much outrage as he could muster.

"I'll ask the questions, if you don't mind, Mister," Clark said authoritatively. "Where are you boys headed?"

"West," Jarvis replied. "What concern is it of yours?"

"What's your name?" Clark asked Jarvis, cocking the hammer on his Colt.

Jarvis was aware many in town had known of his brother and might connect them by the Hutton name. Prominent in his mind was the revenge he sought from Wechsler. He dared not lose the element of surprise he held at the moment.

"Charlie Johnson," Jarvis lied. "And these are my boys. We are headed to New Mexico for work."

"New Mexico, you say?"

"Yeah," Jarvis said.

"Why don't you boys step down from them horses and lay your weapons on the ground."

"Now see here, Sheriff…"

Worley levered a round into the chamber of his rifle. He raised the gun to eye level, training the sites on Jarvis.

"You heard the Sheriff. Step down and unlimber them pistols," he muttered dangerously.

"Do as they say," Jarvis told his men. "This is a mistake, Sheriff."

In short order, the rustlers were taken to the Sheriff's office and locked into the two jail cells.

Three men already occupied one of the two cells.

"Thomas," Clark said to the three men. "You, Gamel, and Roberts got company. This is Mr. Johnson and friends."

Once the locks were turned, Clark went to his desk, collecting paper and a grease pencil.

"You newcomers write your names on this paper. If you can't write, Deputy Worley will write it for you. You are all under arrest for cattle thievery. Turn out your pockets and surrender your belongings to the Deputy for safe keeping in the courthouse safe."

After the din subsided where every man claimed his innocence and denied any wrongdoing. Names were recorded along with a written description of each man. Their personal belongings, including large amounts of currency, were logged on the paper.

"You boys are in possession of a lot of cash for out of work drifters headed to new Mexico," Worley observed, nodding to the pile of cash and coins on Clark's desk.

The Sheriff poked the pile with an index finger, making an informal tally of the amount. Finally, he surveyed the prisoners with a grim look.

"You men will be arraigned in the morning by Judge Hey," Clark announced. "Until then, behave and don't cause me no trouble."

Clark motioned to Worley. They gathered the money and possessions on the desk and placed them into a white sack. They moved to a steel box bolted to the floor.

The man Clark addressed when the others arrived looked at Jarvis. He held out his hand.

"My name is Thomas, MB Thomas," he said in a voice too quiet to be heard by the lawmen.

Jarvis looked at the hand for a moment before he decided to accept the handshake.

"I'm Charlie Johnson."

They shook hands.

Thomas continued the introduction.

This is my partner, Allen Roberts. We own ranches in Llano and Burnet Counties. This man is Tom Gamel, a local man we hired to guide our search."

"Mr. Johnson," Thomas said. "I'm not sure of anything except this county is rustler crazy. We were on a hosted hunt, looking for our lost cattle when the Sheriff and a large posse of men fell upon us and arrested us. There is talk of a lynching party. The charges against you are the same. I recommend you and your men watch your step."

Jarvis said nothing in return. He grimaced and turned to the cell bars.

The Sheriff and Deputy Worley deposited the sack containing the prisoners' money and possessions in the steel box, securing it with a heavy padlock.

The only man who had not lost his loot was Caleb Hall, who had stuffed his money in his boot before they entered the saloon. The hidden coins gave him the appearance of a limp, but otherwise his stash had not been discovered.

Hall sidled over to Jarvis. He spoke to him in a hoarse whisper.

"If that kid is caught, he's going to sing like a bird about the whole operation."

Jarvis looked at Hall with a hard look.

"I expect just that," he said out of the side of his mouth, a peculiar habit affected by most hard time convicts. "That kid is drunk by now and he has been stupid his whole life. We're sunk."

Hall looked at the men around him. The two ranchers and the third man, Gamel, seemed oblivious to their conversation. Jarvis' gang watched their leaders with keen interest, though they remained silent.

Jarvis nodded his head at Hall.

"Keep your head down and your mouth closed. We'll see what opportunity presents itself." Jarvis leaned towards Hall. He whispered, "Be ready for anything. Follow my lead."

Hall nodded and moved to the others.

He spoke amongst the gang then took a seat on the crowded bench.

15

IT WAS WELL AFTER DARK WHEN A staggering Allen Bolt dragged himself into his saddle, the vapors from the liquor befuddling his efforts. He rode from the hotel into the darkness, leaving a boisterous crowd of newly acquired friends behind him. His leather sack was much lightened. Despite the heavy expenditures at the hotel saloon, he was encouraged by the knowledge his coffers would once more be replenished when he reached Williamson's ranch.

The cool air benefited him much towards his revival from the effects of the night's drinking, but not soon enough for his recovering senses to warn him of impending danger. Suddenly, he was surrounded by a dozen men in masks. They converged upon him en masse, encircling him. One member of the group seized his reins while others relieved him of his two pistols. They dragged him from his horse and threw him to the ground.

"Where did you get the money?" one of the masked men asked.

"I earned it at Williamson's ranch. What business is it of yours?"

One of the masked men lifted him by his collar only to deliver a hard blow to his face. He fell back to the dirt, his head bouncing off the hard ground.

"You are a goddam rustling thief."

"I am not," Bolt complained, rubbing the back of his head.

His disclaimer was met with another hard blow to the face. He felt blood leaking onto his cheek.

"Let me go," he complained. "You got no right to beat me. I'm harmin' no one."

"Name your confederates," another masked man demanded.

"I got nothing to say. You are cowards, waylayin' a kid on his way home."

A gunshot scattered the masked men. A red spot spread under the kid's shirt. Another man retrieved the leather money bag from the dying boy's clothes.

The men removed their face coverings.

The man with the money sack handed it to the shooter. The shooter lowered his rifle and removed his mask. Henry Pluenneke hefted the bag.

"Verner," he said as he tossed the money to Koenig. "See that Wolfgang receives what's in this bag for his losses. Anyone have a paper and pencil?"

Silently he was provided with the requested supplies.

He kneeled next to the dead kid and scrawled words on the rumpled paper.

It read "Here lies a noted cow thief."

Using a cactus spine, he pinned it to the back of the kid's shirt. He heaved the kid's corpse onto its face in the dust, the note easily visible for anyone who passed by.

He rose, examining his handiwork.

"He mentioned Williamson," Pluenneke said. "Carl Bader, I need you to get word to your brother in Loyal Valley. They can deal with Williamson."

Bader nodded, his eyes on the dead lad.

"I'll tell Peter," he said in a quavering voice.

They mounted their horses.

16

D EPUTY WORLEY HELD HIS RIFLE AT THE ready at the front of the courtroom. When he saw the door to the Judge's Chambers swing open, he cried "All rise for the judge."

Judge Hey moved towards his desk, his black robes swishing audibly in the silent court room.

The judge took his seat.

Worley called out, "Sit down."

Judge Hey thumbed through the handwritten paperwork provided by the Sheriff's office. He glanced up several times, searching the men before him, associating each with what he read.

Finally, he stacked the papers before him and looked upon the men awaiting his judgment.

"Gentlemen," he began. "This is not a trial. This is an arraignment. When I call your name, you will give me two answers. Both queries require no more than a one-word response. When I ask if you are guilty or not guilty, you will reply with an answer of guilty or not guilty to the crimes with which you are charged.

"This is not a trial, and I don't care to hear your side of the story. I don't want to know about the particulars of your case. I want to hear only if in your view you are guilty of the charges brought against you, or if you are not guilty of the charges brought against you.

"The second question is a yes or no question. I will ask you if you would like to be represented by counsel. Counsel is an attorney. If you would like to be represented by counsel, you will reply yes. If not, you will reply no. Again, I do not want to hear any testimony or any other thoughts you may have about your case. Am I clear?"

His question drew a rising din of murmurs but no intelligible answer.

"Very well." Hey continued. "In no particular order, I will begin calling names from the list of prisoners. Mr. Thomas, please rise."

MB Thomas rose stiffly, his hands to his sides, his back ramrod straight.

"I am MB Thomas, sir," he said in a clear voice. "I am not guilty, and I don't need a lawyer because I am not guilty."

"Mr. Thomas," Judge Hey said with a weariness which was his thin patience. "Please wait for me to read the charges and ask you the questions. You are charged with cattle rustling. Do you plead guilty or not guilty of the charge?"

"I've answered both questions, sir. Asking again will not change my answer. I am a reputable rancher in from Llano County and I resent these proceedings."

"Your answers are noted. Mr. Allen Roberts, please rise."

Roberts rose demonstrating identical outraged indignance.

"Mr. Roberts, you are also charged with cattle rustling. How do you plead?"

"I am not guilty of any crime, your honor. I don't require the help of a lawyer because I am innocent of these charges."

The proceedings continued in roughly the same manner until the last of the nine men charged had answered. All pled not guilty, and none required counsel.

After the last man was reseated, Judge Hey took off his glasses and looked over the men before him.

"Bail is set at $500.00 each. Your court date will be announced as the docket allows. If you fail to post bail, you will stay in jail until your court date."

The prisoners were returned to the two cells in the jail house. Sheriff Clark locked the cell and quieted the men with a gesture.

"Any of you men who can pay their bail step forward."

Voices rose as a general clamor of excited voices were raised in eagerness to post bail.

Once more Clark shushed them with a gesture.

You men arrested last night with a large amount of money on you cannot use that money to post bail. The money has been captured as the state's evidence in your cases.

Jarvis and his men rushed the bars, angry and protesting loudly.

"There is no use in arguing. The judge made the decision, not me. You can bring it up with him in your trial. The rest of you men step forward if you can cover your bail now."

Caleb Hall had hung back during the protest, speaking earnestly with MB Thomas. When called, Hall stepped forward with Thomas and the other two men who had been previously detained.

"Hall," Clark explained. "You are not allowed to use any money we collected from you for bail."

"You didn't collect any money from me because I ain't got any on me."

"I'm covering this man's bail," Thomas said soberly. I have enough among my possessions to cover both of us, and Roberts, and our guide, Tom Gamel."

Clark looked Thomas over suspiciously. His gaze moved to Hall, who stood quietly aside.

"Are you sure that's a good idea Thomas?"

"As I told the judge," Thomas replied. "I don't have a need for counsel, not even you. Take the money and release us at once."

The Sheriff did as he was bidden, and four of the nine inmates walked out of the jail.

Hall nodded at Jarvis with a touch to his nose.

17

TEXAS RANGER CAPTAIN DAN ROBERTS sat on a wooden chair in a dingy white canvas sided tent. He seemed frozen in place as he read a letter written on thick fibrous paper before dropping it on the small table beside him.

Nearby stood a young Ranger. The only feature distinguishing the ranger's appearance from any other frontier boy was a dingy handmade star on his chest. He was tall and spare, a big Navy Colt strapped to his waist. The worn holster was too small for the long pistol which hung bare beyond the leather like a foot sticking out beyond the sheets of a small bed.

"When did this letter arrive?" Captain Roberts asked the youth.

The young Ranger's voice quavered with his nervousness.

"With the evening post, sir."

With an amused eye, Roberts noted the boy's discomfort. The veteran Ranger was well aware of the stories circulating as to his adventures in the service of the state. He rose from the comfort of his chair with a grunt. Though many of those tales were embellished, the scars and their associated aches were not.

Roberts shooed the boy out of the way with a sweeping motion as he moved to the entrance of the tent. The young Ranger moved aside clumsily, nearly falling over the door post.

Captain Roberts was second in command of the Frontier Ranger Battalion, and leader of the famous Company D. He was an icon of Ranger lore, and wildly popular with the men. He was treated as a celebrity and regarded as a hero amongst his subordinates.

Outside, the morning was fresh and cool. Several of his men attended to horses and equipment nearby. The murmuring springs and gentle water falls of San Saba Springs provided a tranquil and serene atmosphere.

Roberts never failed to pause to admire the beauty of the scene. He did so now. He placed his rough hands on his hips and stretched the stiffness from his back and shoulders. He never spoke of it, but these early morning stretches forced him to take stock of the many wounds he had suffered from bullets, knives, and arrows.

Finally, he addressed the young Ranger, his back remaining towards him as he admired the view.

"Is Major Jones still in town?"

"Yessir, at the hotel."

"Send word that I request his presence at his earliest convenience."

The boy saluted and hurried away.

Roberts went to the central fire and poured a cup of coffee from the large pot. He sipped the scalding brew gingerly as he made his rounds, responding to the greetings and comments of his men. He ensured his men were in good form for the Major's visit.

Within the hour Major John B. Jones arrived at Roberts' tent. Roberts dismissed two of his men before stepping outside to greet the Major. They shook hands.

Roberts handed Jones the letter.

Jones read the letter as Roberts spoke.

"Judge Hey out of Mason County sent a letter to Governor Coke requesting assistance with their rustling dilemma. Governor Coke wants us to assemble an expeditionary mission to look into it. What are your orders, sir?"

Roberts waited for Jones to finish reading the entire missive.

The Major was a capable leader, and his manner was thorough. Before his time with the Texas Rangers, Jones had been a highly decorated officer in the Confederate Army. He had been instrumental in assembling the Frontier Ranger Battalion for Governor Coke. He handpicked Roberts before the Ranger unit was formed.

Jones considered Roberts with a thoughtful smile. Roberts could not help but smile in return. The man's humor was contagious. Jones was not a particularly jocular man. Rather, he found great reward from his life of dangerous pursuits and violent means. He was a warrior born to the trade. He approached his work in an offhanded way, tending to underplay the gravity of his actions.

Roberts recalled on many occasions where the Major faced certain death with a devil may care smile. During many of those times, Roberts had stood with the Major as crazed Indians or desperate outlaws attacked them. While the enemy swarmed around them, Roberts never thought to smile in response. Distinctly, he had felt an opposite urge in the moment. Early on, however, he had drawn courage from the Major's appearance of calm acceptance of matters beyond his control.

For Roberts, the lesson was clear. He believed unquestioningly he and his men had survived because a soldier cannot die if he is uncaring or unafraid of his own death.

Roberts stowed his thoughts as he turned his attention to his commander.

Major Jones turned the paper in his hands as if he might find more information than what was written.

"This missive mentions no violence," he said.

His gaze lifted towards the springs. He clasped his hands behind his back, the letter fluttering in the breeze behind him.

"Take three men with you to Mason under the auspices of purchasing supplies for one of our outposts nearby. Assess the situation and report."

"Yessir. I'll leave this morning."

Jones nodded, turning towards the Captain, his hands remaining behind his back.

"You have a fine vista here, Captain. I envy it."

He extended a hand to Roberts. They clasped hands, then Jones moved along up the hill towards the wooden buildings of San Saba.

18

BOYD AWOKE EARLY. He had adopted the habit of sleeping in the stables. Although too low and narrow to be considered a legitimate barn, the hay mow was a space above the ceiling planks where tack and various implements were stored against the elements and theft.

It was a comfortable place to sleep, and because of its height above the ground, warm during cool nights. He lay still for a moment as he gathered his wits from the remnants of his dreams. He heard voices below him. After a moment he recognized them as belonging to Verner Koenig and Ernst Wechsler.

"You killed him?" Ernst asked incredulously.

"He was a rustler, and your father was clear about how we are to handle these thieves.?

"I'm not saying otherwise," Ernst said. "I didn't think killing was in your nature. "What did that kid say about the others."

"He didn't say much, only he was carrying so much money because he collected wages from Williamson."

"Tim Williamson?"

"I guess. I don't know him."

"He's a rancher out of Cold Springs."

"Loyal Valley," Koenig corrected him.

"This ain't a school lesson. Don't counter me, Vern."

Koenig grunted.

"I think we should pay Williamson a visit," Koenig said. "He is probably involved one way or the other."

There was silence for a moment. Finally, Ernst spoke again.

"Where's Boyd?"

"Probably in bed. What do you want with him?"

"I got a bad feeling about this whole mess. Killing is a serious thing, even if it's a rustler who dies. Now that he's carrying a pistol, it might be in our best interest to have Boyd along on the next ride."

"You putting that much faith in his ability with a gun?"

"Of course not. I just want some insurance in case the law comes looking for a killer."

"He's your nephew, Ernst."

"Only half. The rest is as bad as them rustlers we are after. Blood will always tell. He ain't one of us. He's one of them."

"Goddam Ernst. He is still your sister's boy. You are a cold-blooded bastard."

"That's funny coming from the man who gave father the warning when Emma was about to elope."

There was silence for a long moment. Finally, Ernst chuckled as he spoke.

"I thought she was gonna shoot Spears - and with his own gun. Ha ha. I think he nearly pissed hisself."

"Why did the old man stand up for the kid like that? Ain't no love lost far as I can see."

"It would have looked bad if he gave up a man in his family or even the outfit without a fight. No one else knows the truth. He had to save face."

"So, what about going after Williamson?"

"I'll relay what you told me to the old man."

Boyd heard the men depart. He waited motionless until their footfalls were no longer audible. He dressed then lowered himself from the rafters. He dropped to the dirt floor, brushing off remaining hay strands from his clothing.

His thoughts were awash with what he had heard. Why did the family hate him so? Why would they try to hang a murder on him? Who was his father? His mother was to elope?

Years of mistreatment and careless comments replayed in his memory. It was a certainty he was not considered one of them. He was an outsider, maybe less. It was clear they wanted to frame him if murder was done. He was surprised Koenig had admitted to murdering a boy the previous night.

He reviewed recent events more carefully. Is that why Spears called his mother a whore? Was it all connected in some way? What was the secret his mother said caused her to pay more than anyone would ever know? Is that why she rarely went into town?

Whatever the answer, it was dire enough his family plotted to frame him for the ill-deeds they planned for the rustlers.

He felt an overwhelming urge to confront his mother, to get the full truth out of her. He had enough information to force from her the rest of the story he didn't know. He left the stables with purposeful strides. He would make her reveal it all to him.

He entered the kitchen. Finding it unoccupied, he moved into the house.

"Boyd."

He heard his Grandfather's voice calling him from his office. Boyd moved in that direction. He could as easily get the truth from him.

He arrived at the office doorway.

His grandfather sized him up from his seat behind the old desk.

"I thought I heard you bang that back door. I want to talk to you about the gun you hide in the stables."

Boyd didn't answer, trying to summon the courage to confront the Wolf with his new knowledge.

"I've changed my mind about your carrying it here on the ranch. You're old enough to handle a man's work. How good do you think you are with that sidearm?"

Boyd was taken aback. Why was his grandfather reversing his decision about him wearing a gun?

"Are you trying to size me for a hangman's noose, sir?"

"A hangman's noose? What the devil are you talking about? I don't have time for riddles."

"I heard Verner shot a kid last night and I'm to be blamed for it."

"This is the first I've heard of any of this. Where did you hear this?"

"I heard Verner tell Ernst about it this morning."

"Bring them to me immediately. We'll talk about your hanging later."

"Wechsler!"

A loud voice from outside the house froze Boyd where he was. He quickly came out of his surprise and looked at his grandfather. The old man's gaze had not left Boyd.

"Did you hear…?" Boyd began uncertainly.

"I did. Get your uncle and Verner, like I said. Find Klaus too."

Wechsler rose from his chair as Boyd hurried to obey. The Wolf crossed the house to the kitchen door.

Outside, a man sat a horse. He was unshaven and armed. His appearance indicated he had been long on the trail.

The old rancher recognized the man as a member of his Cattlemen's Association.

"You have news, Krause?" Wechsler commanded from inside the house.

"We did as you said, Herr Wechsler. The thieves came back to town. We tipped off the Sheriff and he has a jail full of rustlers."

Verner and Ernst appeared from around the corner of the house. Boyd appeared after a few more minutes bringing Klaus. When they arrived, the newcomer was speaking calmly to Wechsler, Ernst, and Vern.

Boyd waited a distance back from the others, watching the stranger with a keen eye.

The newcomer was midstream in an ongoing conversation with Boyd's grandfather.

"The strangers were carrying a lot of money with them," Krause said. "I don't know the exact amount, but Worley told me it was considerable."

"Go on," Wechsler prompted the rider, sensing there was more to be told.

"So, the Sheriff was in the Southern Hotel talking free and easy about the six new prisoners in his jail. He said he wasn't in fear of no Cattlemen's Association and what they might do. He said the keys to the cells would be safe and sound with deputy Worley."

Wechsler scratched his chin. His sons exchanged looks.

"That almost sounds like an invitation," Verner Koenig noted.

"It does," Wechsler agreed. "Gather the Association. We ride tonight. Klaus, go with Krause. Ernst, you, and Verner come to my office. We have much to discuss."

Wolf looked around until he located Boyd.

"You too," he said to Boyd.

Wechsler led his son and hired man to his office. Boyd followed, lagging behind. In his office, the old man leaned on his desk. He looked at Ernst with a stern eye.

"What is this I hear a boy was killed last night?"

Ernst looked at Verner. Boyd stood behind them, silent and observant.

Verner returned the look before clearing his throat.

"Keiferstein's boy saw a group of mounted men split into two parties a few miles northwest of town. Three men of the group headed east and south of town. The other group of a half dozen men rode into town. Keiferstein's boy lit out and passed the word to the Sheriff, then he found the on-duty Association Posse. I was with them, as you ordered.

"A lookout followed the second group into Mason. They ate and drank at the Southern Hotel. One of the men he saw headed east earlier, a boy, came back to town and entered the hotel. He showed off a lot of money and bought rounds at the bar. The other men didn't tarry but hightailed it when the kid showed up. I'm guessing those are the men in the jail.

"We caught up with the kid later, on the road southeast of town. We braced him and he told us he got all that money working for Williamson out of Loyal Valley. He wouldn't tell us more, so we shot him."

Verner produced the leather sack.

"Here is what he had on him, maybe forty dollars. I kept it to give to you."

He handed the leather bag over.

Wechsler eyed the bag before tossing it on his desk.

"What else?"

"We left a sign on him so thieves would know how we treat rustlers here in Mason County."

"I know Williamson," Wechsler said. "He has a reputation for moving cattle from time to time. Last I heard he was foreman over the Lehmberg Ranch. Carl Lehmberg would have nothing to do with rustlers. He is one of our own.

"The kid rustler said he was working for Williamson. That's all I know."

Wechsler nodded with no pleasure at what he heard. His manner was one accepting of events beyond his ability to control. He could only affect a response. But his response was something to which he was committed with his last breath.

"I have to go to town. Saddle up – both of you. You shall accompany me. You too."

This last was for Boyd. The other two glanced at him with little interest.

Wechsler, Ernst, Boyd, and Verner arrived at the sheriff's office as a lowering sky drove fierce winds and a smattering of rain against them, a spiteful warning of the storm to come.

They dismounted and entered the office.

Inside, Clark sat, drowsing behind his desk. His extravagant comfort was due in no small degree to the security he enjoyed, sheltered from the storm to come. The sturdy brick courthouse was as safe in a violent storm as any building in town. It was said a cyclone couldn't topple it.

Although the jail cells were full, the prisoners seemed to have surrendered to their fate. They remained silent as the Sheriff drowsed.

The newcomers' entry roused the Sheriff. He stood with a snort and a scuffling of his heavy boots dropping to the wooden floor planks. The prisoners looked over the four newcomers with interest.

The Sheriff nodded to the newcomers, sparing only a brief look of disdain for Boyd.

"Hello Herr Wechsler, Ernst, Verner. To what do I owe this unexpected visit?"

"You should have expected it John," Wechsler replied tersely. "There's more than a storm in the wind. The devil is up and busy."

"If you are talking about the Bolton boy found dead on the road this morning, you're right."

"I didn't know about the dead boy," Wechsler lied. "But I lost more than one-hundred head of young stock to rustlers, and it appears you have those rustlers here behind bars. The Städtbewohnen have made much of my grandson's actions here in town, visiting my place twice, once with Judge Hey. I am told you were ill-available."

Clark nodded sympathetically as the storm gained force outside, bludgeoning the building with heavy wind gusts. Smatterings of raindrops struck the windows with the force of flung gravel.

"Verner," Wechsler said loudly so he could be heard over the storm front. "Stable the horses across the street until the storm passes."

Verner hesitated for a moment before he moved to obey. The hired man had the look of one concerned his role in the boy's death might come under discussion while he was away.

Wechsler didn't seem to notice the delay as he continued his conversation with the Sheriff.

"What do you know about Tim Williamson?"

"Not much," Clark replied. "He works for Lehmberg out past Cold Springs. What does he have to do with any of this?"

Wechsler displayed signs of a growing frustration with the slow progress of the conversation.

"I have heard through rumors he is known to round up a stray from time to time. There is some talk he might have been a part of this latest theft. Don't you agree it might be worth a look, if you can fit it into your busy itinerary?"

"I suppose there ain't no such thing as a coincidence," the Sheriff said, shuffling papers on his desk.

He pulled a single sheet with trifold marks.

"I just got this missive today. The state wants me to bring him in on a state warrant for a tax matter. Now I have two reasons to ride to Loyal Valley. I'll head out after the storm."

Wechsler nodded with a small measure of satisfaction. He took a seat opposite the Sheriff at his desk. He glanced at the men in the two cells. Their attention was fully focused upon their conversation.

Clark considered the men in the cell for a long moment before returning his attention to Wechsler.

"Why don't we step outside for a moment, Herr Wechsler."

Both men rose.

Clark pointed at Boyd and Ernst.

"Stay away from them cells until I return."

Once outside, with the door closed, Wechsler spoke in a low tone, but with an authority which nettled Clark.

"I'm certain I don't need to remind you that I got you elected, a man without a past. We put you in office for one purpose, and one purpose only. That purpose did not include men visiting my ranch to remedy some inconsequential town matter. That purpose was to rid this county of the scourge that is the preponderance of rustlers here abouts.

"You gave your word you would commit your time and efforts to that end. Your time is now, Sheriff Clark. I want two things from you. The first is to root out the remaining cattle thieves and bring them to justice. The second is you stay out of my way when the Cattlemen's Association participates."

"Wolf," Clark said with the authority of his office. "I heard about your so-called Cattlemen's Association. I can't stand by while you or anyone else takes the law into his own hands."

"Don't hand me that guff, Sheriff. You are as loyal to your oath of office as the money we add to your salary is regular. I mean no slight when I say you are a chosen man, here particularly because you are not a man who finds refuge in an oath of office. This ends with peace and goodwill in the region. On that matter we both agree. Don't split hairs how we achieve that end, John. Do I have your help, or do I need to pay someone else?"

The rain rattled on the shake roof overhead with a loud staccato as Clark leaned against the brick wall. His face split into an unexpected smile. His demeanor was no longer that of the self-possessed lawman. His manner was more like an outlaw agreeing to a crime.

"Don't work yourself into a lather, Wolfgang. I was just gauging your commitment to what must be done. I have business elsewhere today and tomorrow. The keys to the jail are safely in the hands of Deputy Worley. Even if he goes home, he'll keep the keys with him."

Wechsler nodded, his lip curling as he glimpsed the true vagabond Clark was beneath the Sheriff's badge.

Leave it to an outlaw to do an outlaw's work, he thought.

Inside the Sheriff's office, Boyd surveyed the prisoners. The elder man amongst them caught his attention for two reasons. The primary reason was judging from the deference the others showed him, he appeared to be the leader of the group. The second was the keen attention he paid to Boyd in particular. Boyd was taken by surprise when the prisoner addressed him.

"What's your name kid?" the older prisoner asked, approaching the bars.

Jarvis grabbed the bars in two hands, watching Boyd carefully.

"What's it to you, mister?" Boyd replied.

"Not much," the other said without heat. "You look familiar is all."

"I don't know you," Boyd assured him.

"I'm sure of that. I'd still like to know your name, son."

Boyd hesitated before answering fearlessly.

"My name is Boyd Wechsler."

The older man's reaction to his words was remarkable. He stood straighter, releasing the bars. He seemed to pale a fraction beneath his sun darkened skin. His eyes widened, revealing the whites.

"You said 'Boyd' Wechsler?"

"That's right. I don't know you mister, like I said."

"Did you know your daddy?"

"I don't owe you any more answers."

"He died before you were born, didn't he?"

"How do you know that?"

"You would be interested in what I know."

"What's your name?"

Jarvis hesitated as he hastily reminded himself of the danger he faced if Wolfgang Wechsler learned his true identity.

"I'm Charlie Johnson."

"The name don't ring any bells."

"It wouldn't. But I knew your daddy, Kyle Boyd Hutton. He died before you were born."

"He was a rustler," Ernst snarled suddenly. "That proves you are one too. Were you a part of his gang of thieves too?"

The man claiming to be Charlie Johnson considered the German with a dangerous set to his jaw.

"I wasn't anywhere near when he was lynched."

Boyd raised his hand to his uncle, but his full attention was reserved for the prisoner.

"He was lynched, you say?"

"By your grandfather personally."

"Shut your mouth, prisoner!"

That last came from Wolfgang Wechsler as he and Clark reentered the room.

"Boyd," Wechsler said. "You and Ernst get us a room at the Southern for the night. The storm is coming, and it is a big one."

Ernst obeyed without a second thought, leaving the room immediately.

Boyd seemed reluctant to leave. He searched the prisoner's face, hungry for more information.

The Wolf stepped towards his grandson. He gripped the boy's shoulder, pulling him towards the door.

"Do as I say, boy."

Boyd shrugged off the hand with a gesture.

"Is what he says true, Grandfather?"

Boyd's tone held no innocent doubt or subservience. He was demanding an answer.

Boyd's unexpected rebellion against the Wolf's authority angered the latter, overpowering any restraint he may have relied upon. His response was terse and brutal.

"Your father was a cattle thief and a coward. He stole cattle from me while he tried to steal my daughter. He didn't have the courage to ask my blessing because he knew what he was. He received the justice he deserved. If it hadn't been me, it would have been someone else."

Boyd stared in shock at his grandfather. If anyone had spared a look at Jarvis, they would have seen a similar expression on his lined face. Both recognized a truthful confession. Both felt anguish at the admission.

"Obey me, boy." Wechsler shouted, ashamed of his weakness in a moment of anger.

Boyd shook his head. His eyes glistened with his emotion. The years of poor treatment and careless words flooded in. Ernst's and Verner's conversation that morning in the barn gained context. Boyd knew the truth. The man in the cell was telling the truth. Boyd's grandfather murdered his father in cold blood.

Boyd turned to the Sheriff who had remained silent as he took in the spectacle before him.

"Sheriff," Boyd said bitterly. "Verner Koenig killed that boy on the road last night. He confessed it to Ernst. I was nearby and heard the whole story."

Before the Sheriff could react, Jarvis cried out.

"Did you say Koenig, son?"

Boyd looked at the man called Charlie Johnson with a significant expression. This man had revealed a lifetime of information in a single moment. What more did he know?

"Yes, Verner Koenig."

"Koenig is the man who betrayed your father to the old man because he wanted your mom for himself and wanted your daddy out of the way. Kyle was taking her away that night to elope to San Antonio. The old man told Kyle he would see him dead before he saw him with his daughter. He didn't know she was with child – with you."

Wechsler had been frozen in place but suddenly he rushed to the cell bars.

"I'll kill you, you lying cur."

Jarvis didn't retreat. He didn't even flinch from the angry man's onslaught. Instead, he reached through the bars and pulled the old man roughly against the bars.

"I'll kill you, old man," he growled. "Bank on that."

The Sheriff rushed to Wechsler's aid, his gun drawn.

Jarvis released the old man, shoving him away from the bars. He showed no fear of the Sheriff's gun. He glanced at Boyd and a wry grin stretched his thin lips.

Boyd's face was a study in emotional upheaval. A storm was growing within the boy, not unlike the storm raging outside.

Jarvis chuckled with little mirth as he addressed the old man.

"I may not get out of here before the job is done for me, Wechsler."

He nodded at Boyd with a satisfied grunt.

Boyd turned his head slowly, looking at his grandfather with a deadly glint in his eye. In that moment, the pistol strapped to his waist seemed to grow in its significance to everyone in the room.

As the Sheriff recognized the danger, he aimed his pistol at Boyd.

"Give me that gunbelt, son."

Boyd turned his head towards the sheriff with the same slow deliberateness. His blue eyes were empty of life. The typical spark of a boy's mischief or joy was absent. Instead, there was a darkness where light would never enter.

Rather than dropping the gunbelt, Boyd turned from the sheriff and the gun he trained upon him. He walked to the door, slamming it as he left the room. He strode into the approaching storm.

The Sheriff moved to the cell, holding his pistol on Jarvis.

"Who are you, mister?" he asked.

"I'm Charlie Johnson, just like I said before."

"Why do you seem to know so much about our town?"

"There ain't no secrets a man can keep out here. Word will always go the rounds."

Jarvis looked at Wechsler, standing beyond the Sheriff. The old rancher searched the floorboards, oblivious to those around him. It was apparent his grandson's conduct concerned him. Eventually his wits seemed to return, and he gave Jarvis a long silent survey. Finally, he spoke to the Sheriff.

"Keep these men under lock and key Sheriff."

With that, Wechsler left the Sheriff's office. He made his way towards the Southern hotel, large raindrops striking him with force. The inconsistency of the falling rain was annoying. If the drops struck with regularity, it would be tolerable. Instead. The drops struck haphazardly, hitting the Wolf's ear, then between his shoulders. A raindrop heavy enough to soak a half dollar struck him in the chest, immediately wetting his skin. Wechsler cursed the rain, freshening his pace.

When he arrived at the hotel, the rain was falling with force. Lightning flashed evilly just overhead. Thunder shook the timbers from which the hotel was constructed, threatening to undo what man had endeavored to create.

Boyd completely occupied his thoughts. He had sensed a marked change in the boy as Johnson revealed what Wechsler and Emma had agreed to keep secret for more than a decade and a half. He deemed it necessary to evaluate the boy's disposition and determine if further steps needed to be taken.

Ernst stomped water and mud from his boots as he entered the front door of the hotel.

"Where is Boyd?" Wechsler asked his son.

"He didn't say. He just took his horse and rode off. I didn't see which way. I just finished helping Vern with our horses and came here. What happened after I left, father?"

Wechsler did not respond. He glanced out the nearest window. He could see nothing beyond the pane as water sheeted it, obscuring all but the flashes of lightning.

19

AS IS COMMON WITH VIOLENT WEST Texas storms, after a period of attacking lightning and deafening thunder, rain comes down like an overhead lake emptying onto the ground. Despite the promise of an unceasing deluge, the rain passes quickly.

This one was no exception. A growing distance dimmed the empty threat of receding thunder as it chased the fleeing storm.

In the small house he rented just outside of Mason, Deputy Worley listened to the fading thunder as he watched a comforting fire in his rough stone fireplace.

It was well past his typical bedtime when he finally succumbed to weariness and made his way to the little bedroom, where he slipped into bed beside his wife.

He lay awake for a long time. His wife snored quietly as he waited. Although tired, sleep eluded him as he awaited the men he knew would arrive that night. He waited for no more than half an hour before he heard the expected sounds of horses approaching. He rose carefully and dressed.

His wife stirred.

"What is it, John?" she asked in a sleepy voice.

"Nothing Trudy. Go back to sleep."

Worley pulled up his suspenders as he went to the front door of the little shack. He opened the planked door a fraction.

A large gathering of at least a dozen masked men astride restless horses filled his front yard beyond the front stoop.

"We're gonna need the keys to the jail, Worley," the masked leader demanded.

Worley nodded helplessly.

"I guess you fellas got me dead to rights. I ain't armed and can't very well stop you."

Worley reached into his pocket and produced a metal hoop rattling with dangling keys.

"Here they are. I want you boys to know I don't approve of what you are doing and am in no way to blame."

One of the masked men laughed roughly.

"Yeah, Worley. We get it. You ain't involved in the faintest. Klaus, get them keys while we're young."

One of the riders rode forward, accepting the key ring from the deputy.

"Get some sleep, John," Klaus Wechsler muttered quietly from behind the cloth covering his face.

The door opened fully to reveal Trudy Worley in a wrap, a hand covering her mouth.

"John, what are these men doing at our door in the middle of the night? Did I just hear Fritz Keiferstein behind one of those masks?"

Get back inside woman," Worley said harshly. To the riders he said, "Don't worry boys. We didn't see or hear a thing."

The men wheeled their horses and rode off into the night.

Worley entered the house. Trudy was about to speak when he cut her off.

"You saw nothing, and you didn't hear nothing. Is that understood?"

Trudy nodded.

Jarvis awoke with a start. The jail was dark saving a single candle burning on the windowsill. The door burst open, and the room filled quickly with masked men.

Guns were trained on the prisoners as the cell doors were unlocked. One by one the prisoners were pulled from their cells, their hands bound behind their backs with rough cord rope.

The prisoners gave little resistance to the mob as they were bound then herded outside where other men awaited, leading enough riderless horses to accommodate the mob and the prisoners.

"This is it," Jarvis heard Eli Baccus say to his brother.

"Keep still," one of the hooded men warned. "Or you'll die here in the mud."

The prisoners struggled to mount with tied hands. The hooded men helped them by shoving them roughly into the saddle.

As he was led to his horse, Jarvis fell into a puddle. With a curse, the man leading him lifted him off the ground.

"Clumsy old man," the hooded man complained. "You got my clothes muddy."

The man got Jarvis into the saddle then moved to his own horse.

Jarvis worked his forearms back and forth. He felt the smallest amount of play in the ropes around his wrists as the group moved out. While he was being tied inside the Sheriff's office, he had kept his wrists stiff and slightly apart, an old prisoner's trick. He had purposely tumbled into the puddle. He gambled the water soaking the ropes would soften them enough for him to free his hands: hopefully before they hung him.

At a distance, the lights of Mason burned. The town was not only awake, but the townsfolk trod the streets like festival goers. By contrast, the roads around the courthouse were dark and empty, as if the townspeople purposely avoided that region.

It was plain to Jarvis their fate was known to everyone in town. It was also obvious no one was willing to intervene on their behalf.

The leaders of the lynch mob led the group southeast, the nearest route out of town. The riders, both prisoners and HooDoos, remained mute as they rode.

The rhythmic sound of horses' hooves in the mud was accompanied by a tapping staccato as water tumbled from the tree leaves as a slight breeze disturbed them.

The evening seemed cooler than normal. Jarvis was uncertain whether he was chilled by the rain cooled atmosphere or by a fearful dread of the fate before him and his men.

20

I

T WAS WELL AFTER DARK WHEN CAPTAIN Roberts and his three Rangers entered the outskirts of town. To their surprise, Mason was alive with noise and activity. Every house, and most of the commercial buildings, were aglow with lights. Even at that late hour, townspeople milled about the streets.

Roberts directed his mount towards the center of town where a boisterous group gathered around the hotel. The Rangers tied their horses to the hitching rail. They entered the smoky din of the Southern Hotel saloon. He instructed his three Rangers to stay back and watch from the edges of the room as Roberts entered, pushing through the crowded doorway.

Inside, the lobby and saloon were filled to capacity. Tobacco smoke obscured the ceiling. At the bar, a tightly packed audience paid attention to a central figure whose voice boomed above the din.

"I don't control what happens when I am not here, but that doesn't mean it goes unanswered. Those men deserve what they have coming. I suppose the citizens lack the patience to wait for the slow workings of the law. I am the law here, but the law is no less than an extension of the people."

Captain Roberts shouldered through the crowd. In the center of the throng was Sheriff Clark, elbows on the bar. His features sagged from alcohol consumption as if melting from a hot fire.

"What goes on here?" Roberts demanded. "Sheriff, what have you done?"

Russel Spears pressed forward until he stood beside the Ranger Captain.

"The goddam Prussians organized a vigilance committee. They broke into the jailhouse and took away the prisoners for their own justice. The Sheriff here works for them Germans and is turning a blind eye to the lawlessness of them foreign invaders."

"Is this true, Sheriff?" Roberts demanded, grasping the drunken lawman by his shoulder.

"Don't paw me mister," Clark warned. "What do you expect me to do about it? I don't have the men to go against a mob of angry and armed men."

"I expect you, sir, to do your job. You swore an oath."

Roberts turned to Spears.

"Where did these vigilante's take those men?"

"They rode southeast on the road to Fredericksburg."

Roberts studied Clark with a critical dark scrutiny. He muttered an oath then shoved Clark out of the way with a roughness beyond what might have been necessary.

"Who will volunteer to ride with me and my men?" the Ranger asked loudly.

The room grew silent.

"No one?" Roberts cried. "You men ask the state for help, but you are willing to do nothing to help yourselves?"

Spears crossed his arms and spoke in a casual tone in the now silent room.

"We didn't ask for nothing. Them Germans are taking the law into their own hands. That is your problem. The only thing we want from you is for you to do 'your' job."

Roberts muttered another oath then shoved his way through the crowd towards the door. He joined his men at the edge of the room.

"Mount up, Rangers. We got a job to do."

Two men approached the Rangers on the street.

"Ranger," one of the men said quietly. "I'm Caleb Hall and this is Tom Gamel. We'll join your posse."

Roberts eyed them suspiciously.

Hall took off his hat and wrung it in his hands.

"We were arrested with the others. We paid bail and dodged that mob. We know those men, Ranger. We just want to do what's right."

"You are offering to do a very brave thing, Mr. Hall. I'm Captain Roberts. Get your horses and come with us.

21

THE MASKED VIGILANTES SURROUNDED their prisoners on all sides as they escorted them along the dark trail. The prisoners' horses were chain-tied together.

The masked leader raised a hand as he pulled up his mount.

"This is far enough men."

The masked leader pointed at three of the vigilantes.

"You men take two ropes and locate two good hanging trees."

The masked leader pointed at three other vigilantes.

"You three men pick out two of these rustlers for the first round."

The first three vigilantes produced ropes and rode away to locate adequately appointed trees.

The others dismounted and untied the chain knots from Eli and Pete Baccus' horses, freeing Jarvis', and Abe Wiggins' horses.

The Baccus' were led into the grove of tall trees where the others had gone.

Abe Wiggins began to weep.

Through his emotion he yelled, "I ain't hangin'."

Although his hands were tied behind his back, he kicked his mount in the flanks. The horse snorted as he leapt forward, knocking one of the vigilantes to the ground.

Two of the masked men armed with rifles were ready for the break. They brought their rifles up. Two loud reports sounded as one and Wiggins fell to the ground, rolling from the speed of the fleeing horse. He finally came to a stop, laying limp and lifeless on the cold muddy ground, his head cracked like an egg.

Since leaving the jail, Jarvis had busied himself working at the rope binding his wrists with hopeful effect. The loosening of his bonds had increased during the ride. He only needed a moment more to…

As the rifles sounded Jarvis managed to slip his hands out of the ropes. He kicked the man holding his mount and headed the horse into the darkness going the opposite direction from where Abe Wiggins lay dead on the ground.

More rifle shots peppered the woods around him, but none touched him.

"You two," the leader yelled. "Catch him before he gets away."

Two of them leaped upon horses and gave chase.

As the noise of pursuit faded into the dripping darkness, the leader turned to Turley, who sat his mount impassively.

Bring that man along to the grove.

When they arrived, Eli and Pete Baccus were under separate trees, sitting their horses, ropes draped around their necks.

"Stretch 'em boys," the leader commanded. The hangmen slapped the horses' rumps. The two brothers moved forward with their horses until the ropes pulled taut. They were dragged back over the horses' hindquarters where they swung from the trees, kicking silently, no breath escaping to give voice to their agony.

Once they were dead, Turley was brought forward. The hangmen lifted Eli and removed the noose from his neck. They led Turley's horse into position, tightening the noose around his neck.

"Hang him," the leader commanded.

One of the hangmen slapped the horse's rump. Turley was lifted from his saddle, swinging in the air. His legs kicked and he made a strangled gurgling noise.

"The knot snagged," said one of the hangmen. "He'll dangle a while now."

The sound of horses breaking through the brush caught the vigilantes' attention.

The second hangman called to the leader.

"That can't be them boys bringing back the escaped prisoner. Wrong direction."

"That's law boys," said the leader. "Time to slope."

The vigilantes mounted and fled into the night, away from the sound of the approaching horses.

Captain Roberts and his men thundered into the grove. They saw Turley kicking and choking. Hall and Gamel hurried to him. One grabbed him and lifted him as the other cut the rope. Turley dropped to the muddy ground, gasping and gagging.

Roberts and his three rangers dismounted beside Abe Wiggins, who lay unmoving in a puddle of blood and brains.

Roberts shook his head as he spoke.

"This is bad business, Men."

He looked at the nearest Ranger.

"McCullough," he said, "Help them two men with the live one. Get him back to the jail and call a doctor. Guard your man until we return. The Sheriff is not to be trusted with him."

Jarvis struggled to control the running horse. The lead rope dangled from the neck of the frightened animal, the loose end dragging the ground.

He leaned low across the horse's withers, reaching for the rope's end. Low hanging branches slashed at him, threatening to dislodge him from the saddle. He finally managed to gather the loose end of the rope. He grasped one of the horse's ears and pulled it back. The horse stopped short, whirling in the direction of the pained ear.

Jarvis fashioned the rope into a makeshift hackamore. He resumed his place in the saddle and put his heels to the horse. Two riders thundered to a stop behind him. They held rifles, covering him.

"Hands up, Johnson," one of the men said behind his mask.

Jarvis pulled up his mount. He turned his head towards his captors.

"Ernst," the other man said impatiently. "Finish this piece of shit rustler here and now. We don't need more trouble from him."

"I'm not a murderer, Vern," Ernst said to the other.

Verner Koenig levered a round into the chamber.

"This ain't murder. This is justice."

Verner took aim.

A gunshot cracked from the woods nearby and Verner Koenig fell from his horse, twisting like a snake hit with a shovel.

Boyd stepped from the woods, his pistol on his uncle Ernst.

"Take off your mask, Ernst," Boyd said.

Ernst hesitated but finally removed his face covering.

"You killed Verner, Boyd. Are you one of them now?"

"I don't know what I am, Uncle. I know what I ain't, though. I ain't one of you."

"We already knew that," Ernst said with a hint of condescension.

"I wouldn't say that too loud, Uncle. I haven't decided whether I am one of them or not. You may not like my decision."

Verner stopped writhing and grew quiet.

"Get out of here, Uncle."

Ernst opened his mouth to speak but decided against it. He turned his mount and headed back from where he came.

Boyd approached Jarvis.

"You hit?" he asked the outlaw.

"Not a scratch. You have my thanks."

"Don't mention it Mr. Johnson. You did me a good turn. I just returned the favor."

"My name ain't Johnson," Jarvis said. "I'm Jarvis Hutton. Your daddy was my brother."

Boyd nodded his understanding.

"It had to be something like that," he observed. "You seemed too close to it all."

"You can't get no closer. So, what's next for you Boyd Hutton?"

"I was going to ask you the same question."

"We'd best slope before the one you let go gets word to the others."

They headed their mounts into the darkness, leaving the dead man behind them in the mud.

22

CAPTAIN ROBERTS AND HIS REMAINING two rangers rode back to Mason with three corpses in tow. When they arrived at the courthouse, he checked on Turley who was back in his jail cell. Sheriff Clark sat at his desk as Roberts entered. His face remained flushed from the effects of the alcohol. He made no comment as the ranger approached.

"If this man dies on your watch, Sheriff, I'll see you face murder charges for it."

Clark sneered at Roberts.

"I got business out of town in the morning. I'll alert my deputy of my imminent hanging if this man dies, but I can't wait around here. I'm riding to Loyal Valley directly."

Roberts leaned over the desk towards the lounging Sheriff, his ire up.

"You'll do as I order, Clark. Send your deputy to Loyal Valley if you have to, but you are responsible for this man's life. You will protect him personally. Am I clear?"

Clark frowned at the Ranger's tone.

"You ain't got no authority to tell me…"

"Shut your mouth, Clark," Roberts said in a low menacing tone. "I act on the orders of Governor Coke. I have all of the authority here. How did a mob get the keys to the jail last night?"

"How am I supposed to know that, Ranger? A group of masked men braced my deputy and his wife. They demanded the keys to the jail. My deputy and his wife say they didn't recognize any of them. Their faces were covered, and it was dark."

There ain't more than six hundred people in the whole county. Everyone knows everyone. I ain't buying they didn't even recognize a voice. The chief question, though, is why was your deputy in possession of the keys to the jail at his home?"

Clark made no reply.

Roberts growled his frustration as he stood from his leaning position over the Sheriff's desk.

"I will get to the bottom of this, Clark."

Captain Roberts stepped outside.

Caleb Hall and Tom Gamel rode up to the Ranger Captain.

"You can count on us as witnesses to what happened here," Hall said. "Those dead men were friends of ours. No matter what they may or may not have been guilty of, they didn't deserve what they got."

Gamel added nothing but nodded his agreement.

Roberts mounted his horse. His three rangers approached with supplies loaded on a pack horse.

"I appreciate your efforts men," he said. "My advice to both of you is to put miles between you and this place. Your bail will not protect you from vigilantes. Good luck."

The rangers rode away, leaving the two former rustlers behind.

Gamel glanced behind them at the sheriff's office. Sheriff Clark watched them through the window.

"I'm gonna tell what happened here," Hall said with heat. "What happened last night was cold blooded murder and the Sheriff and his men are behind it."

Gamel touched the other on the arm.

Hall looked at his companion. He saw Gamel was intent on something behind him. He looked in the same direction. He saw Clark watching them through the window.

"Shit," Hall muttered under his breath.

The Sheriff left his place at the window. He appeared at the door. After a lengthy stare at the departing Rangers, he approached the two men.

"Your name is Hall, isn't it?" he asked.

"What's it to you Sheriff?"

"It's a lot, Hall. You are a part of that gang of rustlers we brought in the other night, ain't you?"

"I posted bail, all legal and official."

"Well things have changed since them poor boys got themselves hung. I'm going to place you in protective custody - for your own safety."

"I don't need your protection," Hall said with little strength to his voice. "We'll be movin' on now..."

"Nope," Clark said firmly. "Get off that horse and come with me."

Gamel turned his horse to depart.

The Sheriff made a clucking sound with his tongue.

"Your name is Gamel. Am I right?"

"That's right Sheriff, but I ain't a part of that gang you brought in. I was with them ranchers who were looking for their cattle. I'm leaving the county for good - right now."

Clark narrowed his eyes at the man.

"See that you do. You won't get a second chance."

Gamel rode away without a word.

Clark led Hall to the jail where he locked him in the cell with Tom Turley, a raw band on his neck where the hangman's rope burned him.

"You boys cool your heels here. I expect you won't need to wait long before them HooDoos drop by to finish what they started."

Clark laughed with an ugly sound.

"Them HooDoos," he repeated with emphasis on the term. "HooDoo…that's a good one."

Clark paused, turning to the inmates.

"Well not so good for you two outlaws…but still a good one."

Clark strode from the office.

Hall sat beside Turley on the single bed in the cell.

"How's your neck, Tom?" he asked.

"We gotta get out of here and quick," Turley said with unmistakable gravity. "I don't know what he saw, or heard you say out there, but he cussed pretty strong before he went out and hauled you in here."

"How can we escape before they come for us?"

Turley produced a white cloth with a trace of blood on it.

"The doctor wrapped my neck with this bandage."

Turley worked at something within the folds of the cloth. He produced a stiff wire, bent in a half circle.

"He secured it with this brad wire," Turley continued. "When the time is right, I'll work the lock, then we get the hell out of this."

Hall nodded, his eyes moist with hope.

"If we get out of this, Turley, I'll owe you a big debt. I'm with you."

"You already saved mine when you pulled that noose off my neck."

They clasped hands firmly then waited for their moment.

Sheriff Clark rode to Deputy Worley's house. The deputy stepped onto the front porch before Clark could dismount. He was in his long handles and stocking feet.

"What gives, John?" Worley asked without preamble.

"Texas Rangers are involved now. They broke up the Association's necktie party last night. Three of the rustlers were killed, one got away, and I got two in a cell."

"Rangers, huh?"

"I don't see much coming of it if we keep our mouths shut, but the man in command, Captain Roberts, he was pretty worked up. He wants me to keep an eye on the survivors. He was curious how you happened to have the keys to the jail with you here."

"Goddam John. You said I wouldn't be suspected of nothing if Trudy and me gave the same story."

"You're fine," Clark assured him. "If anything, it might seem a mistake we made trying to head off trouble. We can't be expected to know the mind of a vigilante mob. Just stick with the story no matter what."

"This is getting too big, Sheriff. I don't know if…"

"Keep your nerve, Deputy Worley," Clark commanded. "I need you to throw on your boots and serve this warrant on Tim Williamson over to Loyal Valley."

"Trudy is still shook up about last night, Sheriff. I think its best if I stay close – in case somebody comes by asking questions."

"Get on your horse and handle this warrant, John. I ain't askin', I'm tellin'."

Clark pulled his horse around and loped away from Worley.

The deputy looked over the warrant then, with an oath, turned and entered the house, banging the front door as he did.

Clark's ride back to the jail was filled with dark thoughts. He fought a mounting sense of foreboding. Talk of the Governor being involved in Mason business troubled him.

He tied his horse and stomped the mud from his boots as he entered his office.

"Alright boys," he began.

He stopped short, forgetting to breathe. The cell where he had left his two prisoners was empty, the door wide open.

"Dammit," he exclaimed as he hurried back outside. The road beyond the perimeter fence was empty, and he saw no sign of the escaping prisoners nearby.

"Dammit," he repeated before returning to his office.

He slammed the cell closed then fled from his office. He mounted his horse and spurred the animal towards the southeast, the most likely direction for an escapee, trying to find the quickest way out of town.

Caleb Hall and Tom Turley watched from the thicket behind the courthouse as the Sheriff sped away. They crossed the distance towards the livery at a sprint. Inside were several stabled horses. They indiscriminately selected two and hurriedly saddled them. The Sheriff would not be gone long before he figured out his fugitives were not fleeing for open country towards the southeast.

They led the horses out of the livery, casting worried looks up and down the street. There were few townspeople on the street, probably sleeping off the night's revelry. They mounted and struck a fast pace towards the northeast.

As was his habit, after Jarvis brought them to Mason, Wiggins had done his homework in case a hasty retreat was required. He knew the lay of the land and the best way out. With luck, they would gain the heavily wooded country towards Goldwaithe before he corrected their course west. The muddy ground was problematic, but they had speed and misdirection on their side.

The Sheriff would have to learn of the stolen horses then locate their direction of escape. Those two things would take time.

23

IT WAS NEAR MIDAFTERNOON WHEN Worley arrived at the Williamson Ranch. He tied his horse at the rail and climbed the stairs to the neatly appointed ranch house. Before he could knock, the door opened, and Mary Elizabeth Williamson stood there.

Worley removed his hat.

"I'm Deputy Worley of Mason County, ma'am. Is Tim Williamson about?"

"What's your business with my husband Deputy Worley?"

"Law business, Mrs. Williamson."

Worley produced a folded paper from his jacket pocket.

"I have a warrant for your husband's arrest for failing to pay a tax debt he promised to pay. This is a warrant from the state. I'm to take him into custody and deliver him to officers of the state when they come for him."

"That is preposterous. My husband is not going anywhere with you. If the state has a cause, they can come by if they must."

"Ma'am," Worley began carefully. "I am only doing my job. Is your husband here?"

"It's alright Mary," Tim Williamson called from within the house. "Let me handle this."

Mary turned from the door, retreating into the interior of the house as Williamson appeared in her place.

Williamson stepped onto the porch.

"There must be some mistake, Deputy. This matter was handled weeks ago. I have the receipts to prove it."

"Nevertheless Mr. Williamson, my orders are clear. I am to take you in without fail. You can clear this up with the judge, and if you did take care of this matter, I imagine you will be free to return without delay. So, if you'll come with me, we can avoid any unpleasantness."

"I have a few questions," said another voice from behind Williamson.

An older man with silver hair and bright blue eyes within a sun darkened and lined face took his place beside Williamson.

"I don't know you sir." Worley said warily.

"My name is Carl Lehmberg, Deputy Worley. I own the adjoining ranch. Tim works for me on occasion as fore-man. I sold him this place. I know about the tax records here.

"You sold him the land. I don't see how this is your con-cern if you ain't a law attorney. Come on Williamson. We have wasted enough time here."

"I find it irregular a county officer would serve a state warrant," Lemburg said calmly.

"Like I said," Worley repeated with growing heat. "My orders are clear. I cannot, and will not, parley with you about it. Tell it to the judge."

Williamson raised his hands in a gesture of compliance.

"It's all right Mr. Lehmberg. I appreciate your taking my part. I have business in Mason anyhow. I'll come along peacefully Deputy. Let me grab my hat."

Lehmberg eyed Williamson with concern. He glanced at Worley who made no effort to hide his relief at the averted conflict.

"I'm going along with you in case I am needed, Tim."

Williamson reappeared wearing his hat, Mary just behind him. He kissed Mary and stepped onto the porch. He turned to the older rancher.

"I thank you for your concern, Mr. Lehmberg. That's not necessary."

"It's settled Tim," the rancher returned stubbornly. "I'm coming along."

"Thanks Mr. Lehmberg."

Williamson addressed Worley.

"I need to saddle my horse. I'll be only a moment."

Williamson returned, mounted on his favorite gelding. The other two were already in the saddle when he arrived.

"That's a fine gelding Williamson, "Worley said. "I'm gonna need to trade with you for the trip in."

Both of the other men protested with dismay.

"I'm sorry," Worley explained. "If you make a break, my nag won't be able to catch you."

Lehmberg snorted his ridicule over the concern.

"Despite the dubious nature of your visit, Tim has demonstrated nothing other than a willingness to comply with your demands. Trading horses is out of the question."

"It's either that or he makes the trip in irons," Worley said with a growing menace in his tone.

Williamson's good nature evaporated at the threat. He inhaled to say something more. Worley interrupted him, pulling his pistol from its holster.

"Get off that horse and trade with me. I ain't asking again."

Obviously shocked at the change in the lawman, Williamson obediently dismounted and traded as commanded.

"The judge will hear about this mistreatment," Lehmberg promised.

The three moved out without further comment.

They turned west on the road beyond Williamson's property line. They travelled in discomfort with one another for some time before Williamson broke the silence.

"Look yonder," he said, pointing down the road ahead of them. "That is a large group of riders bearing down on us."

The others looked up from their thoughts. Heading towards them at a gallop was a group of nearly a dozen men.

"I don't see that well," Lehmberg said. "Do you recognize them?"

Williamson made no reply as he squinted to make out the identity of the riders.

"Do you see anyone you know Tim?" Lehmberg repeated with growing alarm.

By this time, the riders had approached near enough where it was plain to see their faces were concealed behind masks. Their weapons were drawn and held threateningly.

"Vigilantes," Williamson cried, turning his horse to flee. "Back to the ranch Mr. Lehmberg."

The old rancher obeyed instantly. He was better mounted than Williamson and quickly outran Williamson and the Deputy. Soon he disappeared beyond a rise in the road.

From behind, Williamson heard a gunshot and his horse faltered then fell. The horse struggled to stay upright as he fell, miraculously allowing Williamson to land on his feet. However, he was unable to maintain his stride at that speed and he fell on his face, sliding to a stop. He looked up in time to see Worley ride by on his gelding, sheathing his pistol.

Shots came from the approaching group. Bullets struck impotently around the Deputy, none coming near enough to threaten his safety. Nonetheless, he rode at a full gallop until he disappeared over the rise beyond which Lehmberg had disappeared.

Williamson got to his feet, dusting off his clothes as the group of masked men pulled rein, surrounding him on all sides.

Worley stopped his mount in front of Lehmberg, who had halted his horse and was wheeling around to return to render aid.

Worley was out of breath when he reined in.

"Where is Tim? Did they shoot him?"

"They got his horse," Worley explained with forced concern. "I was about to stop and help when they began shooting at me. I barely got away with my life."

"We have to help Tim. You're a Deputy Sheriff. Do your duty Worley."

"Hell no!" Worley cried. "We can't help Williamson unless we want to get killed too."

"How do you know they plan to kill Tim?"

Worley stammered as he replied.

"What else do you think they are gonna do? They shot at me. We'd best keep moving so they don't get us too."

Lehmberg shook his head. His struggle with the difficult decision to either try to save his friend or survive was plain in his manner.

A flurry of gunshots made his decision for him. He and Worley spurred their mounts back towards the Wiliamson ranch.

Williamson looked around him at the mounted vigilantes. He recognized one of the horses as belonging to a man he knew. The rider was masked, but Williamson recognized his stocky build.

"Peter Bader," Williamson called to the masked man. "I know you. We have been friendly for many years. Talk to these men. Tell them they are making a mistake. I know your horse, Daniel Hoerster. That paint horse is unmistakable. Men, we go back a ways. Don't do nothing rash."

"This ain't personal Tim," Bader said, his voice muffled behind his mask. He fired his pistol, striking Williamson dead center. The others fired a fusillade spinning Williamson in a tight circle before he fell and lay still.

The riders retreated, heading back from where they came. They pulled alongside one another, removing their face coverings. Their faces were moist with sweat from the Sun's heat beneath the masks.

Bader sidled up to Daniel Hoerster, a man of his middle twenties with a bushy waxed mustache beneath a hawkish nose.

"I advise you change out your mount next time" Peter Bader said. "Pick something these rustlers won't recognize.

"Hell, Pete," Hoerster countered. "He recognized your horse too and that table belly you carry around."

Bader grunted rather than reply to Hoerster's accurate observation.

"Scatter men," Bader called to the others. "Be ready for the next signal."

He nodded to one of the men nearby.

"Pluenneke," Bader said. "Stick by me."

Both men spurred their mounts to a gallop, leaving the group to disperse.

24

B OYD AND JARVIS RODE ABREAST. They topped a grassy knoll just above a heavily bunched oak mott. A roiling storm cloud mass towered over the western horizon, looking dark and bruised.

"Rain coming tonight," Jarvis predicted. "You know how to build a proper lean-to, boy?"

Boyd hesitated before answering.

"A lean-to is a bad idea in a strong storm," he said. "Might as well lay out on the ground."

"Not if you know how to build one…"

"My name ain't boy, and I ain't your roustabout in camp. I just met you and we ain't friends either."

"But we are family," Jarvis argued. "You can't talk that part away."

"We'll see," Boyd said simply. "Follow me. I know of an old-line shack just east of here. We should get there ahead of the rain if we hurry. If no one is there, we can hole up and wait out the weather.

Jarvis nodded compliantly. A line shack was preferable to a leaky lean to, and he didn't want to upset his nephew any more than he had so far. Jarvis sensed there was enough Hutton blood in Boyd he likely harbored an as yet unseen innate danger. It was best to move slowly until he was accepted as family and an ally.

As Boyd predicted, they arrived at the small windowless line shack with the first fat droplets of rain. They sheltered the horses within a dense grove of Live Oaks, taking their saddles and other belongings with them to their small shelter. Inside, they arranged for as much comfort as saddles and saddle blankets could offer. The storm grew to a raging beast, crashing against the thin wooden planks, rendering conversation useless.

For the next two hours they sat silently, listening to the violence outside. They cast glances at the roof and walls as though they could see beyond and gauge their chances of survival from the storm.

As suddenly as it began, the storm ended its assault, leaving behind a strange silence with which the two found difficult to grow accustomed.

After retrieving the horses, they moved to a hillock nearby and built a comfortable fire. The warmth of the modest flames and the calmer weather were a welcome change, distracting them from the discomfort of their hunger pangs. Their only sustenance was a canteen of water and two sticks of hardtack Boyd carried in his pack behind his saddle.

Sitting before the merry fire with his brother's son, Jarvis grew melancholy. The boy favored Kyle enough the old outlaw drifted into a fantasy he shared the fire with his dead brother in fact. Even the boy's manner furthered the caricature of Jarvis' phantasmal imaginings. He retreated fully into the comfort of the waking dream, uncaring of the peril such a fiction might have upon his perception of reality or the rational.

Boyd watched the subtle changes washing over his uncle with a cautious interest. He knew little of the man, but the moist glimmer in his eyes and his unflinching study of Boyd set him ill at ease.

Boyd had little experience with the conduct of outlaws, at least that is how he summarized his newly acquainted kin. Did the ill deeds of the outlaw life result in enough guilt to addle the mind?

Boyd had only that previous night killed a man known to him all of his life. Unsuccessfully, he attempted to press his memories of Verner Koenig from his mind.

Before he died, the taciturn German rancher had occupied little space in Boyd's considerations. Since the man fell to his pistol in the clearing where Boyd saved his uncle's life, his thoughts had room for little else.

He recalled the narrowly averted duel with Russel Spears at his grandfather's ranch. In the moment of conflict, the moral considerations of killing Spears had no place in his determination to shoot the man. Nothing more than a need to feed his rage occupied him. Would Boyd have felt the discomfort he endured now if he had gunned down Spears, or was the source of his current funk his long term, though perfunctory, relationship with Koenig? Whatever the elusive answer to his dilemma, he experienced a decided ache and discomfort at taking the ranch hand's life.

"You remind me too much of your daddy, boy."

Jarvis' observation revived Boyd's strength and he pressed the discomfort of his broodings from him. To his relief, his companion had lost some of the somberness which had occupied him before. Jarvis' eye was clearer. His gaze had lost some of its murkiness and he beheld Boyd with a casual interest easier for the younger man to bear.

"You have his eyes and his looks," Jarvis continued unbidden. "He never saved my life like you did last night. I was generally the one who saved his. It was a habit I had to acquire. That's what kept me from finding you sooner.

I spent nearly twenty years at the Walls taking his medicine for him. I knew he couldn't last inside. In review, he might have been better off locked away. At least there would have been a small chance he would have been here today."

Boyd listened without appearing too interested. He had yet to accept this new revelation about his real identity. He clung to his old life still, although he harbored no lasting loyalty to his grandfather or his clan.

He was reluctant to bring the weight of his judgement upon his mother. He was loathe to begin a review that might impugn her in his assessment of her role in the deception.

"What are your plans now you know the truth?" Jarvis asked.

Boyd surveyed his uncle, comparing him to those who had comprised his former life. He found nothing remarkable or noteworthy in his uncle. The man appeared a saddle tramp. He was an admitted ex-con who had languished in a cell for most of the last two decades. What could he offer Boyd? What would a future with Jarvis look like? Boyd detected too much resigned comfort in the man's acceptance of sleeping on the ground, at large from a society that would see him back in jail.

Although too young to contemplate his future, Boyd found nothing attractive or alluring about a life on the lam. He guessed he could make a better way on his own, free of the mistakes and past misdeeds of his companion.

No sooner had he considered this theory before the memory of Koenig falling beyond the muzzle flash of his pistol dashed his ideals to splinters. He could well be branded a murderer in the eyes of society. It was a certainty his uncle Ernst would not recount the event in a version favorable for Boyd.

Boyd revisited his assessment of his uncle. The irony was not lost upon him, what he saw in the old outlaw could easily be a future version of himself.

Boyd had been in a quiet study for so long the sound of his voice gave the old outlaw a start when he finally replied.

"I don't have a sure answer, uncle," Boyd said, his voice filled with the uncertainty his words confirmed. "It is clear I don't have the family I was raised with. Bad or good, they are all I ever knew."

Jarvis leaned nearer, his face stern and wise.

"You have always had a family you never knew about. Your family is deep in its roots. It is loyal by the nature of its blood. Your family would die for you.

"There is no talk of being bad or good or makin' do. Your family is both bad or good when you need them to be and either one when you want them to be. I heard your so called grandpappy talk to you in the jail. He lied to your face. I heard that Prussian murderer talk down to you in the woods when you saved my skin.

"That ain't how family acts."

Boyd nodded absently. He recalled so many more moments in his life when he was treated as an outsider – as a lesser entity.

"So, my name is Hutton," Boyd mused.

"A name to be proud of, son. Everything is in a name. Your heritage is there, your birthright, your pride: it's the only thing that is yours. It is the only thing no one can take away from you. Everything else is no more than dust, blown by the wind. You are Boyd Hutton. I am Jarvis Hutton. Your pap was Kyle Hutton. Your family come from Scotch, English lineage. Our people settled in Nebraska. Now we call Texas home."

Boyd nodded.

Sitting by a lonely fire in the dark wilderness gave Jarvis' talk a definitive point. His name was indeed all Boyd possessed.

"One more thing," Jarvis said. "Your name is the only thing worth dying for. Your name is your honor. Your honor is sacred. Live by the creed, boy. Live by the creed."

Jarvis wrapped himself in his horse blanket and lay down with a groan. He shifted as near the fire as he could without igniting the horsehair on the blanket.

Boyd stared at his uncle, astonished how quickly the man began snoring peacefully. He thought about the older man's words. He gave some attention to his view of what "the creed" might be. He held to one undeniable truth. This old outlaw, this estranged uncle, this newcomer, showed a dedication and kinship Boyd had never known from people with whom he had spent his whole life. There was a power in that. Boyd had to admit to himself he found comfort in the selfless dedication of another.

Boyd wrapped his blanket tightly around his shoulders, listening to the night sounds. The rise and fall of the songs of the unseen creatures of the night were familiar to him. He clung to the small comfort of the familiar as he grappled with the strange possibilities ahead. He sensed things would change greatly.

Lost in his thoughts, he suddenly noticed his companion no longer snored. Boyd held his breath as he waited to hear the sleeper snore once more.

Without turning towards Boyd, Jarvis spoke, his voice muted.

"You need to get used to the fact that I have to kill old man Wechsler for what he did to my brother – your pap. I don't want that to get between us, but he owes it, and he has to pay."

Boyd made no rejoinder. Jarvis' tone left no room for debate. Besides, The Wolf was no more than a murderer himself.

Boyd remembered his fit of passion at the jail when he learned his grandfather had hung his true father. Murder raised its grisly gaze and fixed him with it for a time. He felt no inclination to defend his grandfather. He felt no desire to protect him – not that he would be able to if he did.

In time Boyd drifted into a troubled sleep.

25

DEPUTY WORLEY RETURNED TO HIS small home and his awaiting Trudy. The hour was advanced, but she prepared a late supper for him. As pots simmered and steam rose from them, Trudy made several attempts at light conversation with her husband. He offered little in response other than an occasional grunt or abbreviated reply to a question.

She filled his plate and laid it before him on their little kitchen table. She sat opposite him, her chin resting in her hand as she watched him eat.

He gave his full attention to emptying the plate, not even sparing her a glance.

"What has happened, John?" she asked finally.

He looked up, favoring her with a fleeting glance and a shake of his shaggy head.

"Nothing."

"By nothing," she pressed. "You mean Tim Williamson is in jail and you are not needed away for a while?"

"That is not what I mean," he replied testily.

Trudy straightened at his terse manner.

"What did you do?" she asked pointedly. "What happened?"

Worley slammed the fork on the table, and he uttered a profane oath.

"They killed him. I had to go along, or they might have killed me too. I had no choice."

"They killed Williamson? Who is they, John?"

"The goddam vigilantes stopped me on the road, about ten miles from Loyal Valley. They knew I was headed to the Wiliamson place and told me to bring him to them, so I did. They told me to run from them after I shot Williamson's horse from under him. They said they would shoot after me to make it look like I wasn't involved."

Trudy's mouth fell open as she processed this news.

"But you are in no danger from the association. You helped them."

"Don't you see woman? They are Prussian and I am Anglo. I am nothing to them. I have value only as long as I am useful. A lot of men are dying at their hands. The stakes are too high for them to put any value on my life. I am a lawman, not a thug."

"You did what they wanted. It won't look like you were involved. There were no witnesses."

"An old rancher, Lehmberg is his name: he was there too. I don't think he believes I wasn't involved. We high-tailed it after we heard shots. When we got back to Lehmberg's place, he asked some direct questions and seemed to doubt my story."

"How can you be certain he doubted you?"

"He said as much. He said he would come to Mason and talk with the Sheriff about the ordeal."

"You've nothing to worry about then. Sheriff Clark is on your side."

"He is in as much hot water as I am. He told me the Texas Rangers are involved. The Governor sent them to sort out this thing."

"Oh, for Gordon's seed, John!" Trudy exclaimed. What are we gonna do?"

"Stick with the plan. We keep our mouths closed and stick to the story if we are pressed. Time will put all of this to rights.

"Unless the Germans press you to act on their behalf again."

Worley frowned at his plate. He was doubtful of his chances with the Germans or the law.

26

WILLIAM SCOTT COOLEY ARRIVED IN Menardville as the Sun reached its highest point. He left the empty buckboard in front of Bradford's Store, a squat but longish planked building. The simple structure housed the general store, a saloon, and a blacksmith shop at the rear.

In earlier days, Bradfords trading post was a popular stop for cattle drives, settlers, and Indian traders. The stores were always well stocked, the saloon offered both whiskey and cold beer, and the blacksmith shop was handy, and often used by passersby.

With the growth of the region, and the advent of other mercantiles opening for trade, business was slower, but Bradford enjoyed a better than necessary clientele. As general stores were judged, his enterprise was still a booming success.

Cooley dropped lightly from the tall buckboard seat to the ground. He stretched his legs as he made for the store entrance.

He entered the dark confines of the mercantile. The long narrow room had no windows. The sources of illumination were the opened door, and kerosene lamps nailed to the center posts supporting the shallow pitched roof structure. Under the low ceiling, shelves, filled with goods, crowded the rough walls.

Adam Bradford, a lean, whiskered man, stocked cans on a shelf towards the back wall. Goods were stacked, filling the front entry of the store, where his weekly delivery from Burnet had been delivered that morning.

"How do?" the proprietor greeted Cooley.

"Mr. Bradford," Cooley returned.

Cooley moved about the store inventory. He selected items from the shelves, placing them on the planked counter at the front of the store. Once his list of goods was filled, he waited at the counter to tender payment.

Bradford placed the final can on a shelf then headed towards the counter. He surveyed Cooley's selections.

"Anything else for you Scott?" he asked unnecessarily.

"That should do it, Mr. Bradford."

The proprietor tallied the total and Cooley handed over the requested sum.

As Cooley transported an armload of goods to the wagon, Bradford locked the money in an iron box. When he returned for the next load Bradford cleared his throat meaningfully.

"Didn't you tell me once you were acquainted with Tim Williamson over Loyal Valley way?" the proprietor asked.

Cooley smiled at the mention of his friend.

"More than acquainted," he replied brightly. "He and Mary are family to me."

"Well, that makes this doubly difficult to say."

Cooley's smile remained, but the rest of his face sagged a fraction at what he predicted would be unwelcome news.

Bradford's expression reflected genuine regret.

"The driver who delivered this lot repeated a story he heard when he made delivery to Ranck's Store in Mason. He heard Tim Williamson was gunned down by a band of vigilantes about a week ago."

Cooley's face clouded, his brow twisting in a storm of emotion.

"What happened?" he asked in a barely audible voice.

"Apparently a Mason County Deputy Sheriff served an arrest warrant on him at his ranch. Tim Williamson, the deputy, and another rancher were jumped by a dozen or so masked men. The deputy and the rancher escaped, but the HooDoos shot Tim's horse out from under him then shot him dead on the road."

"Why would someone murder Tim Williamson?"

"The delivery man mentioned no reason, but I hear Mason county is up in arms about the rustling that has gotten out of hand there. I also heard the local German ranchers formed a cattlemen's association to do something about it. Maybe Williamson got caught in the wrong place at the wrong time, or they mistook him for an outlaw."

Bradford frowned at his insufficient knowledge. He continued in a lower conspiratorial tone.

"I haven't heard any proof of it, but rumor has it the sheriff and deputy are on them German ranchers' payroll. It seems pretty odd to me them HooDoos would jump a lawman and his prisoner on the day that lawman serves a warrant."

"You think the deputy was a part of the murder plot?" Cooley asked in a dangerous tone.

Bradford noticed the drastic change in Cooley's demeanor and thought it best to moderate his accusations.

"I got no opinion one way or another, Scott. I'm just relaying what I heard. That deputy may not have any part in it and was just in the wrong place at the wrong time."

"That's two wrong place wrong times. I don't believe in happenstance," Cooley concluded in an angry tone. "Thanks Mr. Bradford."

Cooley gathered the last of his goods and strode from the store. He stowed the merchandise in his wagon then moved to the saloon. He wanted a drink badly.

His insides felt cramped and twisted up as he entered the door to the watering hole next door.

Inside, the saloon shared the décor of the general store. Instead of shelves, however, it sported a long bar along the back wall, adorned with a poorly painted scene of the entry wall to the room, as though it were a mirror reflecting that side of the saloon.

As his eyes adjusted to the dimness, he saw only three men enjoying the hospitality of the saloon. Two appeared to be cattlemen, talking quietly together at a table near the door. The third man stood at the bar, a foot resting on the long footrail. He held a drink in his left hand. His right hand hung free in telltale fashion.

Cooley approached the bar and ordered a bottle. The bartender brought the bottle and a glass. He filled the glass for Cooley and collected payment before returning to his place a short distance away.

Cooley downed the contents of the glass then poured a second. He looked at the glass judgmentally. He resented the courtesy of a glass slowing his efforts to get drunk. He downed that drink and filled the glass once more.

The stranger at the bar spoke in a joking tone.

"I'll have to charge you if I have to carry you out, friend."

Cooley turned his head towards the man at the bar. He was dressed like any ordinary cowpuncher, except he wore a bone handled pistol in a black rig.

"I can carry myself out if I need to be carried anywhere," Cooley replied curtly.

"Suit yourself," the man said dismissively.

Cooley surveyed the stranger once more.

He realized he was demonstrating poor manners to a potentially dangerous stranger. He had no intention of provoking a gunfight with a peevish stranger just to feed his own grief.

"No offense meant, friend," he said with a softening of his ire. "I just received some unwelcome news and I'm not at my best."

The stranger nodded, downing his drink. He stepped closer to Cooley.

"None taken."

"How about a refill?" Cooley offered, pushing the bottle towards the stranger.

"Thanks," the other replied, then filled his glass.

"I'm Scott Cooley."

Cooley didn't bother to extend his hand. He was familiar with the stranger's type. Handshaking was typically an unwelcome ritual.

"Johnny Ringgold," the stranger returned, offering his hand anyway.

They shook hands as Cooley stood straighter.

"Pleased to make your acquaintance Mr. Ringgold," Cooley said with little joy in the greeting.

"Call me Johnny."

Cooley nodded. He forced himself to be cordial despite his grief.

"Call me Scott."

Ringgold tipped his hat and drank from his glass.

"I've seen men throw on a drunk for a lot of reasons," Ringgold observed. "Most are their own. You seem to be a sensible gent with an expensive buckboard full of newly bought goods. You must have got bad news from the shopkeeper."

"You said a mouthful there, Johnny," Cooley agreed bitterly. "Bradford relayed the news of the murder of a man I considered to be everything but a pa to me. I hear he was waylaid in Mason County and gunned down like a cur."

Cooley gripped the edge of the rough bar until it creaked under the pressure. His eyes clouded, blinding him with grief and rage.

"Other than gettin' outside of this bottle and wrecking the carpentry of this bar," Ringgold said, nodding at Cooley's grip on the wooden bar's edge. "What is your plan from there?"

Cooley looked down at his hands squeezing the bar. He released his hold, withdrawing his big hands as if they acted beyond his control. He rested them on the bar.

"Well, that's where it gets fuzzy," he said vaguely. "I haven't worked out anything past this bottle."

Ringgold stretched an imaginary stiffness out of his joints.

"I wouldn't mind seeing Mason County during the Spring. Maybe we could take a look see for the men who killed your friend."

Cooley considered Ringgold for a long moment. His restraint was weak as wet tissue. It didn't take much to send him on the path he wanted to take – the path he had to take.

"If you're in earnest," Cooley said. "I'll meet you here tomorrow morning and we'll take a look see in Mason County, as you say."

Ringgold grinned broadly. He poured another drink from Cooley's bottle, saluted him, and downed the liquor.

"It's pretty quiet here and I'm already caught up on my sleep. Besides, I got friends in Mason County. It's been too long since I dropped by."

They finished the first bottle, then Ringgold purchased a second.

The new acquaintances moved to a table where they spoke privately.

"It would be a waste of time to say you weren't from here, Johnny," Cooley said. "What brings you to Mernardville, if I'm not being too nosy?"

"I'm headed west. I'm from Missouri by way of California. I've been east for a couple years and feelin' a little homesick. I thought I might see the sights on the way back."

"This trip to Mason County could hurt more than being homesick does. I appreciate your offer, but I wouldn't want to take a man to hell even if I am buying the tickets myself."

Ringgold smiled again. This time his smile failed to make it to his eyes.

"That sounds pretty noble, Scott. I know you mean it to be noble. When men talk about a thing, that's a way to pass the time. When men talk about a thing, commit to a thing, then drink to that thing. That is a promise made. We shook on it, remember?"

"Johnny," Cooley reminded his companion cautiously. "We shook when we met, before we talked about going to Mason."

Ringgold's smile evaporated altogether.

Although Cooley was known as a great Indian scalping Ranger, he felt a twinge of unease at the fire he saw growing in his companion. He sensed he had insulted his new friend, though he wasn't sure how he had done it.

Ringgold looked at the table as he continued.

"The promise I made was to the man, not the work. To wait until the stars line up in your favor before you throw in guarantees only when the work gets rough, the man will crawl. I don't crawl for no man."

Cooley saw a strand of reason in Ringgold's logic. He wasn't sure he could explain it himself, but he was certain he glimpsed the soul of the man, a glimpse revealing how Ringgold conducted his life. Was he a drifter, falling in with anyone who caught his interest, or was he a trail partner waiting for the right companion?

"A promise made is a promise kept," Cooley agreed. He nodded to Ringgold and drank from his glass.

The matter was settled.

Ringgold sat back slowly, his ever-present smile returning like the sun appearing from behind a passing cloud bank.

"I'm not sure why you want to wait for the morning, but if it's to get that buckboard full of goods back home, why don't I help you. We can leave together tomorrow."

Cooley looked at Ringgold with a surprised but pleased expression.

"After we get to the outside of this whiskey," he replied. "I think that will work out."

Ringgold poured another drink then lifted it to his lips. He paused before he drank the contents.

"What's for supper tonight?"

27

I

T WAS EARLY MORNING WHEN JARVIS AND Boyd rode west along the trail towards Menardville. Rounding a heavily shrubbed bend in the road, they came suddenly face to face with two heavily armed men, pushing their mounts.

Boyd and Jarvis pulled up abruptly.

The other riders were Scott Cooley and Johnny Ringgold.

"Clear the road," Cooley demanded with annoyance.

"You might show a little caution about who you order off a road, mister," said Jarvis.

Cooley surveyed Jarvis critically.

Ringgold sat impassively, a ghost of a smile pulling at the corners of his mouth.

Boyd watched the two speakers, sure only of what he would do if their talk led to action.

Cooley frowned, obviously not impressed with Jarvis as a potential foe. He spoke with curt authority.

"I might advise caution on your part, talking up to a stranger before you know his capabilities."

Jarvis relaxed in the saddle, his right hand edging closer to his sidearm.

"I guess you see a worry on me I don't know about."

Cooley shrugged dismissively.

"I don't have time to waste jawing with strangers. I got business in Mason County, and I'd rather save my energy for that."

"With your saucy ways, you can count on business being good for you in Mason. Take a hint and go easy or you may find yourself at the end of a rope.

"Is that so?" Cooley asked peevishly. "I guess you know something about that?"

Jarvis weighed his next words. The two riders were strangers with unknown intentions. They weren't German, and they weren't mounted well enough to be lawmen.

"Since you seem curious about it," Jarvis said candidly. "Yeah. I nearly got hung just being in town. I managed to get away before they stretched me. Some of the other boys in my party weren't so fortunate."

Cooley's manner changed noticeably.

"I might owe you an apology," he said sympathetically. "Was a Mason County Lawman involved in that necktie party?"

Jarvis' eyes narrowed at the unexpected turn in their conversation.

"There's both a deputy and a Sheriff. They seemed pretty respectful of that old German rancher who seems to run all of the deviltry going on with that HooDoo gang."

"HooDoo gang?" Cooley repeated. "Are you talking about a vigilante mob?"

"That's exactly what I'm talking about," Jarvis confirmed.

"Did you know a man named Tim Williamson?"

"I do," Jarvis said. "We have done a bit of business recently. Are you a friend of his?"

"I was," Cooley said bitterly. "I got word a gang of vigilantes killed him a few days ago."

"What?" Jarvis cried with shock. "They killed Williamson?"

"You didn't know?"

"Hell no. I know they killed a kid who worked for him, but I didn't know anything about him being killed."

Cooley studied Jarvis with growing favor. The stranger was obviously troubled by the news, and he seemed to have been friendly with Williamson.

"Well, I'm here to collect a blood debt for his murder. If you can tell me anything about the men who tried to hang you, that might lead me to the men who killed Tim, I'd be beholden'."

Jarvis thought of Wechsler and his own debt requiring collection, as the stranger put it.

"I've got a debt to collect of my own," Jarvis said. "The job is too big for me alone. Maybe we can help each other out and satisfy both of what we want."

"Maybe," Cooley agreed.

Cooley nodded in the direction of Mason, and the four rode that way. Cooley and Jarvis rode in front, abreast of one another. Boyd rode beside Ringgold behind them.

"What do you know about this HooDoo gang and who leads it?" Cooley asked Jarvis.

"I'll tell you what I know, but the one to ask is the boy here, my nephew Boyd. He has lived amongst them all his life."

"Is that right?" Cooley asked, casting a glance at Boyd.

"It is," Jarvis confirmed. "I had a little group of men, and we worked the occasional loose stock up the trail between San Antonio to Mason. We sold some beeves to Williamson and partnered with him on a piece of business. The sheriff tossed us in jail and a lynching party took us down the trail and tried to hang the lot of us. I hear they hung two of our number, then shot another. I didn't see it because I managed to escape. Boyd shot one of the vigilantes who caught up with me. The other was his mother's brother, so Boyd let him go.

"The boy's grandfather is involved in some way. I heard the Sheriff tell the deputy to take the jail keys home for safe keeping. The vigilantes must have gotten the keys from him, for they unlocked the cells with the same keys."

Cooley's lips tightened into a hard pale line.

"Well, that cuts it," he said grimly. "That Deputy served a warrant on Tim Williamson. The HooDoos waylaid them on the road and killed Tim. The Deputy and another man escaped. It is clear to me it was a set up."

Boyd listened to the conversation with keen interest. He knew all of the men including many of the so-called Hoo-Doos, personally. Despite feeling like a disjointed observer to actions beyond his control, he felt a twinge of guilt at his association with the killers. He glanced at Ringgold by chance. The man watched him with a trace of a smile.

"What are you lookin' at?" Boyd challenged him boldly.

"You're a salty kid, aren't you?" Ringgold observed good naturedly. "How deep are you into all of this kid?"

"Who's asking?" Boyd returned.

"My name is Johnny Ringgold, what's yours?"

"Boyd Wech… Hutton," he replied, almost defaulting to the surname he had known all of his life.

"Sounds like a big change," Ringgold said lightly. "We'll see how you hold up."

"I'll hold up just fine," Boyd assured the other.

"You just might," Ringgold agreed with a chuckle. "You just might at that."

"What's your stake in this?" Boyd asked.

"No stake. I'm just along for the ride," Ringgold said. "and the action: sure to be plenty of action."

"Say kid," Cooley called to Boyd. "Do you know much about them lawmen or maybe the gang that ambushed Tim in Loyal Valley?"

Boyd thought about the question. If he provided the requested information, he broke all ties with the Wechsler clan. He would be the catalyst for the actions of these men. He would be one of them. His decision was immediate and deliberate.

"The Deputy's name is Worley. He lives in a shack east of Mason. If your friend was jumped in Loyal Valley, that would be Peter Bader's patrol."

"Patrol?" Cooley asked.

"They set up patrols to watch the roads for rustlers at the last meeting of the Cattlemen's Association."

"How many members are in this Association?" Cooley asked.

"All told, leaders and followers, likely upwards of fifty or sixty men."

Ringgold laughed.

"We're gonna need more men," he said with humor.

Cooley frowned at the task of recruiting more members to their group.

Ringgold nodded his understanding.

"I may know some men who could help," he said. "They are in Loyal Valley."

Cooley nodded, his thoughts running out to the future, towards the dark work ahead.

"Let's pay Deputy Worley a call first," he said.

They picked up their pace as they headed towards Mason.

28

DEPUTY WORLEY PULLED UP HIS suspenders as he walked out the back door.

"You be careful around that well," Trudy cautioned him.

Worley grunted as he stepped off the porch. He took a route around the shack, joining another man beside a crudely built water well.

"What's the verdict Doc?" he asked the man at the well.

"You've nursed this well as long as you can," Doc Harcourt replied with the authority of a tradesman wise to the flaws of a poorly constructed well. "It needs to go deeper and wider. That means somebody has to go down there and dig."

"It don't get easier with time," Worley said with ready humor.

Harcourt shook his shaggy head. His frown was concealed behind a full face of beard so thick only two beady eyes could be seen through the bush.

Worley gripped a dingy rope attached to the pull bucket. Harcourt stepped over the narrow rock pile which comprised the rim of the well. He sunk a foot into the bucket and clutched the rope. Worley lowered him by small degrees, hand over hand, until Harcourt's head descended below the level of the top of the rock wall.

The sounds of horse's hooves on packed soil, and the rattling of tack, stopped Worley's labor as he turned his head to look at the four approaching riders. He recognized Boyd Wechsler and another man – he remembered him as one of the rustlers from jail. The outlaw's name came to him: Charlie Johnson. The other two grim faced men were unfamiliar to him.

He heard Boyd say, "That's Deputy Worley."

Cooley stepped down from his horse, a pistol appearing in his hand.

Worley strained to turn his head to watch the man moving in behind him. Hindered by his grip on the rope supporting Harcourt's weight as he lowered him into the well, he was unable to turn his body.

"I'm Scott Cooley, a friend of Tim Williamson's."

He shot Worley in the center of his back.

Worley arched his back with a cry and lost his grip on the rope.

Harcourt yelled as he descended in a freefall to the bottom of the well, where he struck the moist rocky bottom with a splash and a groan.

Worley clutched his back and side, struggling to draw a breath.

Cooley emptied his pistol into the Deputy. The final shot popped a neat hole in Worley's forehead. Cooley holstered his empty pistol and withdrew a large, broad bladed knife from its scabbard on his belt. He stepped to the dying man and snatched a large handful of hair. He sliced an arc at Worley's hairline above his forehead and pulled the scalp back, slicing muscle and sinew until the scalp came free in Cooley's hand like a soggy rag.

He raised the scalp to the heavens like it was an offering to the gods. He uttered an oath in a foreign tongue Boyd took to be an Indian language.

Cooley turned to the group, surveying each man in turn. Without another word he returned to his horse, then mounted. He stuffed the scalp in a rawhide sack tied to his saddle horn.

Boyd watched in mild shock. Jarvis appeared equally disturbed. Only Ringgold made a comment.

"That's a fine bit of Injun knifework, pardner. Not your first time I see."

Curiously, his habitual smile had never left his face throughout the ordeal.

The four were no further away than out of sight from Worley's cabin when they heard the crying wails of Trudy Worley as she discovered her dead husband.

It was after nightfall when the four arrived at a rickety ranch house near Loyal Valley. Three armed men issued from the front door as the riders approached. Their defensive postures softened as their faces registered recognition.

They grinned at Johnny Ringgold.

"Well, I'll be damned," said one of the men on the porch. "Two visits from Johnny Ringgold in one month. How can we be so lucky?"

"Men," Ringgold announced with a gesture to his riding companions. "This is Mose Baird. That well-fed fella to his left is his brother John. That young man hiding in the back is George Gladden."

Ringgold nodded to the men in Cooley's gang.

"This is Scott Cooley of Mernardville. This is Jarvis Hutton, and the kid is his nephew, Boyd."

Mose Baird raised a welcoming hand.

"If Johnny Ringo vouches for you boys, then step down and grab some chow. We just sat down ourselves."

Boyd saw an uncharacteristic dimming of Ringgold's smile at the misuse of his name. However, the moment passed quickly, and his smile returned once more.

"Turn your mounts loose in the corral for the night," Mose said. Then to Boyd he ordered. "Son, there's hay in the mow and a curry comb in the bin if you're so inclined."

Jarvis looked at Boyd to gauge his reaction to the task assigned in such a way.

Boyd hesitated no more than a second before moving to obey. He was accustomed to filling the roustabout role in the company of his elders. Falling back into the role was not a great affront to him, even amongst men he just met.

He led the four horses to the stables as the others filed into the house to the chorus of crude sallies and hearty laughter.

He unsaddled and brushed down the horses. A portion of his mentoring under Simon Martinez included the importance of caring for a horse. Martinez impressed upon him proper care for a horse yields good health for the animal, and speed, stamina, and a dependable bottom for the man the horse carries. He often said many times a horse was the only thing tipping the balance between the rider and danger.

After distributing a cut of hay to each horse, Boyd returned to the ranch house, entering a hectic environment of loud, jovial conversation under a cloud of cigarette smoke, seasoned by the aroma of freshly served food.

Boyd filled his plate before taking a seat at the long rough table in the center of the single room making up the kitchen and lounging area of the cabin. Most of the men sat before empty plates, leaning back in stiff backed chairs, smoking rolled cigarettes and downing whiskey.

Boyd ate in silence, listening to the talk around him with covert interest.

"The job is too big for the three of us," Ringgold was explaining. "No offense Kid."

Boyd shrugged through a mouthful of beef stew.

"We can't be certain about that," Cooley said, his sober tone a stark contrast to the jovial mood of the gathering. "You know Tim Williamson?"

An unintelligible response of nodding and mumbling greeted the comment. All of them knew about the murder.

"He was like family to me. Honor binds me to this path. I got no choice. According to Boyd here, there are too many of them for me to handle with a small crew. I'm hoping some of you, and others around, might understand what happened to Tim could happen to any man in the county, and be willing to make sure it doesn't. In the short term, if you boys will ride with me and my men over to the

Bader place tomorrow, I'll handle Bader myself. If he ain't alone, we'll have enough men to get out of there in one piece."

Mose Baird cleared his throat.

"Tim was my friend too. The only reason we ain't gone after them goddam Prussians who did for him is exactly what you say. We don't have the numbers to make a fight and defend what's ours. We'll join you. No more needs to be said as far as I'm concerned."

John Baird and George Gladden nodded their agreement, tossing back whiskey shots to seal their commitment to the cause.

The night's festivities lasted only as long as the whiskey held out, which was around midnight. The following morning, they were up with the dawn. Mose Baird led the way towards the Bader place.

Seven riders appeared, riding around the tree lined wind break guarding the southeast side of the Bader's hay pasture. Carl Bader stabilized the deep bladed plowshares as they sliced into the rich black soil. He bawled encouragement to a laboring draft horse.

Carl halted the labor of the big horse, wiping sweat from his brow as the riders approached. He thought they might be members of the Cattlemen's Association until they drew near enough he could see their faces. None were German ranchers. He recognized three as locals he had seen on occasion.

"What's your business here?" Carl demanded impatiently. "I've got work to do."

Cooley spoke for the group.

"Are you Peter Bader, the man who murdered Tim Williamson in cold blood on the road to Mason?"

Carl paled.

"Peter is my brother. I'm Carl Bader. You have no right to come onto our land and make unfounded accusations. Get off my property."

"I'll bet you'll deny being a part of them masked cowards who shot Tim down."

"I don't know what you're talking about."

Cooley dropped lightly from the saddle. The rawhide bag in hand. He withdrew Worley's scalp, now stiff and dry, displaying it for Bader.

"This was Deputy Worley's hair until yesterday. Now it's mine."

"My god, man," Carl exclaimed with a tremor in his voice. "You're an animal."

Cooley pulled his pistol and killed Carl Bader where he stood. Cooley turned to the riders, stuffing the scalp back in the sack.

"What about his hair, Cooley?" Ringgold asked with a tinge of disappointment in his tone.

"He ain't important enough to add to my collection."

"Johnny," Mose said with incredulity. "You still know how to pick colorful friends. That's the first scalp I ever seen. Looks like you boys have this matter in hand. The boys and me are gonna head back."

"Mose," John Baird said. "I'm going with George to his place to lay low. We may see something unfortunate come of today's work. You ought to come too."

"That seems like a good idea," Moses agreed.

The three men departed from the group.

Cooley watched the three riders depart with a combination of disappointment and disfavor.

"What about you three?" Cooley challenged the remaining men, giving Johnny Ringgold a significant look.

If Johnny noticed the critical nature of Cooley's challenge, he didn't show it.

"Why should I want to part ways with a new 'colorful' friend?" Ringgold replied with good humor. "The party's just getting started."

"We still ain't settled my score," Jarvis said. "You ain't done nothing that shocks me yet."

Boyd said nothing. He recognized Cooley's indirect criticism of Ringgold's friends. He was not pleased their leader would show insult to the men who had been with him since the beginning. Although these thoughts crossed Boyd's mind, his demeanor gave away nothing to the others, and Cooley didn't press him for a response. Instead, without a glance for the dead man, he led them back to the road.

29

SHERIFF CLARK WAS SEATED BEHIND HIS desk when Wolf Wechsler arrived. Ernst Wechsler followed closely behind. They pulled two chairs from against the wall and took seats on the opposite side of the Sheriff's desk.

After a moment of silence where the Sheriff said nothing, the Wolf spoke, impatience heavy in his tone.

"What are you going to do about all of these murders?"

"Which murders?" Clark returned defensively. "Are you talking about those your men are doing, or are we talking about whoever is killing those same murderers?"

"Is that what Deputy Worley was, a murderer?"

"I place his death at your feet, Wechsler. He was intercepted on his way to deliver a warrant on Williamson. They forced him to play a role in his murder. He was accosted by your men in the dead of night. They took his keys and lynched them rustlers."

Wechsler sat back in his chair. His face registered genuine surprise. He spoke with the calmness of a parent to a child.

"Do you honestly believe that story will cut muster under scrutiny? If so, you are a bigger fool than I thought you were. Worley went along willingly, even so far as to switch horses with Williamson to preserve the better mount when he shot the horse out from under him. Leaving the keys with your deputy was too simple a plan to be mistaken for genuine..."

"Don't talk to me like that..."

"Shut up and listen to sense, John," the Wolf interrupted impatiently. "You are up to your neck in this. This whole thing is circling you like buzzards around carrion. By your own admission, the Rangers have a keen interest in your involvement in the lynching. Ernst here barely got away alive when one of your escaped prisoners killed my man Verner Koenig."

"That was Boyd," Ernst said, correcting his father's misstatement.

"Be silent jungen," Wechsler said sharply to his son.

He gave Ernst a black look as he reluctantly admitted, "My grandson has joined the outlaws - as I always knew was in his nature."

Wechsler paused for effect before continuing.

"The killing of Deputy Worley and Carl Bader are murders in the name of vengeance, Sheriff. You have to know your name will be on their kill list."

Clark shifted uncomfortably in his chair.

"So, you didn't guess that until now," Wechsler observed significantly. "They scalped Deputy Worley, for god's sake. What do you think they are going to do to you?"

Wechsler paused again, watching his words sink into the Sheriff's understanding.

"Their numbers are growing," Wechsler continued. "I can send more of my men to join your posse if you think it wise."

"A witness identified the Baird brothers and George Gladden riding with four men he didn't recognize. That makes seven. I should have enough men for now."

Wechsler watched the Sheriff expectantly.

"I'm riding out today in pursuit of Deputy Worley's murderers," Clark said emphatically.

Wechsler surveyed the Sheriff with something akin to a look of disgust on his face. When he finally spoke, his tone was grave and threatening.

"This matter does not come to my doorstep, Sheriff. This is your moment. This is why we brought you here. This is what you are being paid for. Root out these brigands and bring them to justice."

Wechsler stood.

Ernst waited in his seat, uncertain of his father's intentions.

"This barbarism can't stand, John."

The Wolf glanced down at Ernst.

"Komst du," he said, turning on his heel, leaving the office without another word.

Ernst followed, sparing a final glance for the Sheriff.

A man entered the office, glancing at the departing Wechsler's. He took off his hat as he entered.

"You sent for me Sheriff?"

"You remember you owe me a favor, don't you Cheney?"

"What's this about, Sheriff?"

"Sit down John," Clark said in a kinder tone.

Cheney took the chair Ernst had occupied.

"Do one thing for me and we are square. Ride to Loyal Valley and look up the Baird boys. They were last seen with George Gladden. Bring 'em here. Tell 'em I'm trying to get to the bottom of the Williamson ambush. He don't have many friends here in Mason and we are trying to add any information that might show his side of what happened."

Cheney shook his head.

"I doubt they were there, Sheriff."

"No doubt they were not there, John," Clark said sarcastically. "They are providing what we call character facts - you know, 'he wasn't the sort of a man to rustle cattle,' 'he was a God-fearing family man' – that sort of thing. We're looking out for the widow and her reputation. Just get 'em here."

"Yes sir," Cheney said meekly. "Why me?"

"You're a gambler ain't you, John? This opens the card games to you again. Just do it with no more questions."

Cheney stood, returning his hat to his balding head.

"I'll head out first thing, Sheriff."

"Go now, John. I want them here in the morning – midday latest."

Cheney nodded and left the office.

Clark watched the front door as if trouble would burst in on him at any moment.

30

IT WAS MIDAFTERNOON WHEN CHENEY arrived at George Gladden's house. Gladden and Mose Baird were seated on opposite sides of a small fire. They smoked cigarettes and tossed stones in the fire, talking about nothing in particular.

Cheney rode into the little clearing encircling the dilapidated shack.

"How do, boys." Cheney called pleasantly. "Hope I'm not catching you at a busy time."

The two offered no hospitality to the newcomer, remaining seated at the fire, unmoving in their scrutiny of Cheney.

Cheney knew both men, but not well. He had been able to locate them only because he had lost money to Gladden in a poker game and had visited the Gladden place when he paid off his debt. He didn't know where Baird's place was.

The Sheriff didn't vouchsafe any details, but Cheney suspected he was sent to draw the two into a trap. The gambler in him sensed subterfuge, but he dared not fail to make good on his commitment to the Sheriff. Nonetheless, he was aware of the dangerous situation in which he found himself.

"You fellas mind if I step down? It's been a long ride."

Gladden nodded.

"I don't remember you owing me any more money John," he said tauntingly.

Cheney's chuckle seemed a bit forced at the remark.

"It's nothing like that George. The Sheriff is looking into the Williamson killing, and he's having trouble finding anyone in Mason who will say anything good about Tim Williamson. You were his friends and he asked if you two might drop in and give a statement. The Sheriff is concerned about how this whole thing is affecting the Williamson widow."

"The man is killed," Mose Baird pointed out. "What does the Sheriff expect Mary will gain in the bargain?"

"Hell, Mose, I don't suppose to guess what the law wants or needs. I only do what I'm told."

He stretched from his long ride, looking around.

"I don't see John here. Is he doing alright today?"

"He's up to his own business. Does the Sheriff want him for some reason?"

Cheney saw the trap in the question. He shrugged.

"I'm not sure how I got on your bad side boys. I thought I was doing you and your friends a good turn by riding all this way to help out. If you don't want to say your piece for Williamson and his widow, I'm not gonna try to make you. I'd better slope anyhow."

Gladden looked at Baird as if to indicate, 'Nobody knows about our part in the Bader killing. Why so touchy?'

Baird stood from his seat.

"Sorry, John. It's true we don't know each other very well, but that ain't no reason to send a man off on a long ride on an empty stomach. We'll go to Mason and make our statement in the morning. Why don't you sit down and eat with us? We got an extra bed - if that's good by you George."

"Sure it is," Gladden agreed.

Cheney nodded his appreciation to the proffered hospitality. His obligation to the Sheriff was fulfilled. Baird and Gladden agreed to go to Mason in the morning. Although John Baird was not going, Gladden would probably suffice if they required two statements.

With Cheney's debt repaid, he was eager to get into a card game as soon as horseflesh could deliver him to one.

"I am obliged boys," Cheney said with genuine gratitude. "I've got a poker game waiting on me at the Southern. Maybe look me up when you're in town tomorrow."

"Suit yourself, Jim," Moses said. "Buy us a drink with your winnings."

Cheney laughed.

"Bring your billfolds boys. I ain't that hospitable."

The others laughed as Cheney rode away.

Mose and George left at sunup. The ride to Mason was long, but the road wound through beautiful country, and the morning was pleasant.

They rode along, discussing their usual subject of interest, how to make a profit in the cattle business with no seed money.

Mose was mid-topic as they topped the rise known as Hedwig's Hill.

"Buying young cattle makes for a longer time to earnings but it costs less at the start. I talked to John about it, and he agrees with me. If you have a better idea, I am all ears."

Both riders heard the sound of breaking branches and approaching hoof falls coming from the woods to the south. They were only a couple of miles east of Mason, but they could determine no reason for a large number of unseen riders to be bearing down upon them from cover.

Mose grunted as he pulled his mount up short, causing the gelding to rear back.

"Hell's in the wind George," he cried and spurred his horse, leading the way towards their backtrail.

George Gladden followed, his faster horse soon taking the lead. The approaching horsemen cleared the woods, the sound of their pursuit growing tenfold. The increased noise spurred Mose, George, and their horses to a higher pace.

From the rear, Mose risked a glance at the pursuing group. They numbered a half dozen. In that glance, he recognized Sheriff Clark and Mose's distant neighbor, Peter Bader, brother of Carl, Scott Cooley's recent victim.

"George," he called to his friend ahead of him. "We've been had. The Sheriff and Peter Bader are among them riders."

Shots rang out from the chasers. Bullets sang past Mose's head like angry hornets. The dirt beneath their horses' hooves spatted dust puffs, and tree branches splintered overhead.

The two riders hunched low over their speeding mounts, clinging desperately to their saddles. Mose felt a bullet enter his back below his vest line. A sharp heavy pain lodged deep inside of him. George caught a slug in the seat of his pants. Neither man was armed and were unable to return fire.

Wounded and desperate, they turned off the road, entering the tight brambles amongst the live oaks bordering the road. They rode with the panic of the lost. By some miracle, with each lunge of their mounts, they heard the pursuit fall further behind. Brambles scraped them, cutting through their clothes and tearing their skin.

Mose felt the world spin up towards him and he fell from his horse. He tried to rise as Gladden returned to see what was wrong.

Gladden's horse pranced nervously. After one attempt, Gladden found his wound prevented him from dismounting.

Mose again tried to rise but his arms and legs had lost strength sufficient to perform the task. He grimaced in pain and the certainty he would not leave that grove.

George saw a lot of blood pooling beneath his friend.

"My god, Mose," he uttered through a tight throat and dread fear. "Please, brother, get on your horse. You gotta be alright. We'll just ride out of this."

Mose grew still, his eyes losing their light.

"We'll just ride out of this." George repeated through his tears.

The sounds of approaching riders, horses breaking brush, rider's cursing the ripping brambles, forced George to abandon his fallen friend. He rode away, hot tears and slapping branches blinding him.

31

I T WAS WELL AFTER DARK WHEN GEORGE Gladden, sagging in the saddle, cautiously walked his horse towards the Baird house. His wound ached nearly beyond his ability to bear the pain. He experienced relief as he recognized Johnny Ringgold's horse among those tied before the house. The men inside weren't a posse or a band of vigilantes.

He pulled up near the front door and called out.

"Hello the house. It's George Gladden."

In an instant, the door was flung open, and John Baird stepped from the light of the interior into the darkness. He squinted, recognizing Gladwell in the saddle.

"Step down, George," he said brightly. "The boys are just sitting down to a drink. Where's Mose?"

"I can't get off my cayuse on my own, John, Can you bear a hand?"

"You can't get off your.... What the hell has come off, George. Where is my brother?"

George began to weep openly, not bothering to cover his shame.

"He got shot. He's dead, John. I'm shot too. I can't get off my horse. Please help me."

By this time, the others were filing out of the house to assess what delayed John and the newcomer. Ringgold was outside when George announced Mose was dead. His smile evaporated, and a deadly light filled his eyes. He squinted as though to dim the illuminance of his rage.

"Mose is dead you say?" Ringgold uttered in a voice hoarse with emotion. "Who shot him – and you, George?"

"Jim Cheney showed up at my place yesterday. He said Sheriff Clark wanted a statement from Mose and me to vouch for Tim Williamson – something about helping Mary. He seemed friendly enough and the request made sense at the time. Mose and me left out this morning. Sheriff Clark, and about a half dozen others, jumped us at Hedwig's Hill near Mason. Peter Bader was in the posse. Before I ran, I recognized a few other faces as German ranchers, but I'm having trouble remembering their names. I think…"

George sagged in his saddle. He would have toppled onto the ground if John Baird hadn't caught him. The others helped carry him into the house.

Hurried hands cleared bottles and glasses out of the way as they laid Gladden on the table.

Cooley moved closer to examine the wounded man. He pulled his knife and cut Gladden's trousers away, revealing the wound.

"The bullet's still in there," Cooley said grimly. "We need a doctor to get it out. It's too deep for me to cut out without him bleeding to death."

Cooley sheathed his knife, looking around the room.

"Boyd," he called. "It has to be you to ride into town and get the doctor. You are the only one who isn't wanted yet, and you know the town. Can you do this thing?"

Boyd looked at Jarvis.

His uncle watched him, giving no indication of what he should do.

It was true Boyd had not been arrested nor had he been included in any plot to get him back to town. That didn't mean he wasn't in danger from the law or the vigilantes. He had killed Verner Koenig. Ernst would have reported that to his grandfather. A pang pierced his heart when he thought about what they would tell his mother about the killing. It was certain his part in the event would be exaggerated to make Ernst and Verner appear blameless.

He looked at the men around him. Each waited for his decision. There was a connection each of these men shared. They were bound to one another by a common cause. More accurately, they were bound by a common fate. If they were captured, they would share the same punishment no matter their role.

Although he was not a major player in Cooley's vendetta, he was as deeply involved as they were. Boyd felt an overwhelming need to belong to this group – this new family in which he had fallen. He had an advantage over the others, but it was unknown to them. His advantage was he knew Doc Traynor and knew where he lived. He doubted if even the locals from Loyal Valley knew Mason as well as he.

"I'll go," he agreed.

Jarvis nodded to his nephew. He was proud of the boy's courage and his willingness to act on behalf of the group.

Boyd grabbed his hat and left the house in a rush. He gathered his gelding's reins and threw a leg over the horse, pulling himself into the saddle.

Inside the house they listened to the sound of his horse's hooves grow dimmer as Boyd made his way west.

"This is recompense for killing Carl Bader," John Baird said bitterly. "Mose didn't kill nobody."

John concealed his sorrow within his ministrations for the wounded man. He covered him and tried to comfort him. Occasionally he could be heard stifling a sob.

"That doesn't matter to them who kill in the name of the law for their own ends," Ringgold said bluntly. "It's the Germans against the Anglos. It was headed that way when I was here last. It just came to a head with the killing of Williamson.

"I know Jim Cheney. We played cards when I was here last trip. The man has the worst fault any gambler can have. He is a sore loser, probably why he is beholden' to the Sheriff. My bet is he did something foolish in a fit of temper and got arrested."

Ringgold brushed his bone-handled Colt free of imaginary dust. The gesture was unintentional as his mind worked.

"He's a dead man. So is the Sheriff, Peter Bader, and whoever else was in that posse."

Cooley nodded.

"The list is getting longer by the day," he agreed.

His words reflected his darkening mood and the murderous intent growing in his breast. Sheriff Clark and the Germans were killing people he knew with impunity. Williamson was not a one off. These men were on a mission to kill anyone who opposed them.

Cooley's teeth ground painfully as hatred filled him so completely, he feared the emotion might kill him.

He struggled to comport himself and resist the desire to flee that place and travel the countryside, killing every German immigrant rancher he found.

Jarvis took a seat near the wounded man who was unconscious on the table. He watched John Baird attend to him. Baird was keeping himself occupied as he tried to find a direction in which to channel his grief over his dead brother.

Jarvis's thoughts darkened as much as the others' in the room. He clenched and unclenched his hands as he imagined killing Wolfgang Wechsler.

His vengeance was of a different nature. He learned patience in prison. When you are helpless to act on your desires, you necessarily develop a strong level of patience. He saw a great benefit in the others acquiring a personal investment in their vendetta.

With a practicality Jarvis did not recognize nor credit to himself, he knew innately, while in the pursuit of vengeance, the more mouths to feed at the revenge trough, the better his chances for help when he finally went after the old rancher.

Ringgold stood suddenly. He was all business. The cause had touched him personally. He was no longer along for the ride. Mose's murder had put him all in. He looked around the room.

"We leave at first light."

He approached Baird until he was close enough to place a comforting hand on his shoulder.

"John, if the Kid isn't back with the doc, stay here with George until he brings him."

Ringgold looked at Cooley who watched him silently.

"This ain't no sightseeing trip for me no more," Ringgold said soberly. "Blood will flow over this treachery. It appears every man in this room has cause to exact a price from those who haunt Mason County. Starting tomorrow, we put a stop to it for the last time."

Boyd pushed his gelding to a rolling canter. The road was smooth and the night air pleasant. A freshening breeze carried upon it the promise of a revisit of cooler temperatures.

His energy and attention elevated by the cool air, and the strangeness of the surrounding darkness. The gelding moved along with a high head, ears erect, alert for unseen dangers hidden by the night.

Boyd patted the gelding's neck, comforting him.

"It's alright boy," he said to the horse. "The danger ain't hidin' out there. It's in plain sight from two legged creatures, and they ain't a danger to you."

Mason slept under a rising crescent moon when he arrived at the outskirts of the little village. He rode along the main road into town, unnoticed.

Doc Trayner and his wife owned a house on the western road at the edge of Mason. They kept a neat house with a well-tended flower bed in front. It wasn't long before he arrived at Doc Traynor's house. A lamp burned inside. It was surprising at that hour, but to Boyd it seemed fortuitous.

Boyd passed by the house, looking around him for undetected witnesses. He concealed the gelding in a grove of trees a small distance from the house. He kept to the woods as he made his way back towards the Doctor's house. He passed Mrs. Traynor's fragrant flower garden, climbing the front steps.

He rapped lightly on the door.

Immediately he heard footfalls inside the home. Doc Trayner opened the door, wearing spectacles at the end of his nose, a book in his hand.

"It's late son," he said.

"It is, Doc," Boyd agreed. "We have a man at the Baird place. He's been shot and the bullet is deep. I've been sent to fetch you if you'll come."

"Son, I know where the Baird place is. It's nearly to Loyal Valley, and it is past midnight. How bad is he shot?"

"He's shot in his tail end and there is a lot of blood."

"How's his color? Is he pale or flushed?"

"Pale I guess."

"Is he conscious?"

"He was when he rode in, but he passed out right away after."

The Doctor struggled with his reluctance. He yearned for the previous solitary moment where he enjoyed a rare moment of respite, reading his book beside the tranquil glow of a fragrant lamp, relaxed in his modest home. Finally, his commitment to his duty and the preservation of human life bested his languor.

"Alright," he said wearily. "I'll get my hat and bag. Do me a favor, son. Saddle that sorrel mare for me in the stall behind the house. I should be there by the time you are done."

"Yes sir."

Boyd leaped from the porch to obey. He ran to where his gelding was hidden, then rode him to the stable. He saddled the mare, and in a quarter of an hour they were underway.

The doctor offered no small talk as they rode through the sleeping town.

Boyd was noticeably alert as they travelled, his head swiveling in every direction. He gave even the most inconspicuous noise and movement his full attention. Doc

Traynor's attention for Boyd's careful vigilance went unnoticed by the youth.

A frontier doctor plies his skills for all comers, whether outlaw or law-abiding. He learned early to quell his curiosity for fear of riling the frequently encountered intemperate outlaw. He didn't know Boyd well, but he seemed innocent enough.

Many of those he helped who ended up being dangerous, started off as pleasant and innocent. He had no desire to press Boyd to change his temperament.

They rode throughout the early morning hours, arriving at the Baird house at dawn's first sign, a light gray tendril stretching along the eastern horizon, like a tangible division between daylight and night. Even at that early hour, the house was alive with movement.

They dismounted and made their way towards the house, passing men saddling and loading packs on horses. Inside, Gladden looked no worse to Boyd than he had the previous night. The doctor appeared concerned, nonetheless.

"Son," he said to Boyd. "Bring me soap and a pan of clear water, and whatever rags you can rummage up."

Boyd clattered through dishes stacked around the room until he found a suitable vessel. He hurried outside to the well. As he filled the pan, Jarvis approached.

"We're headed out," he announced. "Are you keen on going along or do you need to rest after your ride?"

Boyd glanced at Jarvis, the water filling the pan garnering most of his attention.

"I can go along if I can have a fresh horse. Mine needs a rest and a measure of feed."

"That's a good lad," Jarvis said with a lift to his voice. "I knew you wouldn't flag. That's the Hutton in you. I'll see to a fresh horse for you. Turn the doctoring over to the Baird boy. Hurry and gather your gear for a forced march. You can sleep later."

Boyd returned inside with the pan and sat it beside the doctor who had already cut away the rest of Gladden's clothing. Boyd rushed around the cabin, collecting a bar of lye soap and what rags and old clothing he could find.

He provided John Baird with a brief explanation before collecting his bed roll and personal items. He stepped outside where his uncle was already mounted, holding the reins of a rangy chestnut gelding. Nearby, Cooley and Ringgold were in the saddle, appraising their youngest member favorably.

With a nod to Jarvis, Boyd took the reins and mounted up.

Cooley and Ringgold led the way with Jarvis and Boyd just behind. They took the road west towards Mason, covering the same trail Boyd had already travelled twice.

Any sleepiness he suffered was alleviated by the dire nature of their mission. He knew death waited at the end of this trek. Few moments passed without the ghost of Verner Koenig visiting his thoughts. Despite Boyd's efforts to dispel the memory with a strong justification of justice for his father's murder, he often relived the moment he fired his pistol, the bullet striking the German with a meaty thump. Boyd found it uncanny he recalled even the most minute details of the deed. He wondered if he would ever forget.

He dreaded what he believed was the certainty he would kill again for another justifiable reason. He had taken one life. He had heard rumor somewhere the second was easier. He found it hard to believe, but he was in the company of men blooded multiple times in armed conflict. They lived by the credo a life lost required another in return. They followed the rule casually. At least they seemed to give no thought to the consequences beyond this life. To Boyd it appeared a matter of course to them.

Raised under the stern Christianity of the German immigrant, he had been taught the wage of sin is death. Although he resisted spirituality, his ethereal side toyed with the horrific prospect of a damned spirit and an eternity spent paying for his deeds in the white-hot flames of hell.

He shook off his macabre thoughts. The morning was too sunny, his surroundings too familiar to allow grim imaginings made for lonely nights to take hold.

Their mission was one comprised of menial tasks. Those tasks would end in death, but in the light of day, their errand seemed almost normal. He would deal with the dark horrors sure to visit him as they came when he rested at night.

32

JOHN CLARK WAITED IMPATIENTLY AS townspeople milled around the front of the courthouse. Spears once again led the throng, casting meaningful glances towards the Sheriff's office window.

Clark peeked around the frame of the window, awaiting the confrontation to come. He eavesdropped to gain a fraction of an advantage in crafting a response to their inevitable demands.

This time, the crowd was ill content to wait outside while Spears spoke for them. Clark moved to his place behind his desk, standing in readiness. The door to the courthouse banged open, and the angry voices muted by the thin door to his office clamored. His door was thrown open, and the mob entered, led by Spears. The din grew uncomfortably loud within the confines of the small room.

"Clark," Spears said abruptly. "A lot of people are dying, and you don't appear to be doing anything about it. We think the Governor ought to be notified. Rangers must be summoned again so you have reinforcements to help you uphold the law."

The last part was said with bold disdain.

Clark held his hands high before him in an impotent display of authority.

"Everything that can be done is being done."

The crowd grew restive and louder.

Clark frowned, lowering his hands significantly to his waist, close to his pistol. The crowd noticed the gesture. Their voices fell a fraction with their doubt of the intentions and the history of their sheriff.

"The best thing you all can do is to return to your homes and businesses. I've deputized six men as County Deputies and they are following my orders to the letter. We will put an end to the violence in Mason and the surrounding county."

Spears snorted his ridicule.

"Six men?" he scoffed, spreading his arms wide in an invitation for the crowd to join him in his criticism. "You have formed your own vigilante gang with six Dutchmen who are probably guilty of the same killings you are claiming to be investigating."

"Both Germans and Anglos are dying in this violence," Clark said with a hard edge to his words. "Watch what you say, Spears. There are enough rumors and hearsay going the rounds. It does nobody no good to spread more of the same."

Spears shook his head and spit on the floor.

"If you won't do it, we will. We're gonna wire the Governor for help."

Threateningly, Spears narrowed his eyes at the Sheriff.

"You better be on the right side of this thing, John. Otherwise, you could find a rope around your own neck."

Spears turned on his heel and pressed a path through the tightly packed crowd behind him. The room emptied quickly.

Clark returned to the window where he watched Spears lead the townspeople through the courthouse lawn and across the Square to the post office, which also housed the telegraph office.

The Sheriff's mind worked busily at his solution to the growing violence he faced. Mose Baird's friend Gladden had escaped their ambush and was likely spreading the word Sheriff Clark headed the posse. Clark knew little about the newcomers who killed Deputy Worley and Carl Bader. He was certain he hadn't heard the last of them. The information he had on the killers was limited to one source.

Charles "Doc" Harcourt, Worley's neighbor who tumbled down the well, overheard the killer boast his name was Scott Cooley, a friend of Tim Williamson's.

That information was late arriving because Carter was trapped in the well for several hours until he regained consciousness. He was finally able to hold the rope so he could be rescued. He was in a stupor for two days from a head injury sustained in the fall. Only after he recovered his wits did he recall the killer's final words to Worley.

Clark gripped the butt of his holstered colt, his jaw muscles working. The killer scalped Worley – his friend and deputy. He would see this killer, Cooley, die a slow death for the murder. A cursory inquiry had yielded no information about Scott Cooley. The local brand inspector, Daniel Hoerster, said he had heard Williamson mention his name once in passing, but knew nothing about the man other than Williamson said he was from Jack County.

That was a long way north. Clark guessed Cooley must have been close by to have arrived so soon after Williamson's death.

Tracks at Worley's house proved Cooley was not alone. There were signs of at least three others who were present when the deputy was gunned down and scalped.

Six men passed beyond Clark's window as they moved towards the entry door.

Clark returned to his desk where he grabbed his hat, pulling it onto his head. As he looked to his colt, the men entered his office. All of them wore deputy badges. They waited near the doorway, silent and grim.

Without a word, Clark holstered his pistol and strode to the door. The others followed him outside. Horses, including Clark's, were tethered behind the building. They mounted.

Finally, Clark addressed the group.

"We stay off the main road until we are well past the last settlement east of town. Bader, where do we meet up with the rest of the posse?"

Peter Bader had a dark look about him.

"They will rendezvous with us west of Loyal Valley."

"Good," Clark said, putting spur to his mount.

If they had taken the main road, they would have encountered Cooley and his men, who were a mile or so out of town.

Boyd pointed towards a narrow trail off the main road, following the bank of Comanche Creek.

"Cheney's shack is about a quarter mile down that trail on the riverbank."

"Thanks kid," Ringgold said. "Hey, why don't you come along – make sure I don't lose my way?"

Boyd studied Ringgold for a moment. His smile had returned, but his good humor failed to make it to his eyes, which were cold and dreadful to behold.

"Go ahead, son," Jarvis said quietly. "We won't need no help handling the Sheriff. I've seen his layout."

Boyd nodded uncertainly but led the way onto the trail. He glanced behind him where Ringgold followed closely. Just leaving Boyd's view, Cooley and Jarvis continued towards Mason.

Boyd followed the winding trail for some moments before Ringgold spoke.

"How do you happen to know where Cheney lives?" he asked.

"I grew up here, Mr. Ringgold. I know where everyone lives."

"Call me Johnny, kid."

Boyd nodded.

"Call me Boyd," he returned. After a moment he said, "or Hutton."

The name felt strange on his tongue when applied to him. His accepted name, Wechsler, made him just as uncomfortable, but he preferred Hutton and assumed he would grow accustomed to it in time.

"That's the spirit, Kid," Ringgold said with a chuckle. "How much further?"

"Less than a few rods."

"Give me the lead."

Ringgold overtook Boyd and led the way into a small clearing where a ramshackle shed stood, debris and refuse scattered around it; a horse was staked nearby, grazing. It lifted its head and nickered at the approaching horses.

As they drew near the house, Boyd smelled bacon and heard the clanging of cooking items inside. Cheney stepped out the door holding a fork and a dirty rag. He squinted at the two newcomers.

"Your Johnny Ringgold," he said. "And the Wechsler boy. What's the occasion for the visit?"

Ringgold pulled rein some ten feet from the gambler.

"You remember me." Ringgold observed.

"You were awful drunk," Cheney said good naturedly. "You and them Baird boys..."

Cheney's face drooped as he made the connection. He knew he looked at the man who would end his life.

"It was a mistake, Johnny."

"That it was, Cheney," Ringgold agreed.

Boyd had never seen anyone pull a pistol so quickly. The explosion of the shot startled him.

A red hole popped open in the center of the gambler's head, and he fell with his eyes and mouth unnaturally wide.

Ringgold spun the pistol like a performer at a shooting exhibition and holstered it. He turned his horse's head, leading the way back to the main road.

They pushed their horses to a canter, catching up with Cooley and Jarvis in front of the Southern Hotel.

Cooley nodded to Ringgold.

"Did you locate your man?"

Ringgold nodded and tipped his hat.

"And you?" he asked.

"Clark left town unobserved."

"We didn't see him on your back trail," Ringgold said.

"Well, that's a relief," Cooley said sarcastically. "Let's have a bite. Maybe he'll turn up."

They tied their horses and entered the hotel, taking seats at the very table Jarvis and his men had occupied during their last visit. They ate rare steaks and fried eggs, then mopped their plates with heavy biscuits.

Ringgold called for a whiskey bottle and glasses.

Boyd sipped whiskey for the first time. It tasted foreign and bitter to his inexperienced pallet. The warmth, however, was pleasant, and the following moments seemed lighter and more pleasurable as the liquor took hold.

"The kid drinks like a grown man," Ringgold noted with amusement. He poured another for Boyd then sat back in his chair.

"How long you feel like waitin' for the Sheriff?"

This last was for Cooley.

Cooley drained his glass and gestured for the bottle.

"You don't need to stay, Johnny," he began.

"Don't let drink make you forget. We already had this confab. Besides, I want his hide as bad as you do."

Ringgold poured himself a drink. He gestured with his glass as he spoke.

"None of us will be much good if we empty this bottle."

"It's a party as far as I'm concerned," Cooley said, tipping another glass empty. "What's a shindig without a good drunk?"

Ringgold smiled with real amusement, tossing down his own drink.

"So be it," he said graciously.

They were at the bottom of the bottle when two men entered. Ringgold stood with a laugh and welcomed George Gladden and John Baird.

"I thought you was shot, George," Ringgold said with surprise.

"I am shot, Johnny. Doc pulled out the bullet and I feel better enough to be a part of this comeuppance party."

John Baird shrugged helplessly.

"We rode in with the Doc," he explained. "and he didn't protest much."

Baird's expression darkened as his attitude sobered.

"Have you seen my brother's body?"

"The sheriff is not in town, and I don't know where they would keep the dead in this town," Cooley replied.

"I expect the sheriff will know the answer when he returns," Ringgold said. "Sit down if you can and help out with this bottle."

33

SIX ADDITIONAL MEN JOINED CLARK AND his deputies near Mill Creek. Among them were Ernst Wechsler and Henry Pluenneke. The rest were also members of the Cattlemen's Association.

Henry eased his horse to the front of the group.

"We spotted William Coke on Tom Gamel's place. We didn't see Gamel, but Coke wouldn't be there without him."

"I sent Gamel packing," Clark explained. "He don't have courage enough to stay in Mason County."

"What if he does?" Ernst asked.

"I told him what would happen to him if he came back."

"Why would Coke be hanging around Gamel's place if he wasn't expecting him?"

Clark glared at Ernst for a long moment as his mind worked at the potential affront to his authority if Gamel had indeed returned.

"Lead on," Clark said.

Ike Beam, a tall lean cow puncher with a large Adam's Apple closed the gate to the pen outside the weathered planks and broken back of the ranch's stable and hay mow.

William Coke, a cowpuncher with bowed legs and a jutting jaw, giving him a perpetual appearance of disagreement, followed him towards the house.

"I don't guess we'll see Tom again, Bill," Ike observed sadly. "I guess the rumors are true. Clark gave him the bum rush for good."

"Shit," Coke exclaimed. "Speak of the devil."

"What?" Beam asked, turning to his companion.

"Riders," Coke explained with a pointed finger. "That's the Sheriff up front."

Beam turned to look. He saw a group of riders headed their way.

"What should we do?" Beam asked.

"Just keep calm. We ain't done nothing to worry about. They may be checking for Tom."

A dozen riders stopped before the two, fanning out around them.

Ike and Bill eyed each of the riders in turn, finally returning their attention to the Sheriff.

"What's cooking, Sheriff?" Beam asked nervously.

"Where's Tom abouts today?" the Sheriff said, ignoring the question.

"Hell," Coke replied bitterly. "From what I hear, you ought to know."

"I'll have straight answers out of you William Coke, if you know what's good for you."

"You ask a straight question, and you'll get a straight answer."

"He's one of 'em killed my brother," Peter Bader muttered.

"Your brother's dead?" Coke asked with sarcastic innocence. "Too bad."

"You makin' fun of me or my dead brother, Coke?" Bader yelled. He looked ready to pull his rifle.

"Not making fun at all," Coke responded casually. "If truth be said, it's too bad it isn't you rottin' in that field instead of Carl. He never killed Tim Williamson. That was all you and your friends here."

"Goddam you…"

"We're taking you two in for questioning," Sheriff Clark said loudly, ending the discussion.

"We didn't do nothing," Ike Beam complained. "I only foremen this place. I don't know nothing about anything you fellas are mixed up in."

"When was the last time you saw Tom Gamel?" the sheriff insisted.

"Not since he went to town, and I heard you sent him away."

"Do you know Scott Cooley and his gang?"

"Who?" Ike replied innocently.

"Bader," the Sheriff said to the angry German. "You and Henry take these men into custody on suspicion of rustling."

"Who the hell do you think you are you can arrest innocent men and pin bogus charges to 'em?" Coke yelled, his face turning red with rage.

Clark leaned forward menacingly.

"You want to make the trip in shackles, Coke?"

"He's wearin' 'em at any rate," Bader said with a deadly steadiness to his voice.

"I'll see you dead first, Bader," was Coke's response.

Henry Pluenneke sidled up behind Coke, whose attention was reserved only for Bader, and struck him in the back of the head with a rifle butt.

"He ought to be no trouble to chain up now Pete," Ernst observed with a nod to Henry who stowed his rifle in his saddle scabbard.

"Ike," Clark ordered. "Go fetch two horses for the trip. "The rest of you boys come with me. We're going to Loyal Valley to find our scalpin' murderers, Cooley and his gang."

Clark and the others gave spur, hooves thundering as they returned to the main road.

It didn't take Ike Beam long to ready two horses and bring them out.

"Bill's hoss was saddled already," he explained.

"Help him onto his horse," Bader said, nodding towards the groaning Bill Coke who struggled weakly against the irons placed upon him while he was unconscious.

Ike Beam helped him into the saddle then mounted up. The prisoners rode ahead of the two deputies. They turned west on the road towards Mason.

34

COOLEY LED THE OTHERS OUT OF THE Southern Hotel with unsure steps. It was evening, and he had participated in the consumption of three bottles of whiskey while waiting for the Sheriff's return.

Ringgold stepped outside immediately behind him, followed by the others, Boyd bringing up the rear.

As he followed the others, Boyd reached for any solid surface he could find, endeavoring to steady the world spinning beneath him. He lamented silently if only the whirling of his surroundings would spin in one direction, he felt sure he could maintain his equilibrium. Unfortunately, as he leaned into the rotation in one moment, the next found him staggering to bring his weight another way to counter the changing roll of the world around him.

Ringgold, not so steady himself, chuckled at the youngster.

"Ride her Kid," he called good naturedly.

Cooley reached behind him unsteadily. With an effort he managed to grasp Ringgold's coat.

"Ask the Kid who those fellas are?" he slurred. "Maybe they are a part of the gang we're hunting."

Boyd squinted at four men riding by the hotel. He recognized three of the men. He made his way to the front of the group.

Jarvis grabbed his arm, restraining him from moving forward and into harm's way. The older man recognized an impending gun battle coming and he wanted his drunken nephew out of the line of fire.

Boyd tried to shake off his uncle's hand, but changed his mind when he looked up in his eyes. Instead, he returned his gaze to the riders.

"Hey," he yelled drunkenly at the riders.

They pulled up, recognizing some of the men, including Wolf Wechsler's grandson.

Boyd pointed at Bader and Pluenneke then the others as he singled them out.

"I know Peter Bader and Henry Pluenneke," Boyd said with a slur to his words. "That fella with the wide brimmed hat is the Brand Inspector, Mr. Hoerster, but I don't know you."

He pointed at Ike Beam.

John Baird and George Gladden moved forward as one. They had already identified their good friend Ike Beam.

John Baird glared at Peter Bader, who's memory was slowly placing George Gladden as the second rider in their ambush.

"Scott," Baird announced. "Like the kid said, that round faced man on the left is Peter Bader. You already met his brother at their farm. Ike, you better ease on over to the side."

Although shackled, Ike Beam nudged his horse away from the deputies who made no effort to restrain his movements.

The transformation of Scott Cooley was remarkable to see. He seemed suddenly completely sober and steady.

As was his habit, Ringgold's demeanor never changed, with the exception of when he learned of his friend Mose's death. Even in the face of the man who murdered his friend, he still wore his ever-present smile.

He took a step to the right, notably creating distance between Cooley and himself.

"You killed Tim Williamson," Cooley said in a strangely calculating voice. "I'd wager this square-headed fella – Henry – was there too. What about you, Brand Inspector? Did you know Tim Williamson?"

"I did not," Hoerster lied.

"The hell you say," Pluenneke spat nervously. "You were the one who pulled your bond off Williamson and made him an outlaw."

"Shut your mouth," Hoerster snapped.

"Is it your intention to murder me like you did my brother?" Bader asked with a flare of temper.

"Was it yours to kill Tim Williamson?" Cooley returned with anger.

"He was a proved rustler and thief."

Bader went for his pistol. He was unaccustomed to the weapon and his attempt was clumsy. Pluenneke also reached for his colt.

Scott Cooley was not quick on the draw, but he was accurate and his bullet gutted Bader.

Ringgold's draw was delayed a half second behind Colley's, but his was a blur of smooth motion. His pistol reports sounded, rapid and deadly. Pluenneke fell from his horse beside Bader. Hoerster fell backwards, his horse rearing as the dying Brand Inspector held to the reins as he fell. All three died in the dusty street.

Cooley approached Bader's corpse, shooing the dead man's horse out of the way. He pulled his big knife and scalped Bader with practiced efficiency.

Ike Beam watched with horrified interest as Cooley stood straight, displaying the gory rag of skin and hair.

"He killed Bill Coke on the way here," Ike said sadly. "Bader took Bill off the road, and they were gone for a while. Bader returned alone."

George Gladden cursed.

"Bill was a good man. He had nothing to do with any of this."

John clapped him on the shoulder.

"Come on, George. You need to get some rest. I'll release Ike first."

Jarvis let go of Boyd's arm.

His nephew stared at Cooley as the former Ranger tucked Bader's scalp into the sack tied to his saddle horn.

Ringgold replaced the empty casings with fresh cartridges and holstered his pistol.

"I'm thinking, based on the badges they are wearing," Ringgold said. "These are Clark's deputies. If they came from the East, the Sheriff is probably headed back to Loyal Valley to clean up some more of his enemies."

John Baird was beside Ike Beam's horse, unlocking his shackles with a key he had pulled from Bader's corpse.

"That's what the Sheriff said when they arrested me," Ike confirmed. "He said he was looking for a man named Scott Cooley in Loyal Valley."

Ringgold laughed.

"He ain't gonna find him there when he stands right here before you."

Ike looked at Cooley.

"I suspected that might be him when he lifted Pete's hair."

Cooley glanced at Ike blandly. He untied his horse then mounted.

"How many men are in the Sheriff's posse?"

"I counted a dozen," Ike replied. "Now there's two less. What does that come to?"

"I guess we ought to make our scheduled meeting with the Sheriff," Cooley said.

"I'm taking John home," George said to Cooley.

They shook hands.

George turned to Ike Beam.

"Ike you better come with us. You were last seen with these men and now they're dead."

Ike swallowed audibly. He said nothing but followed Baird and Gladwell as they rode away.

Cooley watched the three ride away.

"I'll ride along with 'em until they turn off the trail."

Boyd stepped off of the hotel veranda and untied his horse.

"I have business here abouts. I'll catch up with you fellas," he said.

"I'll join you, son," Jarvis said, moving to his own horse. He had an inkling of what was on his nephew's mind and old accounts still needed to be settled.

"Both of you need to stick with us," Cooley interrupted, pulling on the reins to pause his departure.

Boyd mounted his horse, his jaw set stubbornly.

Before he could argue the point Cooley spoke.

"I rangered for a long time. I pursued a lot of outlaws, and the one thing that always got 'em caught was they split up."

"I gotta go my own way," Boyd said in a faint voice. "I've helped you like you asked. That's all I'm in for."

Cooley smiled kindly.

"I wish it was that easy, boy. You are as guilty of killing those men as if you had pulled the trigger yourself."

"That ain't true," Boyd argued. "I never fired a shot – except when I shot Verner – and that was self-defense."

"He's right son," Jarvis agreed sadly. "You're counting on too many details the law won't take into account. For the law – and lawmen – the simple answer is the one they pick. There ain't no more self-defense after you been party to this many killings. Stick with us until the job is done. We'll slide out of this for Mexico and make a new life for ourselves. We are both safer with these men than on our own until that sheriff is brought to heel."

Ringgold shrugged.

"Tough luck kid," he said. "You're part of our gang now. Someday you'll tell the story of your time here. Until then, you're one of us."

"I'm not happy with this whole thing," Boyd announced to the others.

Ringgold chuckled.

"Wait until you sober up, it's gonna get worse."

Cooley and Ringgold rode after the others. Soon all five were lost to the darkness, leaving Boyd and Jarvis alone.

"It ain't ideal, Boyd," Jarvis said. "but it's all we got. Let's slope."

Jarvis nudged his horse, leaving Boyd behind him for the moment.

Boyd looked towards the direction of the ranch where he had spent his entire life. He yearned to see his mother, to clear the way between them. He wanted to tell her he no longer blamed her. He understood why she hid the truth from him.

Jarvis was swallowed by the night in his turn.

Boyd struggled with his will. Finally, he touched the gelding with a spur, following the others east.

35

SHERIFF CLARK AND HIS MEN ARRIVED AT Meusebach's store after dark. They were delayed by a detour to Baird's place where they found only an empty house with clearly seen clues the occupants had been gone only since that morning.

Inside the saloon they found Meusebach himself serving whiskey to three cowpunchers.

"Sheriff," the proprietor greeted Clark.

"Mr. Meusebach. We're looking for a group of murderers. Their leader goes by the name Scott Cooley. Have you seen anyone who might answer to that name?"

"Been slow today. I've served no murderers I know of. Can I offer you a libation?"

"Thanks," Sheriff Clark replied vacantly as his mind worked at the plan for his next move. "I got ten men in all. Can you put us up for the night? I don't want my posse on the road at night to be ambushed by bushwhackers who know the country better than we do."

"Good thinking," replied Meusebach, seeing an opportunity for unanticipated revenue. "I've got the storage shed out back. The mow has fresh hay, and the rats are friendly this time of year. I'll throw in a supply of grub you boys can use to prepare your evening meal and perhaps a light breakfast in the morning."

"That'll do," Clark said reaching for his money bag. He paid the amount asked and pocketed the rest.

"Tell them boys to use the outhouse," Meusebach warned. "Keep their nightsoil out of my hay mow. The almanac is low on pages, but the corn crib has plenty of cobs."

"I'll tell 'em," Clark said as he left the saloon.

He joined his men where they waited with their horses.

"We will bed down in that shed yonder. We'll pick up our pursuit in the morning. Some of you men prepare a cook fire. I need a couple of you to fetch supplies from the store for the evening meal. I'll see to the condition of our accommodations for the night."

Captain Dan Roberts reviewed his men from horseback. They looked rough as boys off the farm, but they were well trained and tough. With only ten total, his company was such only in name. The life of the Texas Ranger was lonely, filled with hardships. Pay was low, luring few other than those gambling on their last desperate chance to find their way.

It was late for a muster, but not unheard of. Much of a Texas Ranger's work was done with no more light than the moon and stars offered. He had prepared his men for the possibility of night travel. The sound of approaching hoof falls drew his attention.

Major Jones led Captain Worth and his larger company A, comprised of twenty men. Although twice the size of his unit, with more experienced men, their condition was similar to Roberts' Company D men.

Jones drew reign near Roberts.

"The Governor's orders are clear men," Jones said in a crisp voice. "We are to root out a marauding group of vigilantes who are spreading murder and fear throughout Mason County. They have butchered several local farmers, taking their scalps as trophies."

Roberts looked at his saddle horn. He had already read the report and the missive from Governor Coke. The leader of the marauders was none other than Scott Cooley, a former Texas Ranger, and friend. Cooley had served with Roberts for the bulk of his term of service before leaving their ranks.

Several of the more seasoned men in Company A were former acquaintances of Cooley's. Roberts left them and Company A behind when he was given command of the recently created Company D.

Roberts surveyed three men in Worth's company he recognized from those days. They nodded to him the greeting of men who shared a common bond of life and death, and in understanding of the conflicting task they faced in pursuing one of their own.

Roberts learned of Tim Williamson's murder during his last visit to Mason. He had heard Cooley mention the rancher's name on numerous occasions during their time together on the trail. Roberts had not expected Cooley to react so aggressively to the news of his friend's death, but he wasn't overly surprised.

Neither was the scalping a surprise to any man who had ever ridden into conflict with Cooley. It was startling the scalps Cooley collected were those of white men instead of his typical victims, warring Indian braves.

Jones nodded to his two Captains.

"Let's move 'em out Gentlemen."

Roberts and Worth took charge of their men, leading the way towards Mason County. According to reports, the last known actions by Cooley and his gang were in the Loyal Valley region. If they rode throughout the night, they would reach the village by first light.

36

COOLEY HELD UP HIS MEN AT THE EDGE of a bushy hedgerow just beyond Meusebach's Store. They dismounted and eased forward behind the cover provided by the foliage. Beyond the store, tied within a rope pen, were eleven horses. Saddles remained on the horses' back, cinches left loose, for quick action if required.

"The Sheriff plus ten deputies," Ringgold observed. "The math works here."

"Yes it does," Cooley agreed. "I'd like to burn it down around 'em."

"Let's light it," Ringgold said. "We'll shoot whoever runs out. Come with me, kid. You're gonna want to see this."

Ringgold looked at Boyd who moved towards his waiting horse further within the grove.

A movement caught Cooley's eye and he shushed his men with a raised hand.

"I saw movement," he explained. "Everyone stays still. Something's in the wind here."

Boyd and Ringo returned to their hiding places, looking out carefully. They too caught movement in the tree line beyond the big shed, behind the store.

"That's a lot of men," Jarvis said quietly. "Who are they?"

No one answered. Instead, they continued to watch as nearly a score of riders issued into the clearing containing Meusebach's property. They were fully armed, led by men who displayed military bearing, recognizable even in the saddle.

Cooley swore softly.

"Texas Rangers, boys, and a lot of 'em."

"How can you be sure?" Ringgold asked.

"I know some of 'em," Cooley said vacantly. "That's Major Jones leading them, and I know some of the men in his command."

Jarvis looked at Cooley suspiciously.

"Why would you know Texas Rangers?"

"Like I said in Mason, I used to be one of 'em."

Ringgold glanced at Cooley.

"I would hazard a guess you experienced what is called an epiphany somewhere along the way, because you are pure outlaw now."

"Something like that," Cooley said noncommittally.

The Rangers surrounded the shed in a wide circle, taking cover in case the men inside decided to resist.

"Worth crept nearer to Major Jones.

"My men are in position behind and around the building, sir."

"Good," Jones replied.

"These are some poorly led outlaws to hide out in plain sight," Worth observed.

"I agree," Jones said. "That's why I want you and your men to be ready, but not to move until I give the command. We don't know if these are outlaws yet."

"Who else could they be: in a barn, horses rigged for a speedy escape?"

Major Jones raised his voice.

"You in the barn, this is Major John B. Jones. We got twenty Texas Rangers out here. Come out with your hands empty and over your heads. You are surrounded. We will shoot to kill at the first sign of resistance."

A voice sounded from within the shed.

"Don't shoot Major. I'm Mason County Sheriff John Clark, and these men are my posse. We're coming out."

Cooley pulled his pistol.

Ringgold touched his shoulder.

"Not the right time, pardner," he said quietly. "Let's ease on out of this while they are occupied."

Cooley looked at Ringgold with an expression of annoyance which faded as he saw the reasoning in the advice.

"You're right Johhny," he said, clearing his head of any foolish notions. "Back to the horses fellas."

After mounting their horses, Scott Cooley, Johnny Ringgold, Jarvis, and Boyd left the grove from the side opposite the barn and the company of Texas Rangers. They kept to the lower ground of a nearby draw. The deep wash wound along haphazardly as the floods were able to cut through the layered limestone beneath.

Sheriff Clark emerged from the shed with his hands held high enough to show he wasn't a threat, but not so high as to appear under the control of the Rangers. His men followed, their hands kept in plain sight.

"What's this laying siege to lawmen carryin' out their sworn duty?" Clark asked as he approached Major Jones and Captain Worth.

"Recall your Rangers Captain," Major Jones said to Captain Worth. To Clark he said, "I didn't know who you were, Sheriff Clark. I'm Major Jones. How many men do you have in there?"

"We number just under a dozen. The last of them is coming out as we speak. I suppose you are here because of the wire sent by a few of the townsfolk in Mason."

"Governor Coke sent us to put down this range war before anybody else gets killed."

"That's why we're here, Major. We bedded down for the night and were readying to depart when you and your men waylaid us."

Major Jones shook his head in annoyance at the characterization of his actions.

"Have you any idea where this man Cooley and his gang are?"

"He was last seen near here. He has been rumored to say he intends to burn out every last Dutchman in Mason County. We are here to see that doesn't happen."

"I see," Jones said thoughtfully.

Captain Roberts had earlier conveyed the details of his last visit to Mason where the Sheriff was drunk and uncooperative with him and his rangers when they acted to interrupt a lynching. Additionally, it was widely accepted the sheriff was on the payroll of some of the local German ranchers. Jones had read reports where the Sheriff was accused of being involved in questionable acts bordering upon misconduct with women.

Jones doubted Clark was acting solely in the interest of his office. He suspected the Sheriff was doing the bidding of his sponsors.

"Fifteen men?" Clark asked after tallying the total number of Rangers emerging from hiding. "I figured Coke could muster a bigger force than that."

"We have thirty men in all. We divided our forces into two groups of fifteen, if you must know. We have men patrolling the area for hidden forces in case you men weren't the gang we are searching for."

Cooley led his men out of the draw and onto the flat of a broad pastureland, fringed at its far edges by closely bunched trees. They made their way west towards the nearer line of trees.

Boyd scanned the area around them. He felt a gnawing sense of unease, travelling open country as they were. A glance at his riding companions confirmed they were equally uncomfortable.

Cooley pressed the pace, and they covered ground rapidly, entering the shadowy murk within an Elm grove. Cooley pulled up and his men gathered around him.

"We got a goodly sized pack of lawmen looking for us," he said unnecessarily. "It's a long chance, but we ought to lay low and travel by cover of night straight out of Mason County and this hornets' nest."

Jarvis nodded his agreement.

"We can't hide here, Scott," Jarvis said. "We're too exposed. Any ideas Boyd?"

Boyd shook his head.

"I don't know this country as well as I do Mason proper. The only place I know where we could hide out would be a bat cave I know of this side of Hilda. It's no more than five miles or so."

"Have you been there?" Cooley asked.

"No, sir. I've only heard stories about it, but it is easy to find at the base of the mountain yonder."

"Indians used to camp there when they massed for attacks on the white settlements. I can't think of anywhere else to hide."

Cooley considered his options for a moment. Finally, he tightened rein.

"Lead the way, kid."

Boyd rode deeper into the grove, ducking under reaching branches. Soon they reached the western edge of the copse, where they issued from the brambles one at a time. Jarvis was the last to emerge. He pulled up short, causing his horse to snort and rear.

They were surrounded by a large group of Rangers, their badges easily recognizable in the morning light.

Captain Roberts and fifteen men had them surrounded, guns trained on the fugitives.

Cooley sat straighter in the saddle as he recognized his former Captain.

"Dan," he said. "Quite a surprise seeing you here today."

"I'll bet it is, Scott. Who are your friends?"

"Just some fellas I fell in with. You're looking for me. These boys were just on the trail. They don't have anything to do with any of this."

"Reports say you are travelling with a group of three or four. Are you trying to convince me you changed out your gang?"

Cooley hung his head.

"Well," he said sadly. "I'm glad it is a friend who got me."

"You don't remember nobody but Captain Roberts?"

This last sally came from one of three men with grins on their faces, their pistols held empty of a threatening aim.

Scott Cooley smiled at his old friends despite his predicament.

"Of course, I remember you Lambert; you too Jimmy Pitt; and who could forget that red hair and fiery temper McLaughlin hauls around at his own peril. How do boys?"

"Is this about that man you told me about who was murdered – Tim Williamson?" Roberts asked.

"It is, Dan. These German ranchers are hanging men pell-mell. Some of them hung are just ranchers themselves, guilty of nothing but being in the wrong place. I can't sit idly by while my friends are murdered in cold blood."

Roberts gave Jarvis a moment's scrutiny.

"You got the look of a man who's been out of circulation for a long spell. You wanted other than this business here?"

"No sir, Jarvis replied. I came here to collect my dead brother's son here."

He nodded at Boyd before continuing.

"My brother was hung a few years ago by a German rancher too. We're headed for parts more welcoming."

"Is that right Scott?" Roberts asked Cooley.

Cooley hesitated as the image of Clark emerging from the shed haunted him.

"Yeah, Dan," he said finally. "We're done here. No more dead men will bring Tim back."

"I got my duty to perform, Scott. I'm gonna have to take you into cus…"

"Captain," Lambert interrupted. "I know your memory isn't so bad you forgot Scott saved your life – hell, all of our lives many times. He never gave a thought to his own welfare. As I see it, he is only doing for his friend what he would have done for us if we was murdered."

The redheaded McLaughlin leaned forward in the saddle.

"As far as I'm concerned," he said. "We ain't seen anyone on this patrol except some cowpunchers headed home."

Roberts kept his eyes on Cooley, paying him close scrutiny.

"You look tired Scott," he finally said. "You ought to get some rest. I'd keep moving on to where the Rangers can't go. Take a long break there and don't come back. Lambert's right. I owe you my life. After this, though, we are square."

Cooley nodded, his eyes darkening with emotion and gratitude.

"Thanks Dan, fellas," he said, nodding to the others before leading his men away.

Dan watched Cooley and his men disappear beyond a copse of trees.

"What about all your talk about duty and honor?" one of the other rangers asked loudly. "You just let the murderer we are after go."

Lambert and his two comrades turned to look fully at the complaining Ranger.

Lambert spoke softly but with passion.

"When he served, that man was worth the rest of you put together. He was the fiercest and most loyal Ranger I ever met. If you was half the man he was, you'd know we wouldn't have let him go otherwise."

The complaining Ranger looked down at his hands on the saddle horn.

Roberts said, "Keep your teeth together and do as you're told."

Roberts returned his attention to his men.

"Let's complete our patrol and get back to Loyal Valley. I doubt those men in the barn are who we are after."

Jones stood as Roberts and his men rode into the Meusebach clearing.

Roberts recognized Clark and noticed shiny stars on most of his men's chests.

"We ambushed the Sheriff and his deputies," Jones explained. "Any sign of 'em?" Jones asked.

Roberts hesitated and appeared uncomfortable, so Lambert spoke up.

"Only ranchers and cowpunchers, Major. We're all pretty down in the mouth not to find these killers."

Jones nodded but seemed dissatisfied with the report.

"Roberts," he said. "You and your men step down and eat some breakfast. We'll continue the search afterwards."

Roberts hesitated. His guilt was powerful, urging him to confess. If he did, he feared Cooley hadn't had time to mount a large enough lead to stay away from a fresh pursuit.

"Yessir."

37

THEY RODE FOR MOST OF THE remainder of the day before Cooley called a halt. They made camp on the eastern banks of the James River. There was little water flowing, but the cover was thick. They risked a fire and put two cottontails on spits. Ringgold had killed them on the trail with a quick draw.

Cooley passed what was left of the bottle he had carried for several days. It was soon empty, summoning some muttered complaints from Jarvis.

Boyd leaned against a tree, fiddling with a twig as his mind worked. He looked around him at his companions. Other than Ringgold, there appeared a glum feeling about the men in camp. They sat quietly as he stood at a distance.

"What's on your mind, Kid?" Ringgold asked. "You look like your plottin' somethin'."

Boyd shrugged.

"Just remembering this picture so I don't forget what I see; what I learned; how I feel about it."

"Your deep, Kid," Ringgold observed. "There will come a time when you won't be able to turn it off. Don't get in the habit of working it over in your mind. There ain't no use in it."

Boyd wasn't certain what the outlaw meant, but he believed the wisdom sound, and it would make sense someday.

"Thanks, Johnny."

"You're welcome, Kid."

"Sit with us," Cooley said. "It's the end of our vendetta. Let's end it like it started – with no plan and only our wits to guide us. I won't forget how you helped. Thanks, Kid."

They were up with the dawn, saddling their horses and tying their packs. They said nothing until they were in their saddles.

"Me and Johnny are headed west," Cooley announced. "Johnny says Arizona. I'm still not settled on that. I don't care for the desert much, and there is a lot of it between here and there. Wherever we go, you men are welcome to come along."

He eased his horse towards Jarvis and Boyd. He extended his hand to Boyd.

"Thanks again, Kid," he said and shook his hand. He released Boyd's then shook Jarvis' hand. "Take care of him old man."

"I'll do what I can Scott. Keep your eyes open. You too Johnny Ringo."

Jarvis grinned at the gunslinger, letting him know he meant no affront.

Ringgold tipped his hat to the old outlaw with his usual smile. The smile faded a fraction as he turned towards Boyd.

"You're going back to see your ma?"

Boyd said nothing.

Jarvis took a moment to consider Boyd's intentions before he spoke again.

"You'll be walking into a hornet's nest if you go back to that ranch, kid. You don't want to be in that situation alone. I'll watch your back."

Boyd looked fully at his uncle.

"I want to talk to my Ma one last time. I can't share that with you. After that, unleash hell if you want to."

Jarvis nodded his understanding.

All right," he agreed with feeling. "I'll wait. This is the only time I will. Bid her farewell, son. There ain't no future for you anywhere but with me. That ain't a boast. That's a simple fact."

Boyd nodded.

"I understand."

"You want me to tag along?" Ringgold asked Boyd, his expression conveying friendly regard.

"Thanks Johnny," Boyd said with gratitude. "I should be able to handle this on my own."

"Boyd Hutton," he said as though he were memorizing the name. "Don't get killed too young. I get a feeling we will meet again on the trail. Adieu."

Cooley and Ringgold rode away leaving Boyd and his uncle behind in the grove.

Boyd raised his voice to be heard across the growing distance.

"When I'm done, where can we meet up?" Boyd called to Ringgold.

"Follow the bodies," Ringgold replied over his shoulder. "We won't be hard to find."

Ringgold pressed his horse to a trot, following after Cooley.

Boyd turned his horse north towards the Wechsler Ranch.

Jarvis watched him ride into the woods before he clucked to his horse, turning him in the direction towards which Boyd had gone.

Boyd arrived at the Wechsler ranch after dark. He tied his gelding within a copse of Live Oaks behind the stables. He shifted his gun belt, adjusting it for comfort and ready access.

Lights burned inside, brightening several of the windows in the ranch house. Boyd crept across the road between the house and the stables. The moon shone brightly on the bare packed road, providing ample but unnecessary light. Boyd knew the ranch well. He also had a good idea where he might find his mother. His guess was rewarded as he heard her voice through an open window near the front of the house.

"Father," he heard her saying. "This whole affair is getting dangerously out of hand. Adding my only son to your list of wanted outlaws goes beyond anything I thought you capable."

"The boy is no good, just like his father. Blood will always flow true, and it has here. This uncle, what did you say his name is…Jarvis Hutton? The name is acid on my tongue. He is here for revenge, pure and simple. He has, by now, poisoned what small portion of your boy's mind was not already against us."

"I should have never told you his name. Kyle spoke of him often."

"A base criminal; doubtless another murdering thief. How could you go around with your bastard's father after learning the entire family was nothing more than a bunch of cutthroats?"

"If you must know the truth, father, Kyle was the only cutthroat as you say. His brother took the blame for his younger brother's crime. He spent almost two decades in Huntsville for his brother. That means something doesn't it?"

"Do you hear yourself, girl? You are as lost as your son. You boast of honor among criminals as though I would understand and agree. You are half witted if you think I am moved by your story. Get out of my sight!"

Boyd had moved to a vantage where he could see his mother and grandfather clearly but was invisible in the darkness beyond the light within the room. He gripped his pistol as he listened to the discussion inside.

He hesitated a moment as his mother fled the room in tears. He fought the urge to confront his grandfather – to finally have his say. Instead, he backed from the window and made his way to the window outside of his mother's room.

He looked within. She sat on a stiff wooden chair, facing the window, but unseeing anything beyond the pain she fought within herself. Her hair was disheveled, and tears streamed down her cheeks. Her hands hung limply on either side of the chair. Her shoulders slumped in despair.

Boyd felt a sharp pang deep within his breast. His anger with his mother over her secrecy about his father faded, replaced with sympathy and a desire to comfort her.

He pulled the window frame open, stepping silently into the room.

Emma gasped, her hand going to her mouth as if to quell a cry.

"I'm here to say goodbye Mother," he explained. "I don't fault you for your decisions. However, this is not my family. I am leaving instead of exacting a price for what they have done to me; what they did to my father."

"You are in grave danger, son." she said in a hissed whisper. "They have sentries posted in case you return."

Boyd stood with a stiffened back. He had seen no one.

He heard a disturbance outside the window. He spun around to see the source of the noise when a rifle barrel snaked inside through the window and pressed against his forehead.

"Don't move Boyd."

He recognized Ernst's voice before he saw his face. His uncle leered at him.

"Drop the gun belt on the floor."

Boyd obeyed reluctantly. He heard the scuffing of boots outside of his mother's room. The door burst open.

Klaus and two members of the Association entered with their guns trained on Boyd.

"You never should have come back," Klaus said with a shake of his head. "Bind him men."

The two others tied Boyd's hands behind his back.

Emma cried and begged them to release Boyd.

The men ignored her. Ernst entered through the door and pressed Emma back into the chair.

"Be still, woman. This is all your fault. Don't make it worse than it has to be."

They led Boyd from the room, closing the door on Emma. They took him outside to the roadway beyond the kitchen door.

Three more men entered the roadway from the darkness. They led a horse carrying a struggling Jarvis, bound hand and foot, gagged, and draped over the saddle.

Boyd's shoulders sagged as he beheld Jarvis, now in his grandfather's custody. He understood what that meant for his case. Alone, Boyd might have been able to talk himself out of this fix. His uncle's presence made it look like they were working together.

The man leading the horse laughed grimly.

"Look who we found sneakin' around. Charlie Johnson."

Wechsler stepped forward as his men dropped Jarvis from the saddle to the ground, where he landed with a groan.

"That man's name is Jarvis Hutton."

The other men looked down at Jarvis with confusion clear in their expressions.

Wechsler stopped near enough to the fallen man he could have nudged him with a grimy toe.

"He's wanted for the killing of old man Miller near Hye. Witnesses said the man we know as Charlie Johnson was identified riding away from the Miller place the night of his murder. Pick him up."

Jarvis' captors lifted him to his feet.

"This man is Boyd's uncle," Wechsler explained, using a grand gesture to animate the startling revelation.

Jarvis, unable to speak, glared at the old German rancher with hate filled eyes.

Klaus glanced at the equally helpless Boyd before moving closer to his father, leaving Ernst to watch the prisoner.

"So that's why he knew so much about the fate of Emma's rustler beau," Klaus deduced. "I thought he knew too much to have learned it through hearsay."

Boyd's gaze fell upon young Hans, standing on the back porch. The tow-headed sprat's expression was a study in pain and betrayal. Boyd could scarcely imagine how completely he had fallen from grace in the boy's eyes.

He felt a strange pity for Hans. The boy was considered a cracked pane in the family mosaic. He was indeed the runt of the litter and shunned. Boyd had been his sole supporter. None of that mattered now. Hans knew the truth. The cousin he worshipped was not family. He was in fact one of the enemy. Boyd thought the disappointment had to be a crushing blow for the boy.

The Wolf leaned closer towards Jarvis' dirty face; close enough to smell the outlaw's rancid breath.

"I'll see you are a glaring part of this county's history, Hutton," he said with a growl of hate. "You, your dead brother..."

The old man gave a purposeful look at Boyd.

"...and your brother's spawn, will all have a place in our history. The name Hutton will be remembered, not as a family name, but instead as a curse. Your name will be a catch all for everything evil: lowly curs, rustlers, murderers and ne'er do wells. The murders of innocent men will be placed at your feet for all time. Posterity will look upon you and the Hutton name for what you are now and will permanently remain."

Wechsler spat on the ground near Jarvis' feet.

"Put these two in the hog trap and lock it. We'll deal with them when the others have gone to bed."

Emma appeared with a crash of the back door and a cry, fixing them all in place.

"You are not going to hang my son in the dead of night, father."

She halted her frenzied approach before her father, nearly in his face.

"This murder and night terror ends now," she screamed.

She looked around her, eyeing her father's men menacingly. Her eyes were opened wide with a desperate wildness, giving her the appearance of a pale wraith.

Wechsler looked at her silently, his judgement a palpable thing. Finally, he shook his head, and a mirthless smile turned the line of his lips upward.

Furious at his reaction, Emma shoved him mightily. The Wolf staggered backwards two steps before he regained his balance – and his temper.

"Get out of my sight," he thundered at her. "How dare you lay hands upon a man as if you had any right…"

"I have every right," she interrupted with equal fervor. "You have ruined this family. You have turned my brothers into base murderers. You did the same to my son. There is a hot place in hell waiting for you."

Wechsler turned to a group of four men clustered at a distance.

"You men," he commanded. "Take her into the house and lock her there."

"Father," Ernst complained. "You would allow strangers to handle your own daughter – my sister?"

"Your complaint is precisely why I do not depend on you to remove her."

He looked at the four men.

"Obey me now."

As one, the men strode rapidly towards Emma.

Boyd moaned with fury as he struggled against his bonds and Ernst's grip. He managed to free himself, leaning forward to add impetus to his struggling gait as he scrambled towards his mother.

A blow to his head scattered his senses. He fell unconscious.

Four men restrained Emma as she moved to help her son. She wailed as they grabbed her roughly, struggling to drag her to the house.

"Wait," Wechsler said. "Emma!"

Emma grew strangely still at her father's unusual use of her name.

To the others Wechsler said, "Take Boyd to the barn and tie him securely. Put his uncle in the hog trap."

He turned to Emma.

"We will not hang your son tonight. Go peacefully with these men."

Emma's expression indicated she distrusted her father.

"I will honor my word to you," he said loudly. His tone was less assuring than it was authoritative.

Emma ceased her struggle with her captors, allowing them to take her into the house. She was defeated, her strength depleted. As she saw it, her life was over. If not tonight, her son would die soon after. If that happened, she committed herself to the same fate. She would end her own sorrow at her earliest opportunity.

Ernst led a dazed Boyd to the stables.

With a nod from Wechsler, Klaus brought up the rear.

Inside, Klaus lighted a lantern hanging from the center post. They pressed Boyd to the ground and tied him securely to a nearby post.

Once their nephew was sufficiently helpless, they stood, surveying their handiwork.

"He ain't going nowhere," Klaus observed.

"Nope," Ernst agreed. "Well Boyd, I guess blood will always tell. Still, I don't understand why you would turn against the family that raised you. At least half of your blood is the same as ours. You gotta hate that part of you. If you didn't, I believe some part of you would have been loyal."

"Come on Ernst," Klaus urged his brother. "He hates us as much as he hates those he and his gang killed."

Boyd's voice came calmly and evenly.

"I don't hate you," he said. "I don't feel any way about you or Grandfather. You were my family all of my life. That is the only thing that would stop me from killing you if I survived this thing. Killing you all would hurt my mother nearly as bad as your killing me. I can't do that to her."

"You ain't one of us," Klaus said. "You proved that when you killed Verner Koenig, and you and your gang killed so many others."

Boyd grew silent as he remembered the vivid details of Koenig's death. Finally, he looked at his cousins.

"You are right. I ain't one of you. I think I've always known it. I surely know it now. Kill your sister's son. You may still earn the respect of your father."

Boyd shook his head with genuine pity.

"On second thought," he continued. "We all know that ain't the truth, don't we. You and yours can burn in hell for all time. I'll see you when you get there."

Ernst took a half step towards Boyd before Klaus restrained him by grabbing his arm.

"His time will come, brother. You can pull him high with the rope if you like. Save your anger for that time."

Ernst was slow to abandon his desire for vengeance. Finally, he acquiesced and followed his brother out the door, slamming and latching it behind him.

The hog trap sat at the far side of the stables. The device was made of iron and rough wood. It was used to trap then purify the meat of wild hogs. The method of trapping the hogs was self-evident. Bait was tied in the center of the trap. When a hog enters, it springs the door, trapping the animal. The meat is purified by feeding the hogs plants and refuse from household produce for two to three weeks. The process rids the meat of putrefaction and unclean consumables digested from unsupervised rooting in the wild.

Jarvis sat inside. He was untied and his gag was removed. He had a look of despair on his face. Wechsler and the others gazed upon him as they might a Ferrel Hog destined for the butcher's block. Ernst and Klaus joined them in their scrutiny of the condemned man.

"Boyd is tied to a center post, Grandfather," Klaus announced quietly.

His mood was muted by a prescience of what was to become of the two prisoners. Taking a life is always a matter requiring pondering thought and careful justification.

The Wolf glanced at Klaus with a grunt. He considered Jarvis carefully, engaging his full attention.

"They hang at midnight – in the gloom of the witching hour. Sunlight will never shine on their faces again."

Jarvis seemed not to hear. At least he registered no reaction to the announcement of the circumstances of his impending death.

He had been nearly two decades without the sun on his face. At least he had never had any worthwhile time in it during his confinement. This end was not something he had not considered. More accurately, he was surprised he had avoided the gallows as long as he had. It seemed he had always been no more than a step from death since he was old enough to make his own way.

A passing thought of the revenge he would be denied shouldered into the calm of his acceptance of the inevitable. His eyes raised until he stared at the old German rancher.

"You are a murderous old man, ain't you?" he said to Wechsler. "I don't imagine you have given much thought to the price you will pay for the lives you have taken. I admit it. I planned to kill you tonight. But, as you said yourself, I hail from a family of lowly curs, rustlers, murderers and ne'er do wells. How are you any different despite your prattling on about how justified you are to kill in cold blood?"

Wechsler made no reply, but he stood straighter as the meaning of the prisoner's words pressed upon him with an irresistible reasonableness.

"That boy you're about to kill tonight," Jarvis continued. "He didn't do anything. The man he killed was about to murder me. He saved my life only because he knew your man was set to do murder himself. I guess when an important man of your station sets the example, others follow without question."

Jarvis spat on the ground outside the bars.

"I ain't gonna crawl for you or your blind followers. I curse you all for what you are about to do to my nephew. You will all burn in hell for that. He's a kid. You treated him like an outsider, but he still backed you when we talked after your men tried to hang me. He held to a loyalty to you and your family I will never understand."

Jarvis looked around as if expecting a response to his soliloquy. No one spoke as the thoughts his words inspired worked on them.

Jarvis' abrupt laugh was more a deep lunged hack than mirth. He shook his head sadly. The remarkable thing was his sadness was sincere. His sadness was directed towards his captors.

"I take no pride that I will be proved right in what I said about you. I told him his loyalty was misplaced and wasted on you. I shut down his protests with a warning – no – a promise he would see the truth at his own peril. Well, here it is. I should have come sooner and killed every last man of you. I wouldn't mind if I had been killed doing it if that meant the boy's hands were clean and he lived a long life."

With a growled oath, Wechsler stepped to one of his men, yanking a shotgun out of his hands.

He pointed the weapon rapidly and fired. Jarvis jerked backwards from the impact before slumping against the bars, his chin lolling on his chest as he died.

Those around the cage registered varying reactions to the murder. Although dissimilar physically, it was clear to those men gunning down an unarmed and helpless man in a cage was an outrage, even for a condemned rustler.

The Wolf looked at the men around him with a challenge in his manner, daring anyone to question him. With renewed confidence he tossed the shotgun to its owner.

"Get the boy on his horse. He hangs now."

Boyd heard the command clearly from inside the stables. He had also heard his uncle's last words. He heard the shotgun blast that killed him. He struggled with the ropes binding him. His effort was not driven by fear. He was wild with rage. He would kill Wolfgang Wechsler given the slightest chance. He saw no way to do so, but he knew it would require only the smallest mistake of the men coming for him, and the moment would be his. He would die in the process, but the certainty of death did not dissuade him.

The front door opened slowly, uncharacteristic for men entering to take him to die. In the darkness he saw a figure moving towards him, silently but rapidly. When close enough, Boyd recognized Hans.

The boy held a knife before him. He moved behind Boyd and cut the ropes binding him.

Boyd shrugged out of the ropes as Hans returned to face him.

"I don't care what they say, Boyd. I love you. You are my family. I heard what that outlaw said, and he was right. You have always been loyal to me…"

The sound of approaching men leading a horse could be clearly heard.

Hans handed Boyd the knife.

"Get away from here, Boyd. I'll never forget you and when I'm big enough, I'll find you and be your family again."

Boyd grasped little Hans' shoulder in his left hand. He glanced towards the sound of men outside the front door.

"Come on," he said to Hans. "Let me get you out of here. No telling what will happen in the dark."

Boyd led Hans into one of the horse stables. He dropped to his hands and knees and pressed rotting planks away from a small hole in the wall, making the opening large enough to escape through.

He pushed Hans through, then scrambled through himself, scraping his back and arms painfully on the remaining ragged plank ends not softened by water rot.

He heard the door swing open and saw the glow of lantern light through the hole behind them.

"He's gone," a voice yelled from inside.

"This way," another said. "He got out though this hole in the wall."

Boyd led Hans towards the treeline past the large garden. Shots rang out from the direction of the ranch house. There was no light from the crescent moon, and the bullets sang by and beyond them, striking the trees ahead.

Hans nearly tripped on a low stump, cut to make room for the road bordering the garden and the woods beyond. Shots continued to ring out as he dodged left with catlike balance. A stray bullet struck him in the center of his back, and he went down in a heap.

Boyd cried out, lifting the boy, carrying him into the woods. The tightly wooded grove gave them cover. Boyd dared not risk a halt to assess Hans' wound. He didn't need to. He knew a kill shot when he saw one. Tears streamed down his cheeks and sobs came in shudders as he ran.

"Stay with me Hans," he said in the boy's ear. "You're gonna be alright."

"I told you I wasn't small, Boyd," Hans said weakly. Boyd was close enough to make out a forced smile on the dying boy's face.

"And you are right," Boyd said, crying openly now. "You're bigger than all of us. I should have seen it sooner."

Boyd risked a look at Hans. The boy's eyes were opened but they were unmoving. Despite the danger, Boyd stopped, laying Hans on the grass. He listened to his chest. He heard no heartbeat. Boyd pulled Hans to his chest, embracing his limp body.

"I'm sorry, Hans," he said.

He replaced Hans gently in the grass, then, with a final look at the boy's body, he ran on into the darkness.

38

MAJOR JONES AND HIS TEXAS RANGER Frontier Battalion remained in Loyal Valley for another day, but his search provided no clue where Cooley and his men had gone. Despite Captain Robert's and the others' warnings, the complaining ranger in his squad, overcome with his own indignation, waited until after dark to have private counsel with Major Jones.

Jones occupied one of the three rooms in Meusebach's saloon. The Major was poring over paperwork consisting of testimonials and firsthand accounts of the violence occurring in Mason County. Much of what he read attributed the violence as much to Clark and his deputies as was credited to the Cooley gang, or even the mysterious vigilante force.

A knock sounded at the plank door to his modest quarters.

"Enter," Jones called with typical military bearing.

A Ranger entered, his hat in his hands, eyes downward towards the floor. It was obvious the visitor was uncomfortable, either with the reason for his visit, or merely from being in the presence of the famous Jones.

Jones recognized the man but was unable to recall his name.

"What can I do for you Ranger?" he asked, returning the paper from which he read to the tabletop.

"Thank you for seeing me, sir," the Ranger began. "I witnessed something I need to tell you about."

Jones sat straighter in the stiff wooden chair.

"Go on," He said.

"I was with Captain Roberts and his squad yesterday morning when we came across four men making their way across country. We stopped them. Captain Roberts, Pitt, McLaughlin, and Lambert recognized the leader as Tim Cooley. They didn't know the others in the gang. The Rangers I named, and Cooley, had a friendly confab about how this Cooley had been a Ranger and had saved their lives on occasion, then Captain Roberts let them continue on their way with a promise to leave the territory."

Jones' reaction to the story came early on and increased until at the end of the tale he sat ramrod straight in his chair, and his face was as red as if he had held his breath the entire time. A loud exhalation indicated he might have done that very thing.

"And what did you and the others in the squad do about it?"

"Well, Major," he said slowly. "I told Captain Roberts our orders were clear, to capture those outlaws, to which he and the other three told me I knew nothing about honor or loyalty, or I would never see their decision any other way."

"What's your name, Ranger?"

"I'm Calvin Hays, sir."

"Ranger Hays," Jones said with measured control tempering his tone. "Don't mention we had this talk to anyone, is that understood?"

"Yes sir."

"Dismissed."

The following morning Jones called his men to formation in the clearing before Meusebach's barn. Captains Roberts and Worth stood at attention before their respective Ranger companies. Major Jones stood before the formation, surveying the men critically.

He spoke, his voice ringing clearly in the morning coolness.

"Rangers, it has come to my attention there has been a clear breach of duty and disregard for my orders, occurring at the highest positions in this Battalion. Captain Roberts, you, Rangers Lambert, Pitt, and McLaughlin step forward front and center."

Roberts and the other three fell out and took their places before the Major. It was plain they knew why they were being singled out. McLaughlin cast a dangerous look at Hays as he passed him. Once in front of the Major, they awaited his next words.

"Captain Roberts," Jones said. "Did you have Tim Cooley and his gang in your custody two mornings ago then release them?"

"Yes, I did, sir."

Jones addressed the other three men.

"And you three Rangers saw nothing worth reporting at this deliberate refusal to follow orders?"

McCullough shook his head stubbornly.

"Now, sir," he replied. "Tim Cooley served in this very Frontier Battalion. He saved many of the men here from outlaws and redskins at risk of his ow life. No matter the consequences, we back Captain Roberts, sir."

Jones made a step towards the rebellious Ranger, stopping himself from crossing the distance between them.

"Orders be damned, is it?"

"No sir," McCullough replied, nonplussed by the Major's wrath. "A life debt moves some of us to act outside of what might be expected of us. As I recall, major, you too were at that camp in Lost Valley when we were overrun by redskin savages. You are here because Scott Cooley did not pause, but instead acted. You decorated him in the field personally, sir. We repaid him with his own life, sir. I will not be apologizing for it."

McCullough stood straight with a jutting jaw, returning his gaze forward, staring into his memories, uncaring of the consequences of his actions.

Major Jones nodded, his shoulders losing a fraction of their military posture. He looked again at Captain Roberts.

"Major," Roberts said. "I take full responsibility for the actions of my troop."

"You're damn right you will," Jones said, though with less anger than before. "I should have you shot for dereliction of duty and aiding and abetting a dangerous fugitive. I can't afford to lose any more men or a decorated battle experienced officer. You and those who aided you in this crime are hereby temporarily relieved of duty and will report to the garrison at Camp San Saba where you will remain under house arrest until I return from this manhunt."

After being dismissed from formation, Captain Roberts and his three men left for Camp San Saba as Major Jones and the remaining Rangers made for Mason.

Mason was quiet when the Rangers and Clark's posse returned. They were quickly advised of the deaths of Peter Bader, Henry Pluenneke, Brand Inspector, Daniel Hoerster, and the gambler, Jim Cheney.

Despite Clark's protests, Jones commandeered the Sheriff's Office to serve as the headquarters for their mission.

Towards nightfall Jones sent a runner for Sheriff Clark. The Sheriff appeared before the Major who occupied the Sheriff's chair behind his desk. Clark made a wry face but made no further protest.

"You wanted to see me, Major?"

Jones raised a handful of loose papers.

"Sheriff Clark," Major Jones said with gravity. "I have been reading numerous accounts from several witnesses who have made some very serious claims concerning your actions during this range war."

"Range war?"

"What else would you call it?"

"I call it doing my job as best I can, Major. Just like you, I have to make hard choices and they gotta be made on the run. I'm not saying they are all the best choices, but they are made with the law in mind."

"Is that so?" Jones asked, leafing through the papers in his hands.

"That's so," Clark said firmly.

Jones found the page he was searching for and sat back in the chair as he read it silently before speaking again.

"Do you know a man named Moses Baird?"

Clark made no reply.

"What about George Gladden?"

Again, Clark made no reply.

Jones looked up from his reading.

"Nothing, Sheriff?"

Jones paused, sitting straighter in the Sheriff's chair.

"This eyewitness report says you sent a gambler by the name of Jim Cheney to Loyal Valley with a message Baird and Gladden were to return to Mason where you were to take their testimony in respect to the character of the late Tim Williamson, who your late Deputy Worley arrested, and was later killed in his custody. This report claims Baird and Gladden were ambushed by you and your men outside of town. Baird was shot dead and Gladden was wounded but escaped. Do you still have nothing to say?"

"Those men were suspected of rustling and possibly murder. I was trying to take them into custody peaceably. Things got out of hand and shooting broke out."

Jones nodded, although he seemed unmoved by Clark's explanation. He thumbed through the pages until he located another paper.

"You arrested a group of six men on or about the 13th of February. The next day you were observed drunk claiming. 'I don't control what happens when I am not here, but that doesn't mean it goes unanswered. Those men deserve what they have coming. I suppose the citizens lack the patience to wait for the slow workings of the law. I am the law here, but the law is no less than an extension of the people.'"

Jones quickly found another page.

"Another witness claims you made it public knowledge Deputy Worley was in possession of the key to the jail. That same night masked men, according to Mrs. Worley, entered their house and took the jail keys at gunpoint. Those same men spirited five of those six men from the jail and attempted to lynch them, killing three, and wounding one in the process. One escaped."

"That had nothing to do with me, Major. I can't control what the townspeople do when they are massed and in a temper."

"These men were not townspeople, according to those who seem to know more than they are saying. My information reports they are members of a vigilante gang who also killed a boy on the road and hung a sign on him the same night you jailed those six men."

"Enough of these accusations, Major. Let's get down to what you are really saying."

"Let's do that," Major Jones said, nodding to two Rangers loitering behind Clark near the front door.

"Lock up the Sheriff in his own jail cell, subject to Judge Hey's decision whether to charge the Sheriff or not."

"You won't do nothing of the kind," Clark bellowed.

"Stay where you are Sheriff Clark. My men will shoot you down where you stand if you make a move."

Clark was disarmed and locked inside the first of the two cells.

BOYD PULLED HIMSELF DEEPER INTO A web of roots below the bank of a dry wash. Past floods had exposed the tree's roots, leaving a shallow indentation in the bank. Mud clung to his face and stuck to his shirt where a light rain and sweat from the effort of his long flight had soaked him.

For the moment, he had lost his Grandfather's pursuers though he was doubtful the respite would last.

He had gained his greatest lead during the night. Since dawn, under a lowering sky, he kept to the draws and low-lying areas to avoid providing a silhouette against the horizon. He employed every trick he learned from Simon Martinez, but whether it be luck or coincidence, he had been unable to shake his Grandfather's men.

Despite his many switchbacks, and no matter the trail problems he created for them, they accurately predicted his direction of travel. He knew them to be poor trackers and novices on the trail, but because of his tracks upon the muddy ground, he remained dangerously close to capture. Even now he heard voices calling from the searchers, perplexed by his latest trail problem, widely separated, and scattered. scouring a greater area more rapidly.

Boyd was exhausted, thirsty, and hungry. Sorrow for young Hans gnawed at his insides. He was armed only with the knife Hans had given him in the stables. During daylight hours he was at a decided disadvantage against the Germans' guns, even wielded by men with minimal ability with the weapons.

Fortunately, the terrain was rugged, negating the advantage pursuing a man on foot might provide for a man on horseback. During his flight, he led them beyond the rolling hills and scattered tree groves near Comanche Creek into a region of rugged limestone outcroppings, craggy hillocks, and rocky ravines. The region was tightly protected by the bizarre knuckles, and twisted joints of dwarf junipers, and a thick, spiny underbrush skirting of low hanging branches beneath ancient Live Oaks.

In a move of desperation, Boyd followed the rugged bottom of a draw. He would leave no tracks among the rocks, but he was in danger of drowning in a flash flood if the rain fell heavily upstream.

He had finally taken cover amongst the roots, below the brow of the bank. If only he could rest for a while, undetected, he felt certain he could make it to nightfall, where an opportunity to slip away would be more likely.

Voices drew closer, but he heard no breaking of brambles or dislodged stones nearby, which might indicate a pursuer was close enough to discover his hiding place.

He listened intently for a long time. He felt his nerves wound to a tight strain, keenly set to detect the smallest sound or indication of danger.

Boyd did not remember when his senses lapsed into an insensate and exhausted sleep, but when he awoke with a jolt, stubbing his head against a hard root, the daylight was gone, and only impenetrable darkness surrounded him. The rain was replaced by a cool dry breeze.

He listened intently but heard nothing other than the familiar chirps of night birds, and the hum of nature's creatures going about their nocturnal business.

Satisfied no pursuers awaited him nearby, he snaked his way outside of the web of roots, stepping carefully onto the rocky floor of the draw. He again paused, testing the night for any sounds or sign of an enemy in hiding.

He moved silently in the direction from which he had come to this hiding place. Carefully, he climbed a rocky depression where seasonal flood waters rushed into the draw during heavy rainstorms. He gained the top of the runoff and peered carefully around him. After a long moment, he steeled himself, climbing the remainder of the bank until he stood on level ground.

Finding his way through the brambles and dense undergrowth was difficult and, at times, painful when he encountered the occasional thorn or bull nettle.

In this way he made slow progress for several minutes until he detected the faint smell of wood smoke. He paused. The smoke wafted upon the prevailing breeze from the southeast. He stood taller, searching the underbrush ahead for a fire's glow. He saw none and changed his direction until he moved along in a southeasterly direction, picking his way carefully and silently.

He heard the men at the camp before he saw them. They were making no effort to conceal their location. He heard indistinct, but loud talking, and laughter.

The image of little Hans dying in his arms fired a rage in him. Did his family and friends find it so easy to dismiss the killing of a boy – one of their own? Surely, they were present when Jarvis was murdered. These men had recently pursued Boyd with a murderous intent, yet he heard jovial conversation and laughter.

Boyd clenched his jaw until his teeth ached.

Their lax judgement was a mistake. He would make them sorry they made it. Any remaining loyalty or attachment to the people who raised him was quickly dissolving.

Strangely, though his ties to Jarvis were of blood only, Boyd heard his uncle's final entreaty on the behalf of a nephew he hardly knew. He hadn't seen it, but he could imagine his uncle imprisoned in the hog trap. The murder of a helpless man in a cage was fertile ground from which he could yield a mighty and terrible desire to act.

Even Hans, only a half relation to him, fueled his desire to exact justice upon those who so casually undertook his pursuit with no pause for the murder of the little boy.

Boyd knew the vigilantes would underestimate him. He imagined to them he was only a boy, no more a threat than little Hans. Their open disregard for their own safety demonstrated their belief he lacked the will or perhaps the courage to attack full grown men. Their confidence in these false preconceptions angered Boyd further.

Over the low hanging underbrush, Boyd spotted the upper portions of three horses, hobbled outside of the camp: three men.

He was downwind, moving silently, undetected by the animals' keen senses. Remaining out of sight, Boyd moved on hands and knees until he reached a vantage where he could see the men through a mesh of brambles and leaves.

Three members of the Cattleman's Association sat around a fire too large to be built by an experienced woodsman. Boyd recognized old man Keiferstein's boy, Fritz. He failed to identify the other two. The first man was bearded, his mouth protruding only when he spoke. The second was a squat man with heavy sideburns.

Boyd recognized them as members of Peter Bader's patrol but could not recall their names.

At an Association meeting at the ranch, Boyd recognized them as being assigned to the patrol involved in the killing of the rancher, Tim Williamson.

Unaware of his presence, they passed a bottle as they spoke to one another, loudly, carelessly.

Affecting a poor German accent, the man with the beard mocked Wechsler.

"Wolfgang will wake up with a grave sickness. One does not murder his grandson and recover quickly."

Fritz shook his head in disbelief.

"Mr. Wechsler killed Hans?"

The bearded man gave Fritz a condescending look as he mocked him.

"Yes, Mr. Wechsler killed Hans," he said. "He was too keen on shooting Emma's boy as he escaped. The kid must have got in the way."

"He'll find a way to hang that one on Boyd too," the man of the sideburns said with a grin. "We should have guessed he wasn't pure blood. I always thought something was wrong with Emma's boy – in the head I mean."

"He is odd," the bearded man agreed, drinking from the bottle.

"Where do you suppose he is?" Fritz asked.

The bearded man lowered the bottle and considered Fritz through eyes squinting with the heat of the liquor.

"A better question is what do you plan to do with that gun rig?"

Fritz reached for the holstered colt, drawing the pistol slowly from its sheath.

"It's his gun," Fritz said. "He thinks he is some kind of quick draw artist or something. If he makes the mistake of coming here, I'll show him what I can do with a pistol."

Fritz aimed into the darkness, as if he had Boyd in his sights.

The bearded man scoffed at the thought of their quarry confronting them.

"That coward is hiding out," he assured the others. "We'll pick up his trail in the morning as he scurries away like a scared rabbit."

He settled back against his saddle, looking at the fire sleepily.

"Put that thing away. We'll find him and kill him in the morning."

Fritz holstered the weapon.

"Not if the Wolf finds him first," the sideburn man corrected. "He's out for blood and blood he will have."

While the men talked, Boyd had worked his way to his right, around the camp, moving until he faced the camp, opposite where the horses were hobbled. From that angle he would be invisible to the loungers until he was upon them. He gripped the knife, rising from the dirt.

Fritz was laughing at a humorous remark from one of the others when he saw a shadow from the corner of his eye. He turned his head to identify the movement when a knife sunk into his neck to the hilt.

Boyd left the knife in Fritz's neck as he scooped up a rifle leaning against a saddle and pack. He swung the rifle butt, striking the second man in the head.

With a cry, the man of the heavy sideburns fell into Fritz's writhing body.

The bearded man had the presence of mind to use the time Boyd spent on the other two to grab his rifle.

Boyd levered in a cartridge then shot him center mass as the bearded man raised the rifle to shoot.

Boyd shot the sideburn man who was rising after the blow to his head.

All three died within moments.

Boyd dug through their packs, producing hardtack, biscuits, and a tin of apricots. He ate hurriedly until he was full. He drank the apricot juice, then consumed half the contents of one of the canteens before he was satisfied.

He spotted his gunbelt and pistol near Fritz's corpse. He crossed to it, careful to avoid stepping in the widening pool of blood and strapped on the weapon. It felt familiar, comforting.

He glanced at the dark sky as thunder rumbled somewhere in the distance. Another storm was coming.

He gathered ammo for the rifle then saddled the best of the three horses, a dapple-gray gelding. The horse was all points and had girth and leg length indicating endurance and speed.

Without a second look at the dead men around the dying campfire, Boyd mounted, urging the horse forward, headed towards the Wechsler Ranch.

Boyd rode for several hours before arriving at the tree line behind the ranch house. He crossed the distance to the house cautiously. He was just beyond the lush plants of the garden when he heard a voice to his left.

"You were right Klaus. He came back."

The voice he heard belonged to Ernst Wechsler.

"You're covered Boyd. Step down off that horse. Don't make any sudden moves. We have rifles trained on you."

Boyd turned his head towards Ernst.

"You just keep looking straight ahead," Klaus warned. To Ernst he said, "He's wearing a six gun."

"I thought Fritz had that," Ernst began before his voice died away with understanding. "How did you get that gun from Fritz?"

By this time Boyd was on the ground. He turned to face his uncles despite Klaus' warning. To their surprise, Boyd's eyes glistened with his emotion. His voice quavered as he answered.

"You sent men to track me down and kill me like a rabid dog. What do you think I did?"

Ernst's rifle sagged in his hands as he saw the tears in Boyd's eyes and the sadness on his face.

Klaus glanced at his brother before he said, "You killed Vern and now you've murdered Fritz, Benjamin, and Stephen."

He moved to bring his rifle to his shoulder in readiness to shoot Boyd.

With a gesture, the pistol appeared in Boyd's hand. The explosion was blinding to the brothers as Klaus fell to the ground, his rifle's barrel sticking into the mud. The second report came, and Ernst crumpled beside his brother.

He never had time to pull the trigger.

WOLFGANG WECHSLER SAT IN THE chair behind his desk. He paid no attention to the forms and papers strewn across the rich wooden top. His gaze focused inward. His appearance was one of a man haunted by his thoughts – and his conscience.

Thunder rumbled somewhere in the distance. The sound resembled a gunshot. Another sounded. It was a gunshot.

Wechsler cursed, attributing the shot to one of his sons firing at shadows. The boy would never return. He wouldn't dare.

Wechsler groaned. He had never wanted to see the sunrise as much as he did now. He feared the punishment he would face for the two murders he had committed. He did not fear the law. He owned the law. He feared his own retreating sensibilities. His was not the makeup of one who could kill and forget. He guessed that his short temper should have been paired with a stronger sense of justification.

The day had been filled with the lamenting of Ernst's wife Helga. Ernst suffered also, but not as the large German woman did.

After her son's death, Helga cradled Hans' lifeless body throughout the night and into the morning. Ernst struggled to convince her to allow them to bury him.

They buried Hans as a light rain fell, driving the chill of guilt more deeply into the old man. Ernst and Klaus filled the grave. No one left the family burial plot until the grave was completely covered in fresh wet dirt.

After the internment, with no other industry to occupy her sorrow, Helga had exhausted the last of her frenzy upon Wechsler himself.

For the moment, she believed Boyd killed Hans. She believed Boyd had held Hans hostage in order to escape. So far Ernst had gone along with the ruse, but Wechsler feared his son's emotions would ultimately overcome any sense of loyalty to his father and he would confess what he knew.

The passing hours had weakened even the Wolf's resolve. He lingered in a place between self-loathing and regret. The truth would come out soon enough.

As his mood deteriorated, Wechsler believed his desire to save face and his authority as the Patriarch would fade as well. The punishment he visited upon himself was nearly beyond his ability to withstand.

As a flash of lightning struck a stark white light throughout the room, he glanced at the pistol on his desk for the dozenth time, seeing it as a possible avenue of escape.

Emma was gone. She had fled silently sometime during the early morning hours. She left without preamble. Only the missing horse she sometimes rode gave notice of her departure.

The house was empty. Wechsler was alone in a home that once rang with happiness and family joy. Now it echoed hollowly with the approaching storm. It was the realization of his helpless solitude that caused him to start violently when a lightning flash revealed the silent appearance of his former grandson, Boyd Hutton.

The boy stood inside the door frame of the Wolf's office. The next lightning flash clearly showed Boyd's face. He looked as miserable as the Wolf felt. In that brief flash of light, Wechsler thought he detected tears mixed with blood on Boyd's face.

The youth's silent appearance struck the Wolf's depressed mind the same as if the boy had been a wraith, materializing out of nowhere. The next lightning flash, followed closely by a momentous thunderclap, completed the fantasy.

Boyd leaned against the door frame, but his manner was not casual. He seemed exhausted – spent of energy both physically and emotionally. His eyes were wet and hollow; his shoulders stooped.

Boyd's voice came as a croak at first, clearing to a low murmur towards the end.

"Klaus and Ernst are dead. I killed them."

Wechsler's mouth fell open in disbelief.

"They jumped me near the garden."

Boyd's words were jumbled with shudders of emotion. He shook as he stood there, exhausted and in despair. He felt keenly he was being transported by fate. He was no longer in control of what he did.

"I thought about just gathering my things and leaving," he said almost musingly. Then with a sharp look at Wechsler, his voice grew stronger. "But I can't do that now."

Boyd stood straighter despite his weakness, as if lifted by some supernatural force.

"You and your family have killed my only family and tried to kill me. Now I'm gonna kill you, Grandfather."

"I am not your grandfather," Wechsler shouted through tears and sorrow-filled fury. "You have no one."

"Neither do you old man," Boyd said with a dryness to his words. His statement was a verdict – upon both of them.

Wechsler moved as quickly as he could towards the pistol on the desk. He gambled the distance and exhaustion would slow Boyd Hutton. He gambled also the boy, not even a man, would falter and lose in the race for life.

Boyd crossed the short distance with a single large stride. With his bruised left hand, he slammed the pistol in Wechler's hand down hard on the desk. The gun discharged harmlessly into the near wall. With his right, he drove the bloody knife Hans had given him, into the old man's skull.

41

MAJOR JONES GATHERED WHAT remained of his Frontier Battalion before the Sheriff's office. After two full weeks of combing the countryside, they found no sign of Cooley or the remaining members of Cooley's gang. Jones learned the others were the dead Charlie Johnson, AKA Jarvis Hutton, Johnny Ringgold, and Boyd Wechsler. Jones was officially giving the order, calling a halt to the search.

His men gathered around their leader.

"Listen up Rangers," he called to his men. "It is apparent to me we will not be able to apprehend the outlaw Scott Cooley or the surviving members of his gang. The information we have gained from the local townspeople and those in the surrounding areas has dried up. No one is talking now that the Vigilante Gang is disbanded. The Governor is reassigning us to the Mexican Border region to defend against marauders crossing the Rio Bravo."

The rangers grumbled their muted distaste at the news.

"Keep your opinions to yourselves. You swore an oath. This is what you signed up for."

"What about that crooked Sheriff Clark?" one of the rangers asked, causing another rise of muttering from the others.

"He is no longer our concern. After he successfully dodged any and all charges respecting his actions in the line of duty, he disappeared like smoke. No one saw him leave, he's just gone."

"There's a warrant issued for the arrest of the Wechsler boy in the killing of the old rancher and his sons. The remaining killings will be worked over in time. All statements and associated evidence are secured in the courthouse. This won't be the last you men will hear of Mason, Texas. The truth will come out about this unfortunate event and the guilty will be brought to justice."

Jones looked around him at the few buildings making up the town, his gaze lingering on the so-called square. He shook his head with a wry smile. 'Square,' he thought. There was nothing square about it.

"I'm leaving three rangers from Company A to serve as interim lawmen until a Sheriff can be elected or appointed to replace Clark. The rest of you men…Let's get out of this god forsaken town."

The Rangers mounted their horses and rode out of Mason towards the south.

42

SCOTT COOLEY AND JOHNNY RINGGOLD sat silently in the Lampasas County Jail. They wore striped shirts and trousers. The sun had long before set, and a chill settled upon them in the poorly built jailhouse. It was apparent prisoner comfort was not a part of the construction of the stone jail house or the steel barred cells.

"Well Scott," Ringgold said with his customary smile. "One more day behind us and another on the horizon."

"You say that every night Johnny."

"I do indeed."

"We have been found guilty of attempted murder of a peace officer by a jury of our peers. Our days are numbered."

"Everybody's days are numbered, Scott. Only the free men are willing to brag about it."

"We ain't free."

"Not yet, but I believe in luck and the odds of fortune."

Scott Cooley shook his head, smiling despite his belief in a cold reality unaffected by chance.

"See," Ringgold said triumphantly. "I told you it works."

"I ain't showing humor because I agree with you Johnny Ringo. I just enjoy your waving a flag at the enemy."

At such a late hour, the sound of hinges squeaking and straining under the weight of the door to the cell block surprised them. They stood expectantly, though uncertain of the meaning of a late-night visit. Were they to be lynched?

Three men appeared out of the darkness, jingling a ring of keys as they approached.

Ringgold chuckled and shook his head as if he expected the men who approached.

"What took you so long, Kid?" he asked.

Boyd Hutton shook Ringgold's hand through the bars as John Baird and his friend Joe Olney worked the keys into the lock.

The cell door swung open, and the two prisoners followed their liberators into the jailer's office where the lone jailer was tied hand and foot to his chair.

"Adieu, Barrett," Ringgold said to the bound officer.

"Let's get you out of them stripes and into some duds," Baird said.

After a break-in visit to the only dry goods store in town, the five outlaws rode west out of Lampasas. As if from the habit of being so long together, Cooley and Ringgold rode abreast, behind rode Baird and Olney. Boyd followed back of the group.

The road widened and Ringgold nodded Boyd forward to join him and Cooley.

Boyd moved forward until he rode beside Ringgold on the side opposite Cooley.

"How do you and my old friends find yourself on the same road to Lampasas?"

Boyd shrugged.

"Luck I guess," he replied vaguely.

Ringold turned to Cooley.

"Do you believe now, Scott?"

Cooley glanced at his companions, immersed in his own thoughts, but made no reply.

Ringgold returned his attention to Boyd. This time he gave him a long look over.

"Scott," he said with his eyes on the youth. "The Kid is all growed up now, wearing long pants and all."

To Boyd he asked, "How'd you make out seeing your ma that day?"

"That's been more than a year ago, Johnny. I don't think about it anymore."

"I don't blame you," Ringgold agreed. "Ain't no secrets in jail, Kid. The word is out how the Wechsler boy ran amuck before disappearing into thin air."

Boyd focused his attention on the ground before his horse's bobbing head.

"I was sorry to hear about your uncle. I liked him."

Boyd nodded but maintained his silence.

Baird and Olney listened covertly to the conversation with unusual interest. Many of the details of what had come to be known as the Mason County War were still shrouded in mystery. Baird looked over his shoulder at the three riders behind him.

"Not that you asked, Johnny," Baird said. "But Joe and me left Mason County because of the word that is getting out. That judge in Mason is ramrodding an investigation and statewide manhunt for anybody involved with the range war. All the news going the rounds says that courthouse has enough evidence and eyewitness accounts to hang everyone who ever even lived in the county during the dust up.

"Scott, you are named as the chief fugitive. The Kid's uncle and him are listed as accomplices, although they still name the Kid as Wechsler.

"The rumor is Hutton's alias, Charlie Johnson, is alive and well somewhere out west, dodging the law. But the Germans named him as a major player in the game. Poor Mose and me are branded rustlers and accomplices in the murder of Peter Bader. That judge said in a news story he was bound to hang as many men as that hanging judge back in the day at Fort Smith."

"What about me?" Ringgold asked.

"You are only a rumor so far, although your name is familiar to the judge."

"Well," Ringgold said with a strange sound to his voice. "I guess that's something."

"I wouldn't be lamenting a lack of reputation if I was you, Johnny Ringo," Baird continued. "As long as that storeroom in the courthouse is filled with evidence, no one is safe. Judge Hey said in the same story every name would be remembered and made a part of…"

Olney leaned towards Baird and said in a soft voice, "Infamy."

"Infamy," Baird repeated. "What's infamy Johnny?"

"That's the bad side of being famous. That judge means to blacken the name of every man involved, though I imagine the Germans will be excluded in the reputation assassination."

Boyd looked at the men around him before speaking.

"What's the plan then?" he asked Ringgold and Cooley.

Ringgold shrugged noncommittally.

Cooley looked seriously at Boyd.

"We were waiting for Major Jones to take us back to Mason. He and his Frontier Battalion were in Lampasas not long ago working out a peace between the Higgin's gang and the Horrell's."

Ringgold laughed.

"Hell, the Higgins boys broke into the courthouse and made off with all the evidence against them," he said with a smile. "If we had the chance, we should burn down the Mason Courthouse with their piles of evidence. That would clear our names."

Baird laughed.

"Yep," he agreed. "That would do it.

Ringgold sat straighter in the saddle, pulling his hat over his eyes.

"Scott," he announced. "Come with me to Arizona. We'll live longer if we put a state between us and Texas."

"I've been thinking about that since you started talking about it when we were in the Travis County Jail. I've got family in Blanco County. I'll be safer there than traveling roads and through towns in the open. I'm afraid this is where we part, my friend."

Scott Cooley extended his hand to his longtime partner.

Ringgold hesitated before grasping the offered hand.

"I won't forget you Scott," he said with genuine warmth.

Scott nodded his agreement to do the same.

"In time they'll know you even in Arizona, Johnny."

Ringgold chuckled.

"You boys gave me my alias long ago. It's kinda grown on me since then."

Baird laughed heartily.

"I'll be damned," he said through his mirth. "You always hated that name. At least, I thought you were gonna shoot me and Mose every time we used it."

Ringgold shrugged good naturedly.

"I'm glad you survived it John, because I'm beholdin' to you now."

Baird pulled up and waited for Ringgold to come up beside him. He shook the outlaw's hand.

"Well, here's to the good times, Johnny Ringo. Look up your old friend John Baird when you pass by. You will always have a bed and board."

"Thanks, John, but I don't think I'll be back in this life."

"Well," Baird said warmly. "Then this is so long, pardner."

Johnny Ringo shook Joe Olney's hand then turned to Boyd Hutton.

"What do you say Kid?" he asked. "I told you we would ride again. I'm headed west by way of Abilene to avoid that hornet's nest in Mason County. You coming?"

Boyd gauged the outlaw with a serious look.

"Arizona, huh?" he asked.

"After I stretch my legs a little in New Mexico."

Boyd shook his head.

"I got one thing I need to take care of, and I'll catch up with you, Johnny."

"Suit yourself Kid."

Ringo clucked to his horse, leaving the group as he headed north.

Cooley shook Boyd's hand.

"Stay clear of Mason County, Kid," he warned before he headed south.

Boyd watched him go before looking north where Ringo was just topping a rise.

"Hey Johnny," he called to the outlaw. "How will I find you?"

Ringo pulled up with a laugh.

"Follow the bodies, Kid," he replied.

He touched spur to his horse and crossed out of sight past the rise.

43

BEFORE HIS DEATH, THE WOLF TOUTED his life would begin again on January 21,1877. Boyd reflected in a dark humor that he hadn't lived to see it. Just that morning he had learned the secret to the mystery behind the significance of that date. Although his grandfather never made the statement directly to Boyd's face until his last day in the family, he had overheard it enough to ensure the date was the greatest mystery in his young life, next to why he was treated so much differently than the Wolf's other grandsons. He hadn't imagined the two were connected.

The darkness of pre-dawn was giving way to the rising Sun when Boyd Hutton walked out of the front door of the Mason County Courthouse. The smoke billowed from windows, and even wafted between some of the red bricks, reminding him of a brick oven, constraining a growing conflagration.

He fled the courthouse towards the fence at the main road where his horse was tied. He didn't hurry because he was afraid of the townies who would be drawn to the fire. His steps were hurried because a fast-moving wave of expanding heat pursued him. Arriving where his horse was tied, the heat from the fire reached him, growing intolerable.

Boyd mounted the gelding, retreating some distance where the air was cooler. He took a moment to watch the destruction of the iconic building.

Today was January 21,1877 and this was indeed a day as significant as his grandfather had imagined. Boyd pulled an official looking paper from his jacket. He unfolded it. The top line read Birth Certificate. Under the title, the remaining information was filled into blanks in scrawled handwriting. The handwritten information read on January 21, 1859, Boyd Kyle Hutton was born to Emma Mary Wechsler.

The space where the father's information would be recorded read only "deceased."

Boyd pocketed the paper and turned the gelding southeast. He glanced behind him towards town where the sounds of yells and slamming doors warned him of townspeople waking and raising the alarm.

Boyd looked towards the courthouse once more as the gelding, without urging, lifted his pace to a nervous canter. The horse disliked the heat, smoke, and particularly the popping and cracking of structural timbers and finish lumber as the fire consumed it.

The fire was well started. There would be no extinguishing it. Boyd had found the room where the men of the law had gathered and stored information about the details of "The HooDoo War", as many of the boxes were labelled. The box containing information about Scott Cooley and his friends would also disappear for good.

Neither Jarvis Hutton nor the Hutton name would ever be associated with the Mason County War: at least there would be no proof. Boyd guessed rumors would remain for a time. But they would eventually fade with the slow passing of years, becoming distorted and inaccurate. Wolfgang Wechsler's curse before murdering Jarvis Hutton would not come to pass.

Boyd rode for a while until he reached a small rise south of town where he sat comfortably in the saddle. He could see no more than the top of the courthouse, licked by white hot flames. The useless efforts of the townspeople, the Städtbewohnen, to save the building were audible as an unreal dirge of panicked human voices competing with the voice of the fire, roaring its dominance. The noisy battle for the courthouse conjured in Boyd's imagination the shrieks of the damned burning in Hell.

He pulled the paper from his jacket again. This time he didn't take time to read it. He lit it with a match, allowing it to burn in his hand until he could hold it no longer. The flames consumed what was left of the page as it floated to the tawny grass below his horse's feet.

Boyd pulled a brown bottle from his saddle bags. Pulling the cork, he took a long pull from the bottle.

"Happy Birthday," he said. "Eighteen years old. That was the day the old man dreamed about. Burn in hell with your dream."

He replaced the bottle in the saddle bag, glancing at the tall column of smoke rising above the dying building.

Although his thoughts were about his future. he was not given to imaginings and fantasies. His view forward was pragmatic. His horse was well rested, and he was provisioned for a long trek.

He had no plan, but the idea of seeing his friend Johnny Ringo again appealed to him. He would head west for San Angelo. He would trust in fate to guide him.

Ringo had taught him that.

ABOUT THE AUTHOR

Craig Rainey (1962 -) is an American film actor, author, screenwriter, and musician. He was born in San Angelo, Texas, and lives in Austin. His Texas roots hail back to the original Impresario settlers of Coahuila y Tejas under Stephen F. Austin. He is a military veteran, and he cowboyed professionally in south Texas.

www.ingramcontent.com/pod-product-compliance
Lightning Source LLC
Chambersburg PA
CBHW021240190726
48289CB00005B/1406